New Haven Noir

edited by Amy Bloom

Published by Akashic Books
©2017 Akashic Books

Series concept by Tim McLoughlin and Johnny Temple
New Haven map by Sohrab Habibion

ISBN: 978-1-61775-541-5
Library of Congress Control Number: 2016953900
All rights reserved

First printing

Akashic Books
Brooklyn, New York
Twitter: @AkashicBooks
Facebook: AkashicBooks
E-mail: info@akashicbooks.com
Website: www.akashicbooks.com

To New Haven, our town

ALSO IN THE AKASHIC NOIR SERIES

OAKLAND NOIR, edited by JERRY THOMPSON & EDDIE MULLER
ORANGE COUNTY NOIR, edited by GARY PHILLIPS
PARIS NOIR (FRANCE), edited by AURÉLIEN MASSON
PHILADELPHIA NOIR, edited by CARLIN ROMANO
PHOENIX NOIR, edited by PATRICK MILLIKIN
PITTSBURGH NOIR, edited by KATHLEEN GEORGE
PORTLAND NOIR, edited by KEVIN SAMPSELL
PRISON NOIR, edited by JOYCE CAROL OATES
PROVIDENCE NOIR, edited by ANN HOOD
QUEENS NOIR, edited by ROBERT KNIGHTLY
RICHMOND NOIR, edited by ANDREW BLOSSOM, BRIAN CASTLEBERRY & TOM DE HAVEN
RIO NOIR (BRAZIL), edited by TONY BELLOTTO
ROME NOIR (ITALY), edited by CHIARA STANGALINO & MAXIM JAKUBOWSKI
SAN DIEGO NOIR, edited by MARYELIZABETH HART
SAN FRANCISCO NOIR, edited by PETER MARAVELIS
SAN FRANCISCO NOIR 2: THE CLASSICS, edited by PETER MARAVELIS
SAN JUAN NOIR (PUERTO RICO), edited by MAYRA SANTOS-FEBRES
SEATTLE NOIR, edited by CURT COLBERT
SINGAPORE NOIR, edited by CHERYL LU-LIEN TAN
STATEN ISLAND NOIR, edited by PATRICIA SMITH
ST. LOUIS NOIR, edited by SCOTT PHILLIPS
STOCKHOLM NOIR (SWEDEN), edited by NATHAN LARSON & CARL-MICHAEL EDENBORG
ST. PETERSBURG NOIR (RUSSIA), edited by NATALIA SMIRNOVA & JULIA GOUMEN
TEHRAN NOIR (IRAN), edited by SALAR ABDOH
TEL AVIV NOIR (ISRAEL), edited by ETGAR KERET & ASSAF GAVRON
TORONTO NOIR (CANADA), edited by JANINE ARMIN & NATHANIEL G. MOORE
TRINIDAD NOIR (TRINIDAD & TOBAGO), edited by LISA ALLEN-AGOSTINI & JEANNE MASON
TRINIDAD NOIR: THE CLASSICS (TRINIDAD & TOBAGO), edited by EARL LOVELACE & ROBERT ANTONI
TWIN CITIES NOIR, edited by JULIE SCHAPER & STEVEN HORWITZ
USA NOIR, edited by JOHNNY TEMPLE
VENICE NOIR (ITALY), edited by MAXIM JAKUBOWSKI
WALL STREET NOIR, edited by PETER SPIEGELMAN
ZAGREB NOIR (CROATIA), edited by IVAN SRŠEN

FORTHCOMING

ACCRA NOIR (GHANA), edited by NANA-AMA DANQUAH
ADDIS ABABA NOIR (ETHIOPIA), edited by MAAZA MENGISTE
AMSTERDAM NOIR (HOLLAND), edited by RENÉ APPEL & JOSH PACHTER
BAGHDAD NOIR (IRAQ), edited by SAMUEL SHIMON
BERLIN NOIR (GERMANY), edited by THOMAS WÖERTCHE
BOGOTÁ NOIR (COLOMBIA), edited by ANDREA MONTEJO
BUENOS AIRES NOIR (ARGENTINA), edited by ERNESTO MALLO
HOUSTON NOIR, edited by GWENDOLYN ZEPEDA
JERUSALEM NOIR, edited by DROR MISHANI
LAGOS NOIR (NIGERIA), edited by CHRIS ABANI
MARRAKECH NOIR (MOROCCO), edited by YASSIN ADNAN
MONTANA NOIR, edited by JAMES GRADY & KEIR GRAFF
MONTREAL NOIR (CANADA), edited by JOHN McFETRIDGE & JACQUES FILIPPI
PRAGUE NOIR (CZECH REPUBLIC), edited by PAVEL MANDYS
SANTA CRUZ NOIR, edited by SUSIE BRIGHT
SÃO PAULO NOIR (BRAZIL), edited by TONY BELLOTTO
SYDNEY NOIR (AUSTRALIA), edited by JOHN DALE
VANCOUVER NOIR (CANADA), edited by SAM WIEBE

EAST ROCK PARK

DIXWELL AVENUE

EAST ROCK

YALE UNIVERSITY

EDGEWOOD AVENUE

DWIGHT

BRADLEY STREET

BEINECKE LIBRARY

AUDUBON ARTS DISTRICT

CHAPEL STREET

WOOSTER SQUARE

WEST RIVER MEMORIAL PARK

UNION STATION

LONG WHARF

FOOD TERMINAL PLAZA

NEW HAVEN HARBOR

NEW HAVEN

QUINNIPIAC
MEADOWS

ALLING MEMORIAL
GOLF CLUB

FAIR
HAVEN

LAKE
SALTONSTALL
RECREATION
AREA

LIGHTHOUSE
POINT PARK

AST SHORE
PARK

TABLE OF CONTENTS

PART III: DEATH OR GLORY

INTRODUCTION
NOIR HAVEN

New Haven is not a tourist town. You could come for the food trucks down by the harbor, for the loaf of olive sourdough at the Wooster Square farmer's market, for a wild-eyed hockey game at the Whale, for concerts on the Green with entertainers whom you feared were dead. Some people do. More people come for something to do with Yale—students, staff, faculty, spouses of all kinds; the university has long arms—for something to do with the hospitals (split-liver transplant, anyone?), or for something to do with pizza. (I was surprised that the Sally's/Pepe's/Modern Apizza war didn't feature more heavily in this anthology's stories. It's no joke.)

Our history is bound up with the original king-killers, three guys who signed the death warrant for the murder of King Charles I in 1649 and fled to New England, because even then (pre-Connecticut), payback was a bitch. In New Haven, we love Edward, Charles, and John—the regicides. We even have a trail named after them.

We had Billy Grasso, a garden-variety crook and shake-down artist. We had Charlie "the Blade" Tourine, imported from Jersey. The city had a long run of Midge Renault, who was only 5'3" and not any kind of Frenchman (Salvatore Annunziato), and he, short and crazy, was a one-man crime wave for many years. Midge was the kind of guy to track you down, beat you up, run you over with your own car, and then pick you up so he could hit you again. He'd bribed everyone in

New Haven who could be bribed. If you couldn't be bribed, he burned down your house or your restaurant. When he was in jail, the guards let him go home, just to be on the safe side. Everybody knows that story.

If noir is about corruption, absurdity, anxiety, the nightmare of bureaucracy, New Haven, with multiple universities and multiple clinics and multiple, and sometimes clashing, neighborhoods, is a noir town. If it's about sex, money, and revenge, we have a lot of that, played out against the backdrop of the stately homes in East Rock, or the food carts ringing the hospital, or a bocce game played by trash-talking centenarians who believe that murder is a better solution than divorce. New Haven is a noir town.

We invented the first steamboat, the first cotton gin, the lollipop, the hamburger, and the automatic revolver. That's noir country. We have a large, deep harbor and two traprock ridges (East and West Rock). People disappear into and under these geographic features often.

Our murder rate is up only a little, and way down from where it used to be. Our victims range from children to old folks. The number of shots fired is much lower. Our aim has improved. We have our favorite unsolved crimes: Our town's Whitey Tropiano, a mobster shot dead on the street. The Yale senior killed and found on a quiet street corner (various amateurs have devoted years to this search; one guy is pretty sure it's part of a 9/11 conspiracy, but he belongs in a different anthology). A lot of people were riveted by the headless torso found in an abandoned building, the handless arms found near the State Street commuter station. (See Chris Knopf's story, which may owe something to this tragedy.) The pieces were part of a well-liked homeless guy and, eighteen months later, no one knows anything more about it.

In the place where I get coffee:

Guy buying a muffin: "You know the arms with no hands?"
Woman stirring her coffee: "You mean the legs in the train station?"
Man behind the counter: "It was Ray Roberson."
Guy: "Bobo? I know Bobo."
Woman: "Not now. Poor Bobo."

The twelve people in the coffee shop stop what they're doing and a young woman behind the counter starts singing "His Eye Is on the Sparrow," and everyone either joins in or drops their heads. An older man in a suit clasps his hands in prayer.

We may be a noir town but, even though noir usually manages not to, we have heart.

The chance to bring together some of my favorite writers, in my adopted hometown (in every place I bartended, the cook or the manager carried a .38 in his waistband, and I can still make ten kinds of boilermakers), was a joy and a privilege. Every single story is a noir gem, among them:

Alice Mattison breaks the mold. In her Lighthouse Point Park story, she gives the femme fatale a twist from which I hope the genre never recovers. This time, the hopeful, love-sick dim bulb is a young woman and the sexy, manipulative devil with the irresistible body is a man. Mattison throws in a double twist, in which the dreams of glory and money are all at the most unremarkable levels.

Chandra Prasad's "Silhouettes" takes classic 1940s noir for a perverse spin around a drought- and war-addled Wooster Square, far from its modern charms. The young man with a limp is shy. The girls are flirts. The boss does seem to be looking, all the time. The wife doesn't know much. All I can say is,

Strouse Adler Corset factory—and I didn't see that coming.

Michael Cunningham and John Crowley take us to noir-beyond-time, to worlds that have a whiff of the uncanny. Cunningham creates a nightmarish hotel of disturbances, "The Man in Room Eleven." Crowley assaults all of our senses, *Clockwork Orange*–style, in his exploration of a Yale we haven't seen yet.

The writers in this volume find noir in the seventies, the eighties, and the nineties, from college boys to Italian widows. Roxana Robinson finds noir in the world of biographers and Beinecke Library. Classic noir returns to our modern lives in Sarah Pemberton Strong's "Callback," in which we get the no-good dame, theatrical rivalry, and a stage-door romance as well. In "Evening Prayer," Stephen L. Carter lets us see truth emerging as a knife in the heart. In *New Haven Noir*, everyone lies—and when they tell the truth, it's even worse.

If you are an optimist, noir may be an antidote, a crisp, dry balance for your sunny outlook. If you are a pessimist (or, as we say, a realist), noir is your home ground, your tribe. It's not just that you expect ants to come to the picnic; you know damned well that there will be ants at the picnic. When they come, you're relieved. When they crawl up your brother's leg, you're reassured and possibly delighted. But the other side of noir is the moral center. The center may be shabby, frayed, and in serious need of a facelift, but it is a center. It's not necessarily heroic. It's likely to be cynical, and its resilience is not the showy kind. Mean streets, as Raymond Chandler once said, but not mean.

That's New Haven.

Amy Bloom
New Haven, CT
May 2017

PART I

SKULLS & BONES

CROSSING HARRY

BY CHRIS KNOPF

Union Station

People tend to not like me because they think I smell bad, and I talk a lot, though not to them, but to other people they don't know are there. I personally don't see a problem with this, though there's always somebody trying to fix me, or get me inside some building, or stick a bunch of drugs in me to make me better. When I don't even think I'm sick from anything.

Though usually I'm pretty much left alone, because as a general rule people don't even see me.

My house is this nice little spot under the railroad tracks that mostly keeps out the rain and snow. I got it from a guy who died there, and I only had to drag his body out to the street to take possession, and the dead-guy odor went away pretty quickly. I have room for my sleeping bag, books, lantern, some extra clothes for the cold weather, and other things, like a bag of bottles and cans I usually forget to turn in, and a cat that doesn't take up hardly any space at all.

It's not the world's greatest existence, but I'm alive and free to move around the neighborhood, so things could be a lot worse. Eating is a bit of a problem, since I'm not keen on rotting food, which is plentiful but likely to land you in the hospital, where there's a danger the psych people will trundle you off to a place where they feed you full of drugs and bore you with talk, talk, talk.

But I've got maybe a half-dozen restaurant dumpsters around New Haven that serve quite a lovely cuisine, delivered daily, fresh enough, and meticulously prepared. You have to be careful with your timing, though after a few years of this, I'm pretty good at it.

My friend Harry is a most excellent guide. He absolutely knows what gets tossed out, when, and where. Better yet, he never eats anything, since he lives in a different dimension, so I don't have to share. Though I always offer.

My favorite place in the world is Union Station. It's always warm in the winter and cool in the summer and the architecture is so soothing. It only takes about fifteen minutes to walk there from my house under the tracks, but it's always worth the effort. My goal is to sit on the long wooden benches, comfy and smooth on the ass, for at least an hour before one of the transit cops tells me to get lost. I always go quietly, since their German shepherds look so kind and apologetic, and tell me through Harry that I really don't have to worry. They know I'm only enjoying a little of the luxury of the inside world and have no animus toward anyone, man or beast.

It was one of those times, sitting happily on the bench, that the man in the beautiful dark-blue cashmere overcoat came through the doors leading from the tracks. He had excellent posture, and his shoes were very nicely polished. I didn't see a single scuff. He carried an overstuffed canvas bag, zipped closed, on the side of which was a huge logo of a resort in Jamaica. Since it was February, I really liked examining the palm trees and the girl in a bikini, fake as they were.

He had the high cheekbones and swept-back gray hair of a European nobleman, but Harry said there was something wrong with his eyes. I said to him, too blue? He said too empty.

I kept staring at his face as he walked by, but he didn't

look back, probably for the same reason no one else looked at me. Except for the transit cops, who kicked me out of the station soon after that. With nothing else to do, I wandered down Church Street toward New Haven Harbor. Before I got there, I saw the cashmere coat coming toward me. He was carrying his Jamaica bag, though it looked a lot lighter. Harry told me to duck into a doorway and stay out of view. I said to Harry, why do that, since the guy wouldn't see me anyway? Harry got a little testy about that, and told me to just shut up and do it.

It wasn't until spring, when things had warmed up a lot, that I saw the stylish guy again. This time I was down along the harbor's waterline, trying to catch a fish or two for the evening's meal. A tall guy with a full head of gray hair, he was still dressed like a duke, with silk pants and a suede jacket that hung on him like it was draped there. I wondered how he managed to stay so fit, since he could eat anything he wanted, any time he wanted.

Harry reminded me that people like him could afford private fitness instructors, and I said, of course. That's how he did it.

He still had the big canvas bag with the Jamaica tourism logo. I didn't think he'd recognize me, especially since I'd shed my winter ensemble, so I didn't try to hide myself. I just fished and watched him walk up to the edge of the water and open the canvas bag. He knelt down and pulled out a big sous vide bag.

You probably don't know what that is, but one of my favorite dumpster stops is a French restaurant where they toss out these vacuum-packed plastic bags with the planet's best food inside that you just drop in boiling water. I know, you're thinking cheap rice meals and crap from the convenience store. But you'd be wrong. Sous vide is at the other end of the spectrum. It comes from France, a place that knows a thing or two about tasty food.

Thing is, it wasn't even legal then for restaurants to serve food prepared sous vide, and all the health inspector had to do was peak into the dumpster. Just shows you what people like me know about what really goes on in a city. Not that anybody would bother to ask.

I watched the guy take a pair of little scissors out of his pocket and cut open the bag. Then he pulled out the stuff inside—it looked from a distance like nice veal cutlets or chicken marsala—and started chucking it into the water.

This was very intriguing to me. Why throw a perfectly good, gourmet-prepared, sous vide meat course into New Haven Harbor?

I don't know what possessed me—unless it was Harry, who urged me in a pretty imperious way to walk up to the guy and ask him what the hell he was doing. I said no freaking way, but Harry kept at it. So I did, trying not to show how nervous I was.

The guy just looked through me, like the first time I saw him in the train station, though he didn't seem bothered by the question. Maybe because it was being asked by a smelly homeless person.

"I'm concerned about the world's crustaceans," he said, turning back to his task.

"Like crabs?"

"Specifically crabs. They are in danger. Someone has to replenish the stock, return ecological vitality to their environments."

"I didn't know crab food came vacuum packed," I said, pointing at the plastic sous vide bag in his hand.

He turned to peer down at me from his tall, haughty-guy perspective. "It doesn't. I seal it myself. I am a virtuoso of the culinary arts, trained in France. Preparation and preservation is everything."

"Sure thing," I said. "I get it."

He turned back to his work. "Of course you don't," he said. "How could you know that within a few days, all trace of this finely prepared select protein will be utterly consumed? Vanished, irretrievably. Could there be a more elegant, definitive resolution?"

Harry said, "Huh?"

I said, "That must be incredible food."

"Indeed," he said, his voice a low grumble.

I started to walk away, but he grabbed me by the arm, digging strong fingers into my bicep.

"This work is highly confidential," he said, staring at me with those crazy blue eyes. "Not a word to anyone or there will be consequences. You understand?"

He let go of me when I said I did. Then I walked down the beach, acting like it all made sense, which of course it didn't, since I'd studied crustaceans as a biology major at Yale and knew that secretly feeding them gourmet meals in the New Haven Harbor would have little impact on the ultimate survival of species *infraorder Brachyura*.

I began to spend a lot more time around Union Station, watching all the time for the gray-haired guy with the Jamaica tourism bag. This ultimately bore fruit, when one day I was in the station and saw him come through the doors that led from the tracks, holding his canvas bag and looking fresh as a daisy in a light-blue blazer, red-and-white-striped shirt, and pressed white pants.

This time, I didn't want him to see me, so I ducked into

the newsstand and pretended to leaf through the magazines on the big rack. After a few minutes, I was able to follow him down Church Street, keeping about a block between us.

As always, he went to the edge of the harbor, pulled out his sous vide bag, and tossed the contents into the water. I was close enough to hear the *kerplunk*, but far enough away to stay out of eyeshot. I have to admit, I was drooling a little over what was in those vacuum-packed bags, and determined this time to grab some of it before the so-called endangered crabs had a feast.

My clever disguise when he walked by was to turn my back and act like I was staring off into the distance. It apparently worked, because he just kept on walking. As soon as he was out of sight, I ran like mad down to the harbor, pulled off my shoes, and waded right in. Being summer and all, this was not that heroic of a thing to do, though it meant I'd be drenched to the bone on my walk back to my place under the railroad tracks.

Like before, I couldn't find a thing, which didn't surprise me, thinking that meat might be heavier than water, sinking pretty quickly. But I also had my feet, which I used to scrunch around the seabed, like I'd do to find clams. That's how I struck gold, if you want to call it that.

My first thought was chicken. The flesh was slippery, and full of crunchy bones and cartilage. I'm okay with chicken, though I was disappointed, since I'd been hoping for filet mignon or a nice boneless pork cutlet. I took it anyway and searched some more, but that's all I found.

When I got back to the beach, a little sorry that I was now soaking wet with only a hunk of chicken to show for it, I was able to take a closer look. This wasn't any cut of chicken I'd seen before. It had no recognizable shape and the bony stuff was way too big. When I unsealed the bag, it didn't smell like chicken either. In fact, it didn't smell like anything I'd ever smelled before.

I stuck it in a plastic bag I found in a trash can at the edge of the beach. I carried the bag up Church Street, wondering what to do. Making a meal at this point was off the table, so to speak. Partly because my hunger was getting edged out by curiosity. Biology wasn't only my major at Yale—I'd loved it since I was a kid. I'd absolutely be hunched over a lab counter right now if I hadn't had that little hiccup with the voices in my head and the collusion of the Yale Board of Trustees, the United States Chamber of Commerce, and the Satanic Monks of Aquitaine to deprive me of my undergraduate position.

As usual, Harry had a great suggestion: go to the post office and send the bag of meat to my old faculty adviser in the Yale Department of Ecology and Evolutionary Biology.

It was a major hike to the post office, which was on the Yale campus. But when we got there, I realized I needed a box to put the bag in. And an address to write on the box, and the money to pay for postage. I had none of these things. Harry berated me, saying any normal person would have no difficulty managing this situation. The more he yelled at me, the harder it was to think, so I started yelling back at him, which is always a mistake.

I'm a guy people try to ignore, so I can tell you this is a sure-fire way to get a little attention. Definitely the wrong kind.

This got me pretty anxious, so I clamped my hand over my mouth and just kept walking. Pretty soon, I realized I wasn't all that far from the Department of Ecology and Evolutionary Biology itself. Part of me, I admit, just wanted to chuck the bag full of slimy meat into a trash can and walk back to my house under the tracks. But something else pushed me along.

Maybe to prove to Harry that I was capable of completing a project even if I hit a snag or two.

When we arrived, I thought about the lady at the desk near the faculty offices who scheduled time with the professors. I was hoping she didn't remember me when I handed her the bag and told her my old adviser might find the contents interesting. I prayed she wouldn't say something like, he's in his office, just go on back and say hello. Especially after that last class when all those insects were jumping out of the specimen containers and trying to eat my flesh.

No worries there. She took the bag, dropped it on her desk, and told me in so many words to hit the pike. I didn't give her my name, but I had a plan. Wait about a week, then call the professor. Surprise! *It was me that brought in the sample. What the heck is it?*

And that's what I would have done, only I never got around to calling, because a few days later the *New Haven Register* had a headline that said, "Homeless Man Delivers Human Remains to Yale Professor."

I was freaked out of my skull for a few minutes, too freaked to read the newspaper article. But when I did, I learned that neither the chopped-up person nor the chopper-upper had been identified, though an anonymous source close to the case assumed both were homeless people who got into a conflict while drunk, drugged-up, or crazy—or all of the above. Street people driven to unofficial body disposal was not unprecedented, apparently, especially when somebody ODs and panic sets in.

The question of who would pass along a chunk of said chopped-up person to a Yale biology professor was still open to conjecture.

I looked up and saw a transit cop approaching with his

German shepherd. When they kept on walking, I glanced at the giant train schedule on the wall, wondering how far I could get with the little money I'd hidden away. Then I wondered if they'd even let me on the train, or what I would do when I got to wherever I was going. It had taken me a long time to find and perfect my house under the tracks and establish my activities of daily living. How was I going to start over?

Maybe I could just tell the cops what I knew, I thought for a brief second. No way in hell, said Harry, without hesitation. He said, you're the guy who talks to invisible people, and now you're going to accuse a fancy chef of serving selections of vacuum-packed Homo sapiens to our local sea life?

These are the kind of debates I get into with Harry all the time, and I have to admit, he's usually right. But before I could concede to his argument, there was the guy again coming into the station from an arriving train.

I tried to disappear into the wooden bench, but he saw me and stalked right over. He didn't have what you'd call a happy face. He sat on the bench, holding his Jamaica tourism bag in his lap.

"I'm terribly disappointed," he said, watching the busy parade of train passengers.

"About what?" I asked.

"I can hardly promote a revival of the crustacean population if people are going to tamper with the food stock."

"I get that."

"Our work must remain confidential. I told you that. I thought you understood."

"Absolutely. Understood," I said. "Nobody's gonna hear anything from me."

Those lifeless blue eyes suddenly seemed very much alive. "Too late," he said softly. "There will be consequences."

That was when Harry decided to whistle for one of the German shepherds. The dog came over to us, dragging along a transit cop. The cop started to give me his usual polite but firm request that I vacate the premises, but the dog had different ideas, sniffing like crazy at the Jamaica tourism bag. The gray-haired guy tried to sneak away, but the hair along the dog's back stood straight up and it lunged at the guy.

"What's in the bag, sir?" the cop asked, pulling back on the leash.

Harry, by this point, was getting a little shrill and, despite all his talk about keeping our own counsel, started screaming about hacked-up people and sous vide bags and crab food, sounding about as looney as a person can sound.

People around us began to scatter and another cop rushed over. The gray-haired guy said something like, "Enough of this nonsense," and tried again to walk away, but the German shepherd clamped his teeth down on the bag and held on.

By now, the transit cops were shouting things into microphones mounted on their shirtsleeves, and other cops were appearing out of nowhere; one of them grabbed my upper arm, even though I wasn't trying to go anywhere. He unfolded a sketch of someone's face and compared it to mine. It must have been a good match, since he wrenched both hands behind my back and stuck on a set of handcuffs.

They also cuffed the gray-haired guy, but he had his eyes locked on mine. He looked pissed, for sure, but something new was there. A kind of astonishment. A stunned disbelief.

And, for the first time, the whole world could see me.

CALLBACK

BY Sarah Pemberton Strong

Audubon Arts District

I didn't become a plumber because I like lying on my back in crawl spaces while fiberglass insulation and mouse turds fall on my face. I didn't become a plumber because I like getting sprayed with black drain water, either. I became a plumber for the money, and because I like certainty. Plumbing's not an ambiguous job—the pipe either leaks or it doesn't, the toilet is clogged or it isn't. Money and certainty and the satisfaction of a job well done.

I had to keep reminding myself of these reasons as I turned onto Audubon Street. I was on my way to a new customer's house, and it was going to be hard to make a good first impression given that I was still covered in fiberglass and dirt and smelling of *eau de* drain. Once upon a time, being a woman plumber had seemed both transgressive and sexy: think girl driving a truck, think big pipe wrenches, think buff upper arms. But after spending half the morning lying under Lamar and Francine Bowman's rotted pipes, I felt about as transgressive and sexy as a bucket of dirty water. I smelled like a sewer and I had a bad case of the creeps from accidentally grabbing a dead mouse when I reached for my wrench. I'd been wearing rubber gloves, but still. And to make matters worse, the Bowmans were broke, so when I wrote out the bill I charged them only half of what I usually do.

"Isn't that illegal?" Charlotte asked me once when I confessed I gave discounts to poor people. "And besides, how can you tell who's poor, anyway? Some people are millionaire skinflints—while they're alive everyone thinks they're paupers and it's only after they're dead that—"

"I can tell," I interrupted. Charlotte has probably never even *driven* through the Bowmans' neighborhood, not even with the windows rolled up and the doors locked. "Besides," I said, "it's gotta be less illegal than redlining."

Charlotte hates it when I talk like this. Part of my appeal to her is that when she's with me she feels like she's slumming, and if I start going all analytical on her it messes with this. To shut me up that time, she poured me a drink. It was Charlotte who taught me to appreciate extremely good whiskey, which is a problem in that she's no longer my girlfriend and I'm too much of a cheapskate to buy it myself. I also have a rule about drinking alone—I don't. But as I sped away from the Bowmans' that day, it occurred to me for about half a second that I might stop by Charlotte's condo and ask her to let me take a shower. A shower and a splash of her famous Scotch to take away the feeling of having picked up a dead mouse. She lived right in Audubon Court and I knew she'd be there. Charlotte works from home, doing some kind of stock trading from her bedroom. She lies on her bed and looks up at this enormous projection of her laptop screen on the bedroom ceiling and talks on the phone and makes about a zillion dollars an hour. You can tell Charlotte is rich just from the way she talks to people, even if you only happen to overhear her ordering coffee in a Dunkin' Donuts. Except Charlotte would never go into Dunkin' Donuts. She only drinks Willoughby's.

The idea of using her shower was pure fantasy, though. In the first place, I was too filthy—she wouldn't have let me into her bathroom, which has white fluffy everything—and in the second place, there wasn't time. I have a thing about being late—I'm not. Ever. It's OCD, I know, but it's also one of the reasons I don't have to advertise. I looked longingly up at Charlotte's window as I drove through the Lincoln Tunnel, which is what we call the illegal cut-through on Lincoln with the private footbridge arching across it, and I kept going. I'd rather be dirty than late. I turned the corner and parked, then appraised myself in the rearview mirror. Dirty hair, stained hoodie. Spattered jeans, cracked steel-toed boots. I ran my fingers through my fiberglassy hair. I look good in my work clothes, actually, if you like women who look like scruffy teen-age boys, but I didn't smell so hot. I did a hasty cleanup, scrubbing my face and hands with a few baby wipes. Then, hoping I smelled more like baby fragrance than old drains, I went to the door.

Most of the big houses in this neighborhood have been converted into law offices or therapy practices, but not this one, a gorgeous three-story brownstone. And judging from the single nameplate, the Lancasters had the whole place to themselves. The door knocker was a big brass affair that probably weighed as much as my tool bag, and I heard it echo through what must have been a cavernously large hall inside. There was a long wait, during which I banged the knocker again.

The woman who finally answered had a bath towel wrapped around her head. She was wearing a leopard-print dress that looked painted on, though her face put her somewhere in her fifties. She was holding a mascara wand in one hand and her expression said that although she was annoyed at being called to the door in the middle of getting dressed, she was too well bred to say anything about it.

Rich. Very. *You can tell*, I thought again. Then I said, "Mrs. Lancaster? I'm the plumber. Nicky Biglietti."

If she was surprised to see a female plumber, she didn't show it. She invited me in and I followed her through the enormous entrance doors and down the hall. The brownstone's ceilings were a good twelve feet high, and the walls were covered with big, imposing oil paintings in fancy gold frames. Beneath them, lots of antique furniture that looked like the real deal was strewn about.

I followed Mrs. Lancaster up a curving flight of stairs. The way she carried herself reminded me of Charlotte—she took up space like she knew the space liked her taking it. You could practically see the air molecules stepping aside to make room for her. It's a money thing, I think. I followed her through the master bedroom, past an enormous boat of a bed that might have been teak, and finally reached the bathroom door.

"We had a plumber in here just a month ago," she said, stepping aside, "and now the sink's clogged again. She looked at me and smiled. "I couldn't be shedding that much hair, could I?"

I glanced at the towel on her head. "I don't know," I replied, "I haven't seen your hair."

She reached up and pulled the towel off. Dark gold locks, still damp, fell down around her face and rested on her shoulders. I thought for a second about touching a curl. Her hair was thick and wavy and smelled somehow of damp grass.

"Well?" She caught my gaze and held it. I wasn't expecting that, and I looked away.

"I don't know," I said. "I'm just the plumber."

She turned away too then, and her stockinged feet padded out of the room. A moment later I heard the sound of a blow-dryer.

The clog in the drain was hair all right, but something else too. When I pulled my snake out, a thin line of gold was tangled around the end of it, a necklace impossibly knotted up among a tangle of drain-colored hair that might have once been her shade of blond. There was a pendant strung on the chain, a gold heart with one small, clear stone set in it. It looked like the kind of necklace a teenage girl would wear, not a woman in her fifties, but on the other hand, Mrs. Lancaster was doing the leopard-print dress pretty well, not to mention the eye contact. I rinsed off the tangle of hair and chain, and when I did, little flickers of rainbow fire shot out from the jewel in the pendant.

I stuck my head out the door and called to her and the sound of the blow-dryer stopped.

"Look what I found," I said, holding up the necklace as she came back into the bathroom. "It's not every day I get to fish a diamond out of a drain."

She looked at the pendant without touching it. I couldn't say I blamed her. There were still bits of rusty hair tangled in the chain, and the whole thing looked mousy and sad and wretched. She examined it and then she touched her own hair. Now that she had dried it, it was the pale gold color of a little girl's. A very good dye job can do that. She ran her fingers through her hair and the smell of her hair gave way to the scent of her perfume—something with musk in it, the real kind.

"You found that pendant in my drain?" she asked.

I grinned. "I bet you didn't even know it was missing."

She took her bottom lip between her teeth for a moment. "I didn't," she said. "Especially since it isn't mine." And she turned and walked out of the room.

I'm not dumb but it took me the whole time I was putting away my tools and wiping down the sink and washing my hands with some of her very nice sandalwood soap before

I figured it out. I don't suppose there's a good way to find out you've been cheated on, but if there is, the plumber fishing another woman's diamond pendant out of your bathroom drain isn't it.

I found her in the kitchen, writing a check.

"I left the necklace on top of the toilet," I said. "Maybe you can flush it down—accidentally, of course."

She looked up at me and by this time she'd got her smile back on. Not unlike diamond light, that smile.

"You're a quick study," she said. "Have you ever been married?"

"No."

"Cheated on?"

"Yes."

"Then you'll have a drink with me."

I didn't say anything. I didn't need to because it was a command, not an invitation.

"Bourbon all right?" she asked.

"Scotch, if you have it."

"Of course I have it." She opened a kitchen cabinet. "I knew," she said with her back to me, "that there were others. One after the other. But what I didn't know," she turned back toward me and handed me my glass, "is that he's been fucking this one in my bed."

I took a pull of the Scotch. It was even better than Charlotte's. Mrs. Lancaster knocked hers back in a gulp and poured another, then went to the refrigerator and held her glass under the ice maker.

"I'm divorcing him, you know," she said.

"Did you just decide this?"

"No, no. It takes me forever to decide anything. But this time I've had it."

I swirled more of the Scotch around in my mouth and inhaled. Wood smoke and leather, very smooth, and something sweet I couldn't place yet.

"I should have done it years ago. It's my house and my money. I don't need him. And he doesn't need me, clearly. Not when there are so many lovely young grad students running around."

"He's screwing his *students*?"

"Not *his* students. Richard's too smart for that. Nothing quite against the rules, nothing to interfere with his endowed chair. Nothing except me, maybe. But he's married to me, unfortunately, and that was perhaps not so brilliant on his part, but he's a brilliant man, my husband. Oh, yes. A brilliant gentleman and a brilliant *scholar*. It's too bad nobody listens to me—I've been saying things for years. But now I have evidence. Unless I'm just inventing the whole thing, of course. Out of spite. The *whole thing*."

Maybe it was humiliation and anger that was making her voice slide all over the place. Or maybe she was getting sloshed. I didn't say anything. I was just the plumber. She looked at me as if considering something, and then she leaned toward me and her hand came up and pulled gently at the collar of my shirt. I don't blush easily, but when her fingers grazed my neck I did. It was the scent of her. Then her hand came away again, a bit of pink fluff between her thumb and forefinger.

"You have a piece of cotton candy on you," she said.

"It's insulation." I held out my hand, and she laid it on my palm like a gift. Her hand was cleaner than mine would ever be.

"Being a plumber, you must get into some interesting places." She looked me straight in the eye as she said it. She seemed calm again. And very, very focused.

"I do," I responded evenly, but my cheeks flushed some more. She saw it. And she kept her eyes on mine.

"Tell me: what kind of places?"

"What kind of places?" I repeated.

It wasn't the first time this had happened to me on a job. Maybe it's because I'm a stranger in a person's private space—their bedroom, their bathroom—yet I'm also invited. I'm anonymous, yet intimate. It's a turn-on for some people, I guess. Including me.

"Places—places that can get very dirty," I managed. My face was burning up. I put some more Scotch in my mouth and breathed in again and leaned toward her. Wood smoke and leather, and dried cherries, that was it, and Mrs. Lancaster's musky perfume, and her burning sorrow, I could smell that too, and the smell of her mouth that would be a little smoky from the Scotch, and I leaned in toward her mouth and then I smelled something else, the faintest edge of sulfur, a smell that sent a little jolt of fear through me and knocked all the other jolts away.

I put down my glass. "You have a gas leak," I said.

She looked at me blankly.

"I smell gas. You have a gas leak somewhere in your house."

She sat back in her chair, affronted. "I don't smell anything."

"I have an excellent nose." Talk about a buzzkill. Even the greenest apprentice has heard stories of houses blowing up, entire buildings exploding, because of a gas leak. Sometimes it's equipment failure, sometimes a homeowner's bad handiwork. Sometimes it's the plumber's fault, and then careers and lives get ruined. I've seen it happen.

I sniffed the stove burners, opened the oven. Nothing there. "Is that the basement door?"

She nodded, and as soon as I opened it, the smell hit me

stronger. I grabbed my tool bag and went down the stairs without asking and began soaping the gas pipes with leak detector. Upstairs I heard a door close, but it wasn't the basement door. Then I heard Mrs. Lancaster say something, though she wasn't talking to me. Another door closing, another voice, distant. I kept soaping, and after a few minutes I found it: a leak at the union joint near the furnace.

There was a creak on the stairs behind me and a pair of shoes appeared. Not Mrs. Lancaster's size. These were big leather dress shoes, followed by khaki slacks, followed by a blue oxford shirt and a paisley silk tie and, finally, the face of Richard Lancaster, the guy who drills grad students in his wife's bedroom.

"Helene said you smelled gas," he said by way of greeting.

"I found the leak," I replied, since it seemed we were skipping introductions. Nicky Biglietti, the plumber who tries to kiss married women in their kitchens. "Look at this." Big rainbow bubbles were popping up through the leak detector suds.

He got down on his haunches, stiffly, so that his silver head was level with mine. He looked like someone who had an endowed chair: handsome face in a WASPy sort of way, his nose a little too long and bony, but smart blue eyes, good chin, hair that was silvering nicely. Aging but aging well, just like his wife.

"What are all those bubbles?" he asked.

"Soapsuds. If there's a leak, the escaping gas blows bubbles in it. If there's no leak, the suds just sit there—watch." I hoisted my wrenches, gave a turn of the union, and the bubbling stopped. "Now it's tight. I turn it the other way, the bubbles come back, see? Now it's tight again."

"I never smelled any gas leak," he said.

"Your wife didn't either. I'm guessing you don't visit your

basement much." I picked up my bag and started for the stairs.

"Do you often find gas leaks in houses you're working in?"

"It happens."

"Good way to get a little extra money out of the customer, I imagine."

I stopped on the bottom step. "The customer's already paid me," I said. I drew the check out of my breast pocket and unfolded it so he could see. "*Richard and Helene Lancaster.* I've met Helene, so you must be Richard. Mind if I call you dick?"

If I hadn't had the Scotch, maybe I wouldn't have said it. His face worked a little, but nothing came of it. He'd probably heard the crack a million times growing up, which made me feel not great.

"I checked out the gas leak as much for my sake as for yours," I said, attempting to move on. "I used to know a contractor who did sloppy work and blew up an apartment building. He's in jail now. Plumbing's a riskier job than you'd think—"

"I'm sorry," he said suddenly. He shifted in his dress shoes, uncomfortable. "We had another plumber here only last month about that same drain, and when it clogged again I thought maybe he hadn't done it right—you know, hoping for more work. I was still thinking of that when I said . . ." He stopped, embarrassed.

"Skip it," I said. "But he fixed it fine. The clog this time was a necklace."

He let out a huff of exasperation. "Helene should really be more careful."

And that was the point where I should have remembered something Charlotte used to tell me. That I have a smart mouth. Because if I hadn't said what I said next, maybe things would have been different. But I did say it. I stood on the bottom step, and because I am barely 5'2" and he was a nearly a foot taller, our eyes were almost level.

"Your wife said the necklace wasn't hers."

He frowned again. "Well, who else would it belong to?"

The words were barely out of his mouth when a kind of wrinkle passed over his face. I don't know how else to describe it. It was like a wrinkle on a bedspread that you smooth out with your hand until you come to the edge of the mattress and it disappears. It happened so fast it almost didn't happen: half a second later, his face was perfect again. A freshly made bed, everything tucked in just so. With no expression at all.

He looked away first. "Helene says a great many things," he said.

"I've heard some of them," I answered.

And the bed came unmade, just like that. His right eye started twitching and his mouth started to open and then closed up into a tight line instead. His eyes flew up to the door at the top of the stairs behind me and across to the furnace and back to me and I just stood there, not moving and not sure what I was waiting for. Her, maybe.

"You like her?" he asked me.

I hesitated.

"Because lots of people do. Or should I say, she likes a lot of people."

Maybe it was a game they played, each of them telling a stranger about the other's infidelities. But I'd had enough. I hoisted up my tool bag and started up the stairs.

"Wait," he said. "Let me pay you for your extra work on the gas pipe."

"Forget it," I replied over my shoulder. "It only took a minute."

"No," he said forcefully, "we're grateful you found the leak. I'd like to pay you."

"No need," I replied again, and before he could stop me, I was up the basement stairs and through a kitchen that was empty except for two half-drunk glasses of Scotch, and past a couple of living rooms or sitting rooms or whatever they were, and out the front door and gone. I was a little creeped out, to tell you the truth.

I had lunch at Sababa and was walking back to my van when I spotted Cal Watkins on the other side of Whitney. He wasn't wearing his plumbing clothes, which was unusual for a work-day, and he was carrying a bouquet of pink roses wrapped in cellophane, also unusual. I called out to him and he crossed over to my side.

"Nicky Big, what's up?"

"I'm freaked out from a job I just did. But look at you, fancy-dress man." Cal had on a pair of very new-looking blue jeans and a gray blazer. "You buy those flowers for me?"

"Meri's playing in her school concert. Are you busy? You should come with me—it's right there at ECA." He gestured toward a churchy-looking brick building at the end of Audu-bon Street. "You can tell me about your freak-out on the way."

"Are you kidding? Look at me, Cal. I'm filthy and I smell bad."

He sniffed in my direction. "I don't smell anything. Come on, Nicky. Meri's really good, and I'm by myself—Wanda couldn't get off work."

"All right, then." I've known Cal since plumbing school, almost ten years. I was the only woman in the class and he was the only black man, and after a few weeks of no one speaking to either of us, we began speaking to each other. He's older than me by a lot, and became a plumber after he got out of the Army, an experience he refuses to discuss. Like me, Cal works by himself, and we take turns calling on each other for favors.

We sat on the hard seats in the high school auditorium and I told Cal what had happened at the Lancasters'. By the end he was shaking his head.

"Nicky, Nicky, Nicky. Where do you find these people? The guy was trying to bribe you."

"What? When?"

"At the end, when he offered to pay you extra. Since when do rich people do that? It was so you wouldn't say anything about his girlfriends."

"I don't think so. His wife said she's been telling people for years and no one believes her."

The lights went down then, and a handful of teenagers walked onto the stage. I don't know anything about classical music. Cal had to remind me that the instrument Meri was playing was called a cello. But the way she played it made her the only person in the auditorium. The music seemed to be coming out of her body as much as out of the instrument. It made me stop thinking about everything that was swimming around in my head and just listen, as if nothing was happening anywhere except this girl and her music. It got to me.

When the lights came on we went over to her, and watching Cal hug his daughter I realized that "beaming with pride" is not just an expression. Light seemed to be radiating out of his dark eyes, his high cheekbones, his split-open grin.

"Meri, you remember Miss Nicky? She helped me put in our boiler last summer."

"Your playing was amazing," I said.

She thanked me politely, ducking her head down toward the roses, hiding a smile that was just like her dad's.

"I'm coming back tomorrow night to hear her again at the evening concert," Cal said. Wanda and me will *both* be here."

I left them then, excusing myself to go home and take a shower.

The next day was easier work. No drain cleaning, no dead mice, no accusations of infidelity. I had a couple of faucet in-stallations in Fair Haven, got lunch at El Coquí, and then drove over to Prospect Street to investigate a complaint about noisy pipes for a sweet old lady named Mrs. Berger. It was while I was in her basement that Richard Lancaster called.

"Sorry to bother you," he said, "but I still smell gas."

"From the furnace?"

"I don't know where it's coming from. Right now I'm standing in the living room."

No plumber likes a callback. Especially not a callback about a gas leak. And especially not from a customer you don't like. I could have told him to contact the gas company, but on the off chance I'd made some dumb mistake, I wanted to get back there myself and correct it.

"I'll be there in an hour," I said.

"I have to give a lecture in thirty minutes. Can't you come now?"

Some people think I have no customers but them. "No," I said. "I can't come now. I'll be there by three, but not sooner. Isn't Mrs. Lancaster there?"

"I don't know where Helene is. Look, I'll leave a key un-der the mat for you. An hour will be fine."

I tried to hurry up and finish at Mrs. Berger's. I found the bad washer and installed a new one, but when I went to turn the water back on, the main valve broke. It happens in old houses sometimes, and it meant Mrs. Berger would have no water until I replaced it. It would be another hour of work at least, maybe two. I went upstairs and broke the bad news to Mrs. Berger, and then I called Cal.

"Would you have time to do me a favor?"

"Right now I'm sitting in my truck on State Street eating a honey-glazed donut," he said. "But when I finish my donut, I might."

I explained about Richard Lancaster smelling gas.

"All right," he said, "but tell him who's coming." Cal is careful with white customers who don't know him. I know he's had trouble before, but he doesn't like to talk about it. He makes a point of wearing a very official-looking uniform, with *Watkins Plumbing* emblazoned across his jacket in big red letters. I, on the other hand, don't wear a uniform at all.

"I'll tell him," I said, "but he won't be there. The key's under the mat."

I left Mr. Lancaster a message on his cell phone, and for good measure I looked up their home number and left a message there too.

About twenty minutes later, Cal called back. I knew it was him because my cell phone said so. But I almost couldn't recognize the voice because I'd never heard Cal's voice an octave higher than usual and talking so fast he tripped over his words. It scared me just listening to him, because even without being able to understand him it was clear he was terrified.

"Slow down," I said. "Are you all right?" All I could imagine was that one of the Lancasters had been home and thought he was breaking in and pulled a gun on him, and what was I thinking, asking him to check on my customers for me when I knew shit like this could happen? That went through my brain in the half-second it took Cal to catch his breath.

Then he said, still high and fast, "Nicky, you got a fucking body over here, and gas pouring out the basement, and I called 911 and pulled her out but you better get over here NOW, I think she's dead, Nicky, and gas everywhere, oh, here they come."

He hung up, but not before I heard the sirens behind him.

I don't know how I made it there in one piece. I was shaking so bad I could hardly hold the wheel steady and I don't remember driving that half-mile, only that I didn't stop for lights and it was like one of those dreams where you're running but can't move, as if the air has turned into molasses and you're stuck in it. But somehow I was eventually parking behind an ambulance and two fire trucks and running toward the house where a group of firefighters was kneeling in a circle on the front lawn. I could see something on the grass in the center of that circle. Something gold, her hair in the sun, and that gold was the only bright thing on that lawn, almost lost among the dark heavy coats of the men around her. I ran toward her and it was like dream running. It took forever. One of the firemen stood up and then I saw she was lying on her back, and as I ran I saw the gash on her head, the blood drying in a rusty stain across her forehead and into her hair. One of her arms was flung out to the side as if she were pointing. Pointing at me. I ran toward her until someone called my name, and only then did I turn and see the police car.

It was parked on the far side of the fire trucks. There was a cop standing with his back to me, and in front of him, pinned between him and his cruiser, was Cal, jammed spread-eagled against the door, his face turned sideways against the vehicle's roof. The officer was patting him down.

"Nicky," he called again, and my legs worked and I ran up to them, yelling.

"Officer, stop!" I said. "Cal didn't do anything! I sent him over here, I'm the plumber, he's a plumber too, his name's Cal Watkins, see on his jacket, but it's not his job, it's my job, I asked him to check on my job for me, everything was fine yesterday, he didn't do anything, he just got here."

I went on like that while the cop put Cal in handcuffs and told him not to move. Only then did he turn and look at me. Crew cut, blue eyes, baby-faced, still young. We could have gone to high school together.

"Officer." My voice was really shaking. I took a breath and tried to focus. *K. Milner*, his name tag said. "Officer Milner. I was working in that house yesterday and I found a gas leak and fixed it. But the homeowner called me back and said he still smelled it. I was busy and I asked Cal to go. He has nothing to do with this."

"I *told* you," Cal said to the cop, his face still pressed against the top of the cruiser, "I found a lady laying at the bottom of the stairs in a house full of gas and I carried her out. I'm a *veteran*. I'm the one who called *you*."

Milner ignored this. He was looking at me. "You were working in there yesterday?" he asked.

"Yes, but I fixed the gas leak. They couldn't even smell it. I found it and I fixed it and I don't know what happened, but—"

"Nicky," Cal said hoarsely, "stop talking."

It was too late.

"Turn around," Milner said to me. "Hands behind your back."

I didn't move. A sick feeling broke over me like a wave and for a second I thought I might pass out.

"Why?" I asked.

"A lady's dead in a gas-filled basement and you've just admitted you're the one who worked on the gas." Milner's baby face looked harder suddenly. "Hands behind your back," he repeated. "You're under arrest for criminally negligent homicide."

I saw a flash of silver in his hands, and a flash of light zigzagging off the silver like the beginnings of a migraine. I'd never been in real handcuffs before, and they hurt.

He left us in the back of the cruiser while he went to talk to the firefighters. I was crying and shaking and couldn't stop doing either. Cal was silent and rigid beside me.

"Cal," I tried through chattering teeth, "I am so sorry."

"I don't need your apologies, Nicky, I need your lawyer."

"I swear there was no gas leak when I left yesterday. I tested it and everything."

"All I know is, I knock on that fancy door and nobody answers, I let myself in like you said, and the smell of gas is so bad my eyes water. I open the basement door and the gas just about knocks me over, and at the bottom of the stairs is a lady lying crumpled in a heap. So I run down the stairs coughing my lungs out and carry her out of there and dump her on the lawn and call 911 and now I'm in cuffs in the back of a cop car. Meri's concert is tonight, Nicky. Am I gonna see Wanda and Meri again?"

"Of course you are, Cal. I promise. It's my fault you—"

"It might be your fault, but you can't promise anything. Once they separate us down at the station, anything can happen. To me, not to you." He shook his head. "You don't know."

"I know I fixed that leak, Cal. I know I—"

"You think that matters? When a few months ago I'm working and a guy calls the cops and says there's a black man impersonating a plumber breaking into his neighbor's house? Lucky for me the customer was home to explain to the cops I was her actual fucking plumber, but you understand what I'm saying? *Anything* can happen, Nicky, to *me*. And right now I'm sitting here in cuffs for trying to save a lady I never saw before in my life. Am I gonna get out of this? Alive? That's on you."

I couldn't answer.

We sat there on the vinyl seats of the cop car, staring out the window, watching the paramedics load Helene Lancaster onto a stretcher. I saw again her blond hair smeared with blood as they covered her up.

We sat on the vinyl seats and I wanted to believe the cops would realize there was no way I could have left gas pouring out like that. And that Cal had nothing to do with it. And that the person who should really be arrested wasn't sitting in the back of the police car. I wanted to believe that Cal would be safe, that I would be safe. I like certainty. I wanted to look at the back of Milner's neck as he drove us downtown and feel certain that like me, he wanted to do a job he could be proud of, and that once he'd done it, if something wasn't right he would go back and fix it.

But I didn't feel certain at all.

Some things you can tell just by looking at a person.

Some things you can't.

A WOE FOR EVERY SEASON

BY HIRSH SAWHNEY

Dwight

I used to want to be a writer. But then life happened. Now I just teach. I'm a plain old high school English teacher. Nothing fancy, like Jenny and her academic friends—if you can call them friends, with all their backstabbing and five-syllable words. I sleep easy at night knowing I work at a real-deal public high school. Wilbur Cross on Cold Spring. I sleep easy despite the yes-men administrators and all that George W. Obama testing. But something happened the other day, a conversation with my old friend Josh Kagan. It worked me up and pissed me off. Jenny said, Talk it out, baby; I'm here if you wanna talk. I told her there was nothing to say, and she said, What a shocker. I said, Who's being passive-aggressive now? and then took off with Ralphie. When I got home, she'd already left for the library. The next morning, she's snoring when I roll out of bed. I go down to the kitchen and there's a brand-new leather notebook in a red bow on the counter—a granite countertop, mind you, yet another amenity made possible by Jenny's perfect job. A note on top says, *A little something to get it all flowing.* I shake my head and grin. Maybe she still cares. Maybe there's still hope for us. But this story isn't about me and Jenny. It's about Josh Kagan and James Farrell. It's about the three of us and a kid named Ink.

Me and Josh and James grew up a few miles away in the burbs. Lots of Catholics and Jews; Italians, Poles, and Irish.

And then there was my sore-thumb family, half-Muslim, half-Hindu, all curry. (Yes, Jenny, self-loathing trickles through my veins.) Now I live in the Westville section of New Haven, in a sweet little Cape Cod. A $240K mortgage with $60,000 down, mostly paid for by Stale University, the imperialist overlords of Elm City, thanks to Jenny's assistant professorship. We've got a hammock and a gas-powered grill, something my dad would have blown up if he'd pawed it with his immigrant hands. We've got a nice little patch of lawn that I cut with a hand-powered mower. And even though little Ralphie could easily do all his shitting and pissing at home, I take him for a long walk every morning. Ralphie's our little mutt—part corgi, part dachshund, all monster. Our miscarriage dog, I call him. Like so many of the couples around us—straight, in their thirties—we got him after Jenny lost a fetus.

So it's a Saturday, my least favorite day to walk the dog. All the doctors and lawyers and corporate warriors are out with their perfect pooches, all smiley and self-contented about living in such a beautiful area and having worked hard all week to make the world a better place. And they're starving for small talk. But I'm walking Ralphie anyway, because Jenny's presenting a paper at some coma-inducing conference. And who comes hulking toward me with his dopey, sweaty beast of a dog? Josh Kagan. Josh was one of my best friends between the ages of fourteen and eighteen. Despite his unabating addiction to Xanax and whiskey, he has recently come into a fair amount of cash working as a foreman at a company that installs solar panels on the roofs of gullible elderly suburbanites. Ralphie goes berserk on Josh's dumb-ass English mastiff, and Josh says something like, Guess you never ended up calling that dog trainer. I'm like, Josh, maybe if my dog cost five thousand dollars he wouldn't bark as much, and by the way, I still can't figure out how you managed to turn into such a fucking asshole. But of course I don't say that. What I really say, is, My Ralphie, he's still a bit traumatized from his shelter days. And guess what comes out of my mouth next: I say, Yo, if you got any training tips, I'm all ears. As soon as I utter those words, I want to barf my eggs and masala chai all over Josh and his dog, and Jenny's voice starts buzzing in my head. Maybe she's right. Maybe being the child of immigrants has me choking on my own shame. Nah, fuck her victimizing bullshit. All humans suffer, even the 1 percent.

Josh gets talking the usual sleepwalker middle-age crap. He'll move to Canada if Trump gets elected. He tells me I should have bought a two-family house; the rental market's gonna boom because middle-class people can no longer afford homes. And then he gets started on *the* topic, the one that lately leaves a lump in my throat, though I'd never say so to Jenny. He talks about his two chubby brats and how fast they're growing up. Next comes the state of the schools, as if he's a Noble Prize–winning educationalist. He says he hates to be *that guy*, but he's gonna switch his kids to private schools. He gets that it's wrong, but his hands are tied. I lie, tell him I get it, and this is a green light for him to putter down Racist White Guy Boulevard.

The thing is, Josh tells me, the New Haven public schools aren't like the ones we went to; the students in these schools are different. It's not their fault, he clarifies. It's their families. These families, they're not like ours. *They* don't care about their kids. *They* don't know how to support them. So the kids around here, *they* grow up like a bunch of *animals*.

I'm standing there staring at Ralphie, who has condescended to let Josh Kagan's dunce of a dog sniff his asshole. And I'm absolutely livid. I'm thinking, Josh, what you're really saying is that you think you're better than black people, but you don't even have the balls to say your ugly feelings out loud. I'm thinking, Do you remember how we grew up? Do you remember the things that we did? The tanks of nitrous oxide? The quarter-pounds of BC bud? What about what we got up to right here in New Haven, just a short walk away? Do you remember Ink? Do you ever think about him when you drive by the corner of Gilbert and Sherman in your tank-sized pickup? I must have started smirking or something, because Josh says, What's so funny? I keep this all to myself though and tell him I gotta run—wifey's waiting, or some sexist tidbit like that. As I walk away, he says, Yo, you talk to James lately?

James Farrell was the third member of our little posse, in and out of rehab for as long as I can remember. I didn't take his last couple of calls as I no longer have the stomach for quotations from the AA handbook or pipe-dream plans. Josh tells me that James is clean. Again. That he has a good job selling insurance. He even has a girlfriend. She's Thai and actually went to college. Ralphie's pissing on some freshly planted petunias. I yank the leash and shake my head. The thought of James Farrell in a dress shirt and slacks makes me wanna hurl for a second time. If one of my students did what he's done, you know what would happen to him? Kid would be rotting in a prison cell alongside ten thousand other black kids, stuck inside the slammer until he's too old to do any good or harm. I feel like punching Josh. I'd punch James, but then I'd actually have to see him.

I knew pint-size James Farrell well before I met gigantic Josh Kagan. His dad was an old-school New Haven Italian whose grandparents had worked the gun factories way back when. James's father made his money selling Cold War widgets for some forgettable corporation—the kind of deadening white-collar job that doesn't really exist anymore, which rewards talentless upper-middle-class white people for being just that. His mother was a dental hygienist who smiled all the time, ever since she found a Protestant Jesus. James and I coughed on our first Camel Lights together back in elementary school, lifted our first *Playboys* from the bookshop in the Post Mall when we were twelve or thirteen. Why did we fall head over heels for ganja, that five-fingered green goddess? I dunno. Pot was easier than booze. It was easier to get your hands on, and easier to transport with our parents driving us around. It was a hobby, an extracurricular activity—a sport for two kids who were scrawny, shy, and not especially good-looking.

Me and James Farrell, we liked each other's company because together we could embrace the goofiness and apathy that came so naturally to us both. And if I'm being totally honest with myself, it was easy to be around him because he was so passive. He was such a shy, quiet kid. He did have his talents—he could fix anything with his hands, from the carburetor on my rusty old Civic to his grouchy old Italian grandfather's hearing aid—but various undiagnosed learning disabilities condemned him to a high school career of Cs and Ds in level 3 classes. Let me come out and just say it then: being around Josh made me feel smart. Smart and in control.

James and I met Josh Kagan during the first couple weeks of tenth grade, when we were sparking up a shitty metal bowl full of seeds and stems underneath the bleachers at a high school football game. Josh said, Yo, you shrimps better share that shit, unless you want a beating. Or something along those lines. He was flashing his irresistible Judas Biden smile, so we hoped that he was joking.

Josh was my first Jewish friend, or my first good one at least. His ancestors had ended up in New Haven via Stalin's gulags and then London, or at least that's what he told us. Josh's father was an optometrist and his mother a realtor, and yet they were always broker than a junkie on payday. We're talking six credit cards perpetually maxed out and the power being shut off on more than one occasion. They squandered their dough on leather interiors for their luxury sedans, and saunas and hot tubs that Josh and us weren't even allowed to breathe on—things my good immigrant parents would never have dreamed of getting.

During Josh's ninth-grade year, before we'd even met him, he'd already tongued more than a hundred tabs of acid, and then he dropped out of school. When he returned for tenth grade, they placed him in the alternative high school, for kids who were less bright and more fucked up than he was. But he still read more than anyone else I knew, except possibly my own father. He got me hooked on Kesey and Kerouac. He got me thinking about what *Brave New World* had to say about capitalist America and its retarded culture of media. And the fact that he could talk so smoothly about books had a way of legitimizing all the illegal and immoral shit we got up to back then. James and books, though, were like oil and water. Yes, James might have been able to grow out his dirty white-boy dreads when my parents would have shit bricks if I'd have tried the same thing. He might have been game to try Special K when I was too scared. But James hadn't read a book since Dr. Seuss on the knee of his Jesus-loving mother.

Josh was 6'3" and handsome, and the girls, they really liked him. Even though he was crude and rude. Even though he'd deflowered several young women without ever speaking to them again. Yeah, Josh, he got lots of sex. Jenny insists his stories are boyish exaggerations. But they're not, and I know that for a fact. I used to wake up drunk in the middle of the night, on the floor of some kid's basement next to a Ping-Pong table, or the sofa of some kid's older sibling's apartment in the Taft Building—don't get me started on that racist bastard of a Supreme Court justice—and I'd see Josh sitting there getting a blowjob, or doing some girl from behind, and he'd give me that Biden grin. I'd smile back and shake my head, and for a few moments it was as if I were the one who was getting the girl. I, of course, never got the girl. Josh got girls, and even little James got laid by the second month of eleventh grade. But not me. The girls would be my friends, but they didn't want my body. Jenny used to say it's because I signified so differently from their pasty-ass fathers and brothers. That she would have wanted to jump my bones had she known me in high school. These days, she doesn't come close to jumping my bones. She says there's too much distance. That I oscillate between three modes of repugnant behavior: shutdown, passive-aggressive, and just plain mean. Unlike her, who has only one mode: ass-kissing schmoozer.

Forgive me for rambling. Old wounds run deep. The one thing you do need to know about Josh—Josh back then, at least—was that when he was around, you felt safe. You always felt like you were a part of something bigger, part of a weird newfangled family or something. (Or maybe it was more like a cult?) With Josh Kagan in our lives, James and I got to walk around our suburban school with a don't-even-think-about-fucking-with-us swagger. So when Josh suggested the three of us start selling a little pot to fund our weekends of beer and bong hits, neither one of us said, Really, Josh, do you think that's wise? No, in fact, I got a notebook from my L.L. Bean backpack and started crunching numbers, like the good subcontinental that I am. I figured that if we got an ounce of pot and sold half that ounce as eighths, and a few stray grams at ridiculously high prices, we could smoke the other half for free and still have some money to spend on ales and stouts, on cheeseburgers at Paulie's Lunch, where we ended most of our weekend nights. How's that for immigrant ingenuity?

We had a nice system going by the middle of eleventh grade. Before we met Ink down on Gilbert, there was this dealer, Nick DeLuca, who Josh called DeMookfuck. James's older sister Beverly used to date him, and now he was selling weight so that he could live large while taking classes at UNH, where my father taught civil engineering. DeMookfuck rented an old colonial on Fountain Street, near Dayton Street Apizza, which used to serve decent pie. Speaking of pie, let me be clear about something: I'm a Sally's man all the way, no corporate or soggy pie for me. The Stalies may put up with those two other spots, but not someone who knows their ass from their elbow when it comes to New Haven pizza.

Anyhow, our trio would stop by DeMookfuck's apartment on most Fridays. He'd smoke a bowl with us out of one of his many handblown glass pipes, which we found both impressive and cheesy. Then he'd front us an ounce of midgrade seedless greens. We'd sell the stuff cheap to a few friends, and rip off a few athletes or girls. The following week we'd bring DeMookfuck back his money, and he'd hand us over another fat satchel of pot. Once he'd gotten to know us, he'd always throw in a bonus. A small bag of mushrooms or little yellow pills that were allegedly made of THC. The funny thing about the whole situation was that after a while DeMookfuck only wanted to deal with me. He only made eye contact with me, and he would only accept cash from my hands. No wonder I got so deep in that world. It was the only club that wanted me, that didn't make me feel like some *Jungle Book* pariah.

Shit. That's Jenny's voice again. I wish I could get it to stop. The point is, our little business came to a standstill when DeMookfuck got busted. All he got was ten thousand hours of community service, probably because he was white. Back then the rumor was that he had ratted out some big dealers above him in exchange for a light sentence. All we were sure of that summer was that we couldn't even get our hands on a single nickel bag of Mexican schwag. We couldn't get stoned, and neither could our friends. We had no funds for our weekend antics. This got old after a couple of weeks, and eventually Josh says, Yo, Ray—that's me, it's short for Rehan—we should drive down to Gilbert Street to score some weed.

This was one of the worst I ideas I'd ever heard, but I just shrugged and said, Sure. Why not?

Gilbert Avenue is in West River section of Dwight, but for some reason, in the drug-addled suburbs where we grew up, the dumb-ass dope-smoking kids called it Gilbert Street. The other kids—the straight ones—didn't call it anything, because they didn't know it even existed. When they drove down Congress Avenue through that part of New Haven, they locked their car doors to avoid one of the mythic carjackings their parents had warned them about; their parents had learned about the carjackings from trashy movies like *Grand Canyon*. When I walk Ralphie around this neighborhood now, on one my forget-about-miscarriages-and-failing-school-systems walks, I can't help but gawk at its hundred-year-old homes, most of them Victorians, most decaying or in a state of total disrepair. You stare at these elegant monsters, and you think, What a utopia this all must have been. Where did it all go?

Why did it all vanish? America's best days have passed, but we all just showed up to the dance. And you wonder why Trump has gotten them so fired up.

Don't get me wrong, Dwight's a bit cleaner these days, thanks to a local mosque, which has slowly but surely spruced up the neighborhood. (What do you Trump fascists think about that?) You can tell that some bureaucrats have been holding meetings about beautification and development. I notice an attempt to rebrand parts of the neighborhood *West of Chapel,* or some Waspy shit like that. And there are also big posters of allegedly local celebrities hanging from neighborhood buildings. There's this one of Paul Giamatti, whose father was some bigwig at Stale. I can't help but roll my eyes when I see Giamatti's ugly mug grinning down upon the streets of Dwight. If I was a kid from the ghetto, I'd throw a bucket of paint on that face. I'd throw a bucket of the paint on the dumb bureaucrats who used taxpayer money to put up those bloody posters.

Stale University will probably wanna take some credit for cleaning up the area, though no bona fide New Havenite would agree with them. Stale, for example, recently took over St. Rafael's Hospital, where yours truly slithered out into this world, and now the snotty Stale crest—a shield with the words *Light and Truth*—has been ironically stamped onto the placard in front of the place. My neighbor, who has a tough little beagle with a missing leg, is a nurse at St. Raf's; she tells me that things have gone from dawn to dusk since the coming of Stale—that the university has no respect for its employees or their wisdom. You see, we are all really sick of our tax-exempt imperialist overlords here in New Haven. But when they get wind of our words, what do they say? They say, Quiet down, plebs of New Haven; the gold in our East India Company coffers is what keeps you from becoming Bridgeport. And if you're batting above double digits in the IQ department, you'll have to admit that the Stale folks have a point.

Back in the day, when we got up to no good down in Dwight, things were much worse. It was on the corner of Gilbert and Greenwood that I saw my first real-life prostitute. It was a total shock to me that she looked nothing like Julia Roberts. It was down by the delis on Dwight, where we'd stop to buy Snapples or rolling papers after scoring, that I learned that food stamps looked nothing like actual postage—that those fake flowers—the ones that come in little glass vases—they're not for decoration, they're crack pipes.

The first time we go to buy drugs down on Gilbert, my hands get cold and clammy as I steer the Civic across Ella T. Grasso Boulevard, which marks the unofficial end of suburbia. I know this is all wrong. I know we're gonna get busted and I can imagine my stern-eyed immigrant father picking me up at the police station in one of his dust mite–infested tweed jackets, one with patches on the elbows. Josh tells us we got nothing to worry about though. He says they only bust dealers. I say, Yeah, Josh, but don't we sell drugs? Little James chimes in here, says, Kid, we're not real dealers. I'm outnumbered, I have no choice but to keep on driving. I pull up to a corner where a bunch of black kids are standing—some are older than us, but a few haven't even hit puberty yet. This is all sad and troubling, but I don't do much thinking about social ills at this point in my life. No, racist little me is waiting for a gun to be pointed at my face. For sirens to start wailing. Josh rolls down his window, and one of the older black kids approaches. He says, I got dimes and nickels, what do you want? Josh hands him two tens rolled up in a tight cylinder. I turn to my left, and a twerpy little black kid is standing there looking at me with a no-nonsense face. I think, This is it. This is when they rob us. The dealer on Josh's side says, Yo, white boy, roll down your window. It takes me a few seconds to realize he's talking to me, but then I roll down my window a few inches, and the little hopper outside throws two tiny bags onto my lap. The bags are blue and stuffed fat with schwag. The older guy, the main dealer, says, We all good then?

Josh says, I got a question for you, homey.

Oh yeah, *homey,* says the dealer. And what's that?

I'm not thinking about Josh's inappropriate use of the word, about how the dealer called him out on it. All I can think about is how cool and great Josh is. I'm like, How can he be so natural right now? Where did he learn how to do this? My fear fades, and I'm just proud—proud that Josh Kagan has agreed to let me be a part of his life. It feels like being friends with a movie star.

Josh says, I'm wondering, brother, can you get us some weight?

The dealer says, Kid, next time you're down here, come straight to me. Ask for Ink, that's what they call me. We don't do weight, but I'll take good care of you.

We got to know Ink well that summer. Or maybe that's not accurate. I never did learn anything about his parents, if he had any brothers and sisters or anything. But I did find out that he was eighteen years old, because on his eighteenth birthday—July 4—he gave us an extra nickel bag of *something special,* free of charge. After a while, whenever we showed up on Gilbert, the hoppers would start yelling, Go get Ink! or, Ink's white boys are here! before we'd even rolled down our windows.

Doug E. Fresh high-top fades were still popular among black men back then, but Ink's head was totally shaved. He had a quarter-sized blotch of a birthmark on one of his cheeks, I can't remember which one, but I'm assuming that's where he got his nickname from, though I never had the balls to ask. He wore two pieces of jewelry around his neck: a ropelike silver chain and a black leather string with a few beads on it, beads that had something to do with Rastafari, I think. Ink was a bit overweight, and he always had a smile for us. We'd sell his five-dollar nickels of schwag—which Josh said got you fucked up because they were dipped in something funky, maybe formaldehyde—for twenty bucks to the kids in the burbs. Which meant we were on easy street again, smoking and drinking for free, with plenty of money to spend on Sally's pie or Paulie's burgers.

We'd be so baked by the time we got to Paulie's that Donny, the owner's son, would say, You clowns, in the back right now, pointing toward a dimly lit room reserved for parties and VIPs. It's not that we were important; he just wanted to keep us away from the cops who frequented his business. We'd go back there and pound the cans of Guinness we'd smuggled in, smiling and laughing at nothing whatsoever. We felt so alive, that we knew so much more than everyone else about the world—more than the people on the news, our teachers, our parents. They were all living on the surface; we were down deep in the fucking marrow.

Ink would always have a word for us about that music that was playing in my car. He once said, *Sgt. Pepper's Lonely Hearts*. Now there's something I can dig.

I remember being surprised that a young black guy listened to the Beatles. I remember being surprised that he even knew who the Beatles were. I'm not proud of my gerbil-brained perspectives. But you develop strange and distorted notions of black people when you grow up in a whiter-than-snow world.

Especially when you're the only brown kid there. Ink didn't like the Grateful Dead. He called them a bunch of thieves. But he was impressed when I once had a Miles Davis CD playing on my portable Panasonic Discman.

The next time we came down, just two days later, he dropped a cassette on my lap with the words *Bitches Brew* on the label in neat, bubbly handwriting. He said, You fucking white boys gonna bust a nut for this shit. His gift made me smile, but what really had me pumped was that he kept on calling me *white boy*. I was so pleased that he couldn't smell the curry wafting from my pores. That to him I was just another white kid from suburbia.

It's been six whole days since I've written a single word. Thanks to Jenny. Fucking Jenny. She read my notebook, a gift she had supposedly given to me so that I could have a place to dispose of my most private and perturbed thoughts. What did I expect? Privacy is the purple unicorn of the land of long-term relationships. I walked into the kitchen, and there she was, gawking at my prose. I said, What the fuck are you doing? Nothing, she said. I knew her brain was going wild with opinions and criticism, so I told her to just come out and spill it. She said, Things seem to stop working when I say what I really think. And don't swear at me. She was giving me that squinty-eyed glare to let me know I'd fucked up, and all I could think was: You read my private shit, and *I'm* supposed to be sorry?

She sighed, then told me she was proud that I'd picked up my pen. Relieved that I was finally opening up about the miscarriage. She said, If you want this marriage to last, you're gonna have to start dealing with that. I slapped my hand against my forehead. Marriage? Miscarriage? Jenny, I said, I wrote something about James and Jimmy and how they're a bunch of assholes.

For the next part of her speech, she switched into cold, condescending professor mode. She was impressed, she told me. Impressed that I was finally willing to take an honest look at my childhood. Impressed that I was—and here's some classic Jenny bullshit—willing to finally look at the way being an immigrant exacerbated my feelings of teenage marginalization. And you did that with a nice touch of subtlety, she said. Her praise stopped there though. Surprise, surprise, she had big problems with Ink. She said, New Haven is filled with middle-class black families going about their business, trying to make ends meet. Why'd you choose to make your black character a drug dealer? Why do you have to perpetuate that stereotype? And there was more. Why did Ink have to be into music? Why did Ink have to *teach* you something about music? Can't you see how you're exoticizing him? Haven't you ever heard of the magical Negro trope?

What the fuck?

I wanted to tell Jenny that this wasn't a piece of fiction—it was the goddamned truth. Ink was real, so how could I change him? And if Ink being a drug dealer is a problem, it's not my problem. It's society's problem. It's a big bummer that the only way three well-heeled seventeen-year-olds from the suburbs can interact with a black kid from New Haven is through a financial transaction involving drugs. But at least the three of us—Josh, James, and me—we were pushing past our boundaries. Do you think the captain of our football team had anything to do with black kids from New Haven? Do you think our school's honor society had any black members? We were integrating, I'd like to think. We were experiencing a form of multiculturalism that some pole-up-her-ass lit professor could only dream of.

Well, Jenny, there was this one time when we did try to take our relationship with Ink beyond the realm of commerce. One Friday that August, we drove down to Gilbert as usual, and it was nasty out. Humid, hazy air hanging over the asphalt, you couldn't imagine that snow would coat these roads in just a few months. A couple of hydrants had been opened up, and all the city kids were jumping in and out of the spraying water. We'd only seen that in the movies, even though we lived six miles away; people cooled down in their pools out where we lived. Ink was at the corner with his hands on his wide hips and wearing a Red Sox cap. It was as if he was waiting for us, and he probably was—he definitely enjoyed the chitchat, and we were his best customers.

Once the day's transaction was over, Ink said, So, ladies, any big plans this weekend? Josh said, Actually, there's a party going on tonight, right here in New Haven. Ink said, A party? With actual people? I thought you guys just sat around getting high. Josh said, Yo, why don't you join us, Ink? I'll get you a little piece of blond pussy. As I write this, I remember being mortified by Josh's statement—no, Jenny, not the fact that he had spoken about females in that despicable manner. But that he had so openly alluded to the race thing.

Later that night, we headed back to New Haven, to the East Rock section, an apartheid neighborhood mainly filled with Stalies. Close to a million bucks for a Victorian these days, and twenty thousand in taxes. Pay attention, Donald Trump: You don't need real walls in postindustrial America. The economics of it all puts up perfectly suitable metaphoric ones. I should be honest though: I may mock those ponce East Rock phonies, but the second Jenny gets her tenure, I'm gonna use her raise to get us into a sweet two-family on the right side of Orange Street.

So this kid Fran—Greg Franford—was having a party, because his Stale professor parents were away for the weekend. Fran went to Snobkins, an ancient and prissy New Haven private school, and Josh knew him from Jewish camp. His dad was a real hotshot in the history department, and I actually read one of his books a couple of years ago—your basic justification for the righteousness of Euro-American rape, plunder, and pillaging, which is no surprise; that's how academics earned their keep in the eighties. These days it's the total opposite. You get promoted by talking about the undeniable awfulness of white people. Two sides of an elite and simplistic coin. I'm finding it harder and harder to fathom how Jenny can dedicate her life to all that drivel. Maybe that's the problem. She still has faith in me, in what I do and who I can be. But I look at her and her colleagues and I see them for what they are—a bunch of conniving, careerist drones. They don't care about art. About knowledge. They just care about grant money. About keeping their jobs and fertilizing their CVs.

So about twenty, twenty-five kids are smoking up and drinking down in Fran's father's mahogany-laden, enormous third-floor library, which has ornately framed paintings of dead white men on the walls. There's also a painting of some natives near a bunch of huts, and someone tells me it's a million-dollar painting by some guy named Gauguin. I don't give a shit about art. I'm just worried that someone's gonna see the link between my curried ass and those natives in the painting. Some cool dub music is playing, stuff that Fran probably picked up on a fancy teen tour in Paris or Amsterdam, stuff that me and my crew wouldn't get our hands on for another decade or so. I'm sitting on an ancient Persian rug, rather awestruck by all these good-looking, cool, and precocious kids—boys *and* girls. Josh, James, and I have two friends who are girls—Caron and Olivia. They're pretty, but total alcoholic waste products. Olivia, for example, thought she was pregnant in ninth grade—perhaps with Josh's baby—so she drank an entire case of Natural Light to force a miscarriage. These girls here are different. They're talking about French movies and punk concerts at underground clubs in New York City. James is next to me, packing bong hits for them, and they're willing to talk to us so that they can ingest our free weed and learn how to work James's TobaccoMaster. And then Josh walks in with Ink and a friend of Ink's who I've never seen before.

I'd like to tell you that our attempts at socializing together went well. Maybe some literary journal would publish this story if I lied and said that we got together for a hike and found a sliver of something in common despite being from different sides of the tracks. But that's not the way life works. That's not the way it happened.

Ink is wearing an untucked polo shirt and a sun visor, the kind of thing someone would wear playing golf. His friend is tall and skinny, wearing a Malcolm X T-shirt and surprisingly tight-fitting jeans. I watch Josh introduce these kids to our host, Fran, who greets them with smiles and half-hug handshakes. Ink takes out a fat blunt, sparks it up, and passes it to Fran. Ink's Malcolm X friend leaves the library. I'm wondering where he's gone. Fran, Ink, and Josh are passing the blunt back and forth without talking, and slowly, the chatter of the party dies down. Everyone's staring at them or trying really hard not to. I have to help be a host, I think. Josh has the balls to make Ink feel at home, so I should too. I get up, slap him five. I don't know what to say away from Gilbert Street, so I'm like, Ink, mad kids here wanna buy bud; you're gonna make some serious cash tonight. He raises one of his eyebrows and gives me a glance that I can't really read, then places a hand on my shoulder. He says, Ray, no business tonight. Tonight's about having fun.

And then everyone loosens up for a while, and it looks like, for a bit at least, tonight's gonna be okay. A group of boys and girls start dancing in a corner of the library, and I wish I could join them. But I just stand beside Ink and keep on smoking. Some white girls go up to Ink and his friend and flirt with them. Josh has his arm dangling over Ink's shoulder at one point. But then I see something weird out of the corner of my eye. Fran is whispering in Josh's ear all seriously. Fran's blue eyes are sharp and angry. Josh is listening intently, and he keeps brushing his brown locks behind his ear. That's what he does when he's nervous, which isn't often, at least that's what I used to think at the time.

Josh comes over to us and says, Look, Ink, Fran knows about the car. Ink says, What car? Some dumb-ass model car, Josh tells him, then pauses. I can tell he's trying to choose his words wisely. Josh says, Some dumb-ass model car that's gone missing. Ink says, Oh, a model car's missing. What's it gotta do with me?

My cotton mouth goes from New Mexico to the Sahara desert. I'm waiting for Ink to get belligerent; if Josh were in his position, he would definitely get belligerent. But Ink shouts, in a loud but calm voice, Hey, Franfuck!

Everyone stops talking and stares at Ink. I look over at little James, who's still on the floor with the TobaccoMaster between the legs of his corduroys, which have been stitched up with paisley hippie patches. We exchange a commiserating glance. I think, James and I, we feel the same thing right now. We're both afraid of Ink, but we both feel bad for him too. In that moment, I feel closer to James than I have ever felt before.

Ink says, Franfuck—that's your name, right? You got something to say to me? Fran says, Why don't we take this outside? Outside? says Ink. You wanna fight me? Fran tells him that he doesn't want to fight. He just wants to talk. In private. Ink says, I got nothing to talk about with you. Fran looks down, grasps his neck, looks back up. Fran says, Yo, you can't be disrespecting people like that in their own homes. Says, I know people, people you don't wanna be messing with.

I'm wondering what the hell Fran is talking about. The toughest kid that this Snobkins son-of-a-Stalie knows is Josh Kagan. Ink looks dead serious. I can practically see the smoke coming out of his ears. I'm sure he's gonna do something. Charge at Fran. Pull out a knife. A gun. But he just lets out a disgruntled scoff. Shakes his head, takes off his cap. And leaves without saying a word. His tall skinny friend follows behind him. After they leave, I find out Fran's famous father collects die-cast model cars, and his favorite one, a Rolls-Royce Silver Ghost, has disappeared.

The vibes are horrible at the party now, so me and my posse decide to leave. We get in my Civic, and since we're in New Haven, we head toward Paulie's for a couple of quick cheeseburgers to lift our spirits. As we're driving, Josh, who's in the backseat, says he feels rough, that he needs a quick bowl to chill out. He grabs James's Jansport, but James starts bugging out. Says, Yo, pass me my bag, I'll pack it up for you. But James can't stop Josh, who's digging around the bag looking for a lighter. But Josh doesn't find a lighter. Instead he pulls out a model car, Fran's father's pint-size Rolls-Royce. Josh says, Are you fucking kidding me, James? You little fucking rat. James says, Fran's a fucking prick; he deserved it.

I wish I could write about how Josh explained to James that it was wrong of him to let Ink take the blame, that

James was torn up with guilt for the rest of the night. But none of that happened; we just drove in silence. When we got to the Green, which was desolate except for the sleeping drunkards and crazies, Josh rolled down his window and chucked the Silver Ghost onto the sidewalk, in front of one of those ancient churches.

I didn't want to write in this diary ever again. Writing's stupid. All it does is make you feel important for a second, when you're really not. But then that decision came out, about the fat black guy in Staten Island. Eric Garner. And I felt so deeply bad about it. How could I tell my kids—my students, that is, because Jenny and I don't have any kids—how could I tell my students to dream and hope and try when Eric Garner got murdered and his society said, Too bad you were black, better luck next lifetime.

I broached the subject in my first-period class yesterday, and more than half of them hadn't even heard of Eric Garner. A few of the girls were aghast, though, and talked about making the world a better place. I smiled and nodded and tried to make them feel that I felt what they were saying. But a voice inside of me wanted to tell them, Girls, don't even bother trying. One of my kids, Anthony—super smart and always getting into trouble—he says, Teacher, this isn't anything new. Cops been beating on black folk since the beginning of time.

Now I definitely don't have a problem with policemen. My neighbor's a cop and he's the most helpful guy in the world. Votes Democrat, opposes the NRA, which is the most you can hope for someone in this fucked-up postindustrial world. But Anthony was right. And the first time I learned the truth he was speaking was the last time I ever saw Ink.

The last time we ever saw Ink was during the second week

of our senior year, a Friday in September. Since that East Rock party at Franfuck's house, we'd been down to Gilbert two or three times. Things had definitely cooled with Ink. He still sold to us, still cut us the deal that had been previously arranged. But there were no niceties anymore. No more chit-chat about food, music, or girls. It was an unpleasant change, but we got used to it quickly. As we rolled into Dwight that Friday, I didn't notice anything strange in the air. I didn't think that the gray van parked at the end of the block in front of a boarded-up Victorian was at all conspicuous. There were a couple kids throwing a football on the sidewalk. A cracked-out prostitute hobbled down the street in high heels, hopefully on her way to a shelter. I was ready for some fun after a boring week of my AP classes, and I honestly wouldn't have wanted to be anywhere else in the world besides Gilbert Street with my boys Josh and James. I no longer felt any nerves about copping drugs down here. Anything becomes normal when you do it with some regularity. That's why immorality is the norm, not the exception. That's why genocide occurs.

Ink comes to Josh's backseat window. Josh hands him the money, just two twenty-dollar bills today. They mutter a few words to each other, and Ink's little helper drops the baggies of marijuana onto James's lap. Ink starts walking away. And then there's a boom, the sound of the rear door of that gray Chevy van bursting open.

Three plainclothes cops jump out. They're wearing bulletproof vests; their medallions are dangling around their necks by strings of beads. Oh fuck, I think. Oh fuck, I really am fucked. I can still remember my childish, selfish thought processes so clearly. My father is going to find out about my secret life, the life that I have so carefully kept hidden. He is going to have a heart attack. He will die. My mother and sister will be sad and alone. They'll be all alone, and I'll have to care for them. If only I knew then how the justice system works in this country. If I knew then what I know now, I would have realized I had nothing to worry about.

One cop stands in front of my Civic and yells at us to stay put right where we are, hands on our heads, of course. Meanwhile, the other two cops pin down Ink. They grind his face into the gravel, give him a few kicks to the gut. His face puckers from the pain. It looks like he's howling, but no sound comes out. That's what happens when you get the wind knocked out of you, though maybe you haven't gotten the wind knocked out of you since your days of playground tom-foolery. Our cop joins the other two, and it doesn't seem at all weird to me that he has left us unattended. Together the three cops rough Ink up for what seems like a long while. But it's probably just a minute. Then they stand him up and cuff him, and he's all coughing and drooling.

I sit there frozen, barely breathing. I'm wondering if I would rather die than face my parents at a police station. I look around and see how I might be able to end everything right now, but the only people with any deadly weapons are the cops. Josh says, from the backseat, Throw the bags out of the car; get rid of them. But thankfully I know better than to listen to him in this moment. Josh reaches over my seat to grab the pot, and as soon as he does, our cop is back. And this time his gun is out. He's telling Josh to freeze. He says, Out of the car, you dumb fucks, and keep your hands on your head. We get out, he pats us down. He tells us to keep our hands on the hood of my Civic. The hood is burning hot, but we have no choice but to keep our hands there. I glance around and notice a whole bunch of people are star-ing at us like we're the worst people in the world—not just the hoppers and prostitutes, but a grandmother with a baby carriage.

Our cop grabs the dime bags from the car. I don't see what he does with them. He grabs all my Grateful Dead and Phish bootlegs, even the *Bitches Brew* CD from Ink. He dumps them on the road and crushes them with his black boot. He takes out my Panasonic portable CD player, a birthday gift from my parents, and does the same thing with it. I'm thinking he's gonna go for our backpacks, which have all sorts of booze, bongs, and bowls in them, but he lets them sit there. I shoot a glance at Ink. His cheeks are bloody, covered in sand, and he keeps on bending over and spitting out blood. He looks at me for a second, then goes back to his coughing and spitting.

The two cops with Ink are white and black. Our cop is white, but he might have a touch of color in him. He gets very close to my face. I can smell his stale breath, and yes, it does smell like coffee. He says, Listen very clearly. You little shits are gonna get in that shitty car. You're gonna get the fuck out of here and never come back. And if I ever see any of you little brats again, you'll be shitting from your mouth and pissing from your assholes for the rest of time.

Ink stops his coughing and stares at us. He says, You're letting them go?

The cop who's standing behind him and holding his cuffed wrists pulls something out—a bobby club maybe, I can't really remember. All I know is that he pulls something out and whacks Ink hard across the face with it. And then on his chest. Ink keels over again, gritting his teeth and growling. We get in our car and drive away. And we never go back to Gilbert Street to score drugs.

I sometimes wonder what happened to Ink. Did he straighten out? Become a music producer? Stranger things have happened. But we all know the statistics. We all know that the sociologists' models predict something different.

There was a time last year after some book came out when Jenny's colleagues would talk about the prison-industrial complex at their eighteen-dollar-bottles-of-wine cocktail parties. They talked about the undying legacy of Jim Crow, something they might have read about but never actually experienced. During these Stalie convos, I took long sips of beer and tried not too think too hard about Ink and those fucked-up years. Luckily for me, all this talk only lasted a couple months—a surprisingly long time for these people. Soon they were onto a new topic. Syrian refugees maybe? Or no, it was the plight of Mexican tomato farmers. In Jenny's world, there's a woe for every season.

SURE THING

BY DAVID RICH

Long Wharf

I f a leopard had strolled up the stairs and into the big room, or a giggling leprechaun had slid down a light beam, the reactions of the patrons at Sports Haven could not have been any stronger. Friends, who had sat next to each other through countless losses and victories and drinks and smoke breaks but never knew the color of each other's eyes, checked now for confirmation that the vision was real and to show their own special, personal appreciation of it.

She was shorter than I expected, and leaner, but the muscle definition was there in her arms and her stride was long and cushioned. I turned away as she approached the bar, checked the ice for anything that needed killing, checked the glasses for the weather—partly cloudy—but that only took a few seconds. I didn't have to check her progress anyway—I could watch Lou and Jerry at the end of the bar, as gape-mouthed and riveted as kids at the finish line at Saratoga.

At the sound of the chair scrape I turned and slid a napkin in front of her and met her eyes: blue, but not cool and not calm, and I was thankful for that flaw.

"Hi. What would you like?"

"What kind of wine do you have?"

"The kind that used to be red when I opened it three weeks ago and the kind that used to be white."

"When was that one opened?" She had a way of playing straight as if she was confident of a payoff.

"No one is sure. It's just always been here. Like them." I nodded toward Jerry and Lou, each holding onto his beer for stability.

"Pour me something I won't remember," she said. "Maybe you have a specialty."

I held up a bottle of Bud. She smiled and shrugged, then turned on the stool to look around. The eyeballs did not seem to bother her. I opened the bottle and placed a glass beside it. She asked to run a tab and said, "That the only door?"

"The only entrance. There's a back way out through the kitchen if you need it."

"I'm meeting someone."

I knew who she was and suddenly it seemed important not to let her know that. I remembered seeing her in *Transmission*, *Stiletto*, and *I Can't Help You*, all of them on DVD while killing time at various spots around the Middle East. None more recent than five years ago. In the movies, Addie Tarrant wore thigh-high boots with six-inch heels and eyelashes almost that long, and delivered devastating kicks to guys who just couldn't decide to shoot her quickly enough. She drove fast, wore shiny dresses with slits up the side, flirted with confidence and impunity, and mastered many exotic and arcane weapons. She posed in colorful wigs. She purred.

She looked around for a moment, then said, "I've had a house in Connecticut, just down the road, for five, six years, and never knew we had off-track betting. I suppose most of the towns would rather we didn't know."

"Well, there're casinos up the road and hedge funds down. This is just sort of a rest stop. I suggested they put that on the sign, but . . ."

The place sat next to I-95. It had been built for smokers, a big barn with a thirty-foot ceiling that dwarfed the enormous screens lining the catwalk and walls. Not that it mattered: the world's biggest screen, curved with ten trillion pixels, wouldn't have moved the plungers to a show of awe or appreciation. No matter the size of the presentation, they managed to find the exact dose of hope and disappointment required to keep them upright.

Jerry signaled for another beer. I brought it and said, "That's number five, Jerry."

"Thanks, Pete. Listen . . ." Instead of grabbing the beer as he usually did, he grabbed my wrist. His watery eyes oozed hope, the way they did when he touted a horse based on his great insight and drunken perspicacity. "That's your girl, right?"

I shook my head. "But leave her alone anyway, Jerry."

"Really?" He turned to Lou. "She went right to him."

"That's number five, Jerry."

He nodded, obedient now because of my apparent magnetism, and limped to the men's room. The signal inside him had been permanently muted, and a bartender who relied on Jerry's own tally was usually sorry.

Addie Tarrant had barely touched her beer. I offered to replace it. She shook her head. "Can you show me how to bet?"

"Sure. There're two ways to do this: you can open an account and place bets using your phone, or you can use cash."

"What do you recommend?"

"Are you lonely enough to want to spend five or six hours on the phone with a guy not named Joe Smith in Mumbai?"

"So, cash?"

The screen to my left showed the feed from Santa Anita. Next to it was Golden Gate Fields. I laid out a racing form and turned to the Santa Anita pages. The fourth was going off in a few minutes. I began explaining how to read the form, check the past results, the class, the opening odds versus the real-time odds on the screen, the jockey and trainer standings.

She was watching me.

"Or you could simply choose a name you like. It works just as well."

"I'd like to pick a sure thing," she said.

"Doesn't exist."

"One of them is going to win."

"You're an optimist. There are no winners. There are horses that pay off, but the money just goes back in the system. You just prolong the agony."

"A philosopher too."

I walked her over to the teller and she bet a hundred dollars on Holyshirt to win. The odds were 25–1. As she slid over the money and waited for the ticket, she put her hand on my arm as if to steady herself.

"What do you usually do for good luck?"

"I kiss the ticket." I hesitated and said unhappily, "I never told anyone that."

She kissed the ticket and then made me do it.

"Do you really do that?" she asked.

"No."

She looked me up and down as if she were considering casting me in one of her B movies. "You're confident, aren't you?"

"Not enough to keep me from wondering where that came from."

"Too strong? It's just that I'm around people faking it for a living, so when I see the real thing, I'm impressed."

Real or fake, the openness and honesty was drowning my skepticism. Maybe she was a better actress than she was given credit for. When we turned we bumped against each other. She was looking at the ticket and I was looking back at the bar, so I saw the guy she was waiting for before she did. He was short, about her height. Muscles under a T-shirt and a tight cream-colored sport coat. His hair was carefully tousled.

He stopped and waited until she spotted him. She went to him quickly.

"What's this?" His voice was breathy and low as if he had to struggle to get the words out.

"I just bet on a race at Santa Anita."

"I've been waiting for you outside. I've been sitting there like an asshole."

"I just assumed . . ."

He took her arm roughly and guided her to a table by the far wall. Then he turned and barked something at Shannon, the waitress, who promptly came to her station with the order. I went back and filled it and watched while she delivered it. The man swigged his drink. He said something and smiled with his mouth closed and his eyes narrowed. I lifted the gate to the bar. Addie stood. The man stood too and grabbed her. Addie slapped him and the man slapped her back. She staggered but caught herself and moved at him, pushing with two hands against his chest.

I caught his arm before he could slap again. I twisted it behind his back and pulled hard so it hurt. With my other hand I gripped his throat. I liked the sound of him straining to breathe and pressed for more. I was just pointing him toward the door when I felt the pounding on my back and heard her voice, shrill now and angry.

"Let him go! Let him go!"

Still holding him, I turned to her dumbly. She hit me on the jaw, but I hardly felt it. I let him go. She stepped past me and put an arm around him while he squeezed out a few curses in my direction. They were gone by the time I got back behind the bar.

I don't know what anyone else saw, but I saw my anger get ahold of me and I didn't like it. I knew that for the second time that night eyeballs had detached from the screens, all except mine. I glanced up at the finish of the fourth at Santa Anita.

"You gonna see her again? 'Cause they didn't pay me," Shannon said.

I laid a twenty down on her tray.

By dawn I was able to close my eyes and I pretended to sleep until morning passed me by. I deleted two messages from my day-job employer and went for a run. The black sedan settled in behind me not long after I passed the train station. I led it under the highway down to the water. It's a filthy run. The path along the harbor—what the city of New Haven calls Long Wharf Park—is just an open trash can. The tide was out and seagulls stood on the marshy mud which somehow never clung to their feet or delayed their takeoffs. I ran west to the end of the path and turned back toward the pier. The sedan passed me and parked. There were three other cars in the lot, all empty. I ignored the sedan, ran until I reached the pier, then walked out past the *Amistad* to the end.

Two men got out of the sedan. They hesitated at the beginning of the pier. Behind them was the highway and beyond that, to the right, loomed the big red *Sports Haven* sign. If anyone was watching I should have been able to spot them. But no cars so much as slowed down. It took almost a minute for the men to reach a decision; one came toward me, one stayed put.

Dan Haley was a US attorney from the District of Columbia. His suit, too large as always, flapped in the wind and rustled his curly hair. He was a skinny guy with glasses—the type people think they can push around only to find out too late how wrong they were.

"Why are you following me, Haley? I'm on your side, remember?"

"I don't hear from you. You don't answer my calls. You're supposed to check in. Are you going soft on me?"

"Just tell me when you're ready to go to trial and I'll be there. Just like I told you I would be."

He didn't answer.

I said, "But you're not here because you're worried I'm backing out. It's something else." I knew what else it was, but I wanted him to say it.

"There's been a leak. We think there's been a leak. We think they might know your name. Know you're my witness. It won't be long before they find you."

"Who's he?" I nodded toward the burly bald man Haley had left at the other end of the pier.

"US marshal."

"And now you're going to tell me to come with the two of you and you'll put me somewhere safe . . ."

"It's all arranged."

"And when that leaks? I didn't want to rely on you to keep me safe to start, and I certainly don't now that you've proven how secure your office is. I told you how to contact me. Get me the court dates and I'll show up."

"I have no case without you, Petersen."

"Then stay away from me, Haley."

He was a control freak and I could see the struggle inside him. He knew I was right, but trusting me was another matter. The case was against SteelShield, supplier of private soldiers and most everything else that can be sold in a war zone, and six of their contractors in Iraq. They were charged with raping teenage girls, imprisoning them, and eventually, and inevitably, torturing them. I saw it, spent about a minute considering who to report it to—even considered going to the owner and founder, Ian Finch—but decided I wanted to live, so I waited the two months until I got out of Iraq and then went to the US attorney when I returned home. I played a game with Haley from the start, meeting in cars, then in an apartment in Baltimore, all designed to show him that I was serious about keeping my identity secret. But I knew I would give in despite my doubts about Haley and his office. The vision of that makeshift prison nagged me with vicious, pinpoint insinuations that I could not escape. I doubted justice or peace would result from the prosecution of those six thugs or the company, but vengeance holds some satisfaction no matter what the philosophers claim.

Haley tried again to get me to come with him. I brushed past him. "They'll be following you, Haley. Don't bring them to me."

I had come to New Haven to work as a research assistant for a professor whose specialty was post–WWII mercenaries. He had plenty of theories about the supply and flow of fighters for hire, and I was one of two assistants charged with tracking down evidence that tended to support his theories. As soon as Haley was out of sight, I called the professor and told him I wouldn't be available for a few days. He didn't seem to mind.

That night and the next day at Sports Haven, I kept an eye on the door and told myself it was out of fear rather than hope. No one came in who didn't look like he belonged. A few of the regulars tried to bring up "the fight," but I refused to answer them and their curiosity was muted by races going off every few minutes.

* * *

Marsha was counting the cash, wearing her waitress uniform and her don't-mess-with-me smile, when the door at Cody's Diner opened. It wasn't supposed to. She was six feet and close to 250 pounds, but her hands were quick and the gun within reach under the counter.

"We're closed. Get out."

Addie stopped. She showed her hands and pointed toward the back of the long, narrow room to the last orange booth where I sat. Marsha looked at me and I nodded.

Addie slid onto the bench across from me. "Holyshirt won. Paid 22–1. And you said there were no sure things."

"Maybe see it this way: the other six horses were sure things. Yours was a happy accident."

"Jerry told me I'd find you here."

I didn't say anything.

"You look alarmed."

"You would too if Jerry knew where to find you."

She pointed to the book I had been reading. "What's that?"

"*The Assassination of Lumumba*," I said. I told her about my research job. Her left cheek showed just a faint redness. Her eyes had lost their humor. Uncertainty ruled. Marsha set a cup of coffee in front of Addie and a piece of pumpkin pie in the middle of the table. She walked away before we could react.

"That means she likes you . . . unless it's poisoned. Sometimes I misread people."

Addie sipped her coffee. "I didn't go to Sports Haven just to cash the ticket . . . That pie for you or me?"

"Whoever's first to it."

She pulled it toward her and took a bite. "You seem like the type of guy who doesn't want an apology."

"Only when there's something to apologize for."

"I'd feel better if you let me explain."

I said I wanted her to feel better. She started by telling who she was and I didn't let on that I already knew. She had come to New Haven because her movie career was in the dumps—her last picture had flopped, even in Argentina—and she thought she could change the industry's perception of her by going onstage. Tommy—that was the guy—got her an audition at the Long Wharf.

"He produced my first two movies. We used to be together. I ended it last year. I should have known . . . how he is. I knew what I was doing. Thing is—"

"Tommy thinks he got a second chance and has no intention of losing out again."

She nodded.

"And you want to give me a second chance too. Where is he? Tommy."

She wasn't sure. She had ditched him to get here. Last night he tried to break into her house.

"Is he armed?"

She shrugged.

"I am. We can go back there if you want."

"I thought maybe we could hang out for a while."

Had anyone ever said no? I don't know how to measure cruelty, but it seemed best to limit her humiliation. I said, "It was the slaps that gave you away. Yours was okay, but you leaned in to take his."

Her eyes squinted as if a sharp pain hit behind them.

"I like the script, though. Audition at the Long Wharf? Was that meant to make you seem within reach?"

She looked around. I thought she might run. She should have run. She seemed like a young kid caught after curfew.

"Is it Finch himself? Did he put you up to this?" I said. "What'd he promise you? Something better than an audition in New Haven, I hope."

Her mouth opened but the words wouldn't form. At last she said, "They just want to talk to you. That's all." She mustered all the conviction of a drunk sipping her second glass of water.

I laughed. "These guys? They don't want to talk to anyone. They want to fuck you and kill me—and if that means talking a little first, they'll play along. They won't want witnesses, no matter what they told you. Finch could make any promise because he knows you won't be around to call him on it. They sent you into Sports Haven so people could see us together. When you're found dead in my bed, it'll make sense."

"To who?"

"To anyone who knows me or anyone who knows you."

She sighed and pushed the pie away and looked down long enough to make a decision. "It's down to which horse to bet on again, isn't it? You want something so much, you talk yourself into believing people. Lying off the lies. Finch said he was going to finance a new movie and I wanted to believe it. Funny thing is, if he told me the sky was blue I'd look up to check. Well, I've been taking improv classes. Here I go off script: don't go back to your apartment. I'm supposed to take you there, leave the door unlocked. The rest is probably more like you said than what they said. I'm sorry."

I checked my watch. "I have a train to catch."

Addie caught my arm and turned briefly to look back at Marsha, who was watching closely. "For what it's worth, I couldn't have gone through with it."

"Because I'm so . . . what? Charming? Confident?"

"Even if it was Jerry."

I liked hearing that and believing it too.

Marsha was careful to lock up after us. Outside, Addie pulled me close. Her voice was just a soft whisper: "Where's your train ticket? A kiss for good luck . . ."

I didn't bother with the ticket.

It was just up Union and left on Water Street, under the viaduct, to the train station. Easy enough for an ambush, but I didn't think Finch wanted my death to look like a hit. I made a quick phone call to my professor to inform him that I wouldn't be around for a while. I told him I was taking a train out of town right away.

The station was quiet. A family of four was being escorted down the stairway toward the platform by a big man—one of Finch's mercs, one of my former colleagues. Two more mercs flanked the stairway. Two more came inside behind me and guarded the door. The only other person in the huge, high-ceilinged hall was a bull-necked, crew-cut man sitting with his back to me on the middle bench. Finch. Owner of SteelShield. More petty tyrant commandeering the station than the great and humble general he wanted the world to see him as.

I checked the board: my train wasn't due for almost ten minutes. I went back to the bench, as Finch knew I would.

"Sit down for a while, Pete," he said, as if I'd run into him at lunch. His eyes were two dark threats and he had long since forgotten the difference between a smile and a sneer. I declined the invitation, though standing there only made me a better target. "I want you to take a vacation for a while. On me."

"Overseas?"

"We take requests . . . when we can."

"Let it go, Finch. It wasn't you who tortured those women. Just let it go. A few bad apples."

He had become world-famous. And he built the fortune on his own. What started out as a newsletter for former servicemen had turned into a behemoth stoking the ever-expanding demands of the government at war. Mergers had brought on-site services—food and lodging, transport and entertainment—into the fold, but mercenaries remained the top priority. He didn't do it by letting go.

"Well, you've gotten to the heart of it, Pete. It's about loyalty. I have to stand by my men. You don't seem to get that concept. You could have come to me. Directly to me. And I would have taken care of the problem. The boys let off some steam. They're under pressure. Not everyone reacts the way you and I do. But—"

"You would have done what you're doing now—tried to kill me."

"I don't want to kill you, Pete. But I can't let you testify, either. The company is too big for that now."

"I have a train to catch. C'mon. You'll walk me out there."

I reached back and brought out my gun and pointed it at him. I didn't try to hide it from anyone.

Finch was not impressed. He stood. He was about my height but had gotten thick through the middle. For some reason it dawned on me that he was close to sixty years old.

"Arms up?" he asked.

"If you want to."

He raised his right hand. It was a signal. One of the men at the door went outside for a moment and seconds later two of his comrades escorted Addie inside.

"They have their orders," Finch said.

I maneuvered Finch toward the stairs, keeping his men in

front of me. Addie was working to hide her fear. This was the moment for her slick moves, vicious flying kicks. The moment for me to shoot five men before they could shoot me. Neither of us thought we could pull it off.

"Let her go, Finch. You don't want to die in this train station. Not your style."

I ordered the two mercs guarding the stairs to move aside. I gripped Finch tighter and stood with my back to the staircase facing the other mercs. The one with the gun on Addie had sleepy, calm eyes, the kind that don't panic.

Finch said, "Hold her. Just hold her. He has to catch his train and he's not going to shoot me like this. Not Pete. He's not up to it."

The clock was out of sight and that was fine because I had no idea how to proceed. I listened, hoping the train would arrive and force me into a decision. Instead, I heard footsteps behind me. Coming closer. Coming up the stairs. I remembered the merc who had escorted the family downstairs but couldn't remember seeing him come up.

"Go ahead, Pete, prove me wrong. Show the boys you're better than them," Finch said. "You'll save the girl. Give yourself up to save her." But it seemed more for the mercs' sake than mine.

The footsteps came closer. More than one set. I'm sure Finch heard them too. I don't know what they did to him but each step was like an ice pick creeping up my spine disc by disc.

Suddenly the mercs lowered their guns and the front doors opened and four men with *US Marshal* windbreakers swept in.

From behind me, a hand rested on my shoulder and I heard Haley say, "Thanks for the tip, Pete. We'll take it from here."

My grip on Finch had gone rigid and the US marshals had to yank him free.

Addie stood alone, in limbo, looking at me, but before I got to her, Haley pulled me aside. "How did you know the professor would contact me?"

"C'mon, Haley. Who tipped you I was in New Haven? I have to go now."

"Where?"

I stepped away. He grabbed my arm.

"And what about her?"

I shook my head and avoided her eyes. "She doesn't know anything. They told her to go to Sports Haven and wait for that little jerk. She came around tonight on her own to apologize to me. They caught her and tried to use her. That's all."

Addie reached me at the top of the stairs. I took her hand and we walked down and then out to the platform. The red lights began blinking. The tracks curved just out of the station so I couldn't see the light of the train yet. Now I hoped it would be late.

"You didn't look scared," I said.

"I tried not to lean in too much. Do they sell tickets on the train?"

I shook my head. "I have to try to lay low. Running around with a beautiful movie star is probably not the best way."

The train came in sight but we both turned back to each other at the same moment.

"Maybe when it's all over I'll look you up. If you're still interested . . ."

"Count on it," she said. "It's a sure thing."

I boarded that train and rode a long way wondering whether I wanted the trial to come soon so I could find out if she was right, or to come later so I could hope she was.

I'VE NEVER BEEN TO PARIS

BY AMY BLOOM

East Rock

I liked her right away. Or, I saw that she liked me right away, and I liked that. It'd been a bad year and any little expression of enthusiasm was gratifying. We walked into the East Rock Café at the same time, women in our thirties, double-knotted summer scarves and flat sandals on our dirty feet. We ordered identical lattes and avocado on toast. We rolled our eyes at the always likable yet glacially slow counter girl and took note of each other. She claimed a shaky little table and managed to drop her latte, step on her backpack, and trip over her pile of papers. I handed her a wad of napkins, smiled, and sat down at the opposite table, laying out David Gates in front of me, Khloe Kardashian's secret heartache next to my latte, and the second section of the *New York Times* to my left. Who wouldn't like me?

She glanced at my newspaper. "My God," she said, "Oliver Bullfinch was killed. I knew him. I mean, I worked with him." She looked tense and queasy. She told me he was her colleague, a lovable old coot. What a terrible, terrible thing, she said.

It *was* a terrible thing. It was also not a surprising thing. People had been hating Oliver Bullfinch for forty years (not always the same group of people, but always a robust cohort of colleagues and students and probably waitresses, bookstore clerks, and garage mechanics). I'd been hanging around New Haven for a long time and I'd never heard anyone call him *lov-*

able. I had taken a class with him ("Whales and Wilderness," properly known as Melville and Thoreau, nineteenth-century American literary blah-blah) a million years ago. I'd sat in the same office in which Bullfinch had been found (310 Linsley-Chittenden, on High Street) while his grad student gave me an unmistakable smile and an A on a paper I'd written in the time it took to type it. I accepted the A. I returned the smile and my senior year was more fun than I'd expected.

"It says here bludgeoned to death with a bronze bust—" I began.

"Of Melville," she interrupted flatly.

I liked the flatness. "—of Herman Melville. Yesterday afternoon. I mean, they're guesstimating, I'm sure."

"How are you sure?"

This was the embarrassing part. "I'm, like, I mean . . . I'm a private investigator. Custody, corporate stuff. Unfit parents, paranoid bosses. Not murder. I mean, I'm interested, but—"

"You're a private eye?" Her eyes got warm and swimmy. "That's cool."

I liked that too. It didn't feel cool. It felt pathetic. It felt hand-me-down, which it was. I have a PhD in psychology and I had a job at Wesleyan and then I made a series of errors in judgment (sexual, alcoholic, and vehicular) and did not get tenure. Worse than that, but let's stick to the essentials. My Uncle Luis saw me through the bad times and, having used me to run his office and all googling since I was twelve, he died and left me Luis Gutierrez Private Investigations. So, boom. I had an office and a license and a copier from the eighties, and every once in a while people who had known my uncle called me for a job. *Once in a while* is the important phrase here. I needed an in with the police. I needed my fifteen minutes. I needed to pay my rent.

She held her phone to mine and we exchanged details. Then her phone beeped a reminder and she jumped up. "Jesus, that's all I need. Late for my own class. Allison Marx."

"Dell Chandler," I mumbled.

I didn't see her for a week. I made myself call three divorce lawyers about possible work, in a fast-paced game of Who's the Better Bottom-Feeder? I let a nervous young wife know that her suspicions about her husband were well founded (that what he'd done to her predecessor, he was now doing to her) and I sent her to a better lawyer than the ones who used me. I played gin with Big Betty, making enough money to pay for one of her pulled pork platters, and I followed the Bullfinch case the way I read *Travel and Leisure*: glamorous places I wanted to go and delightful experiences I wanted to have (in this case, a regionally famous homicide investigation)—but couldn't. I snooped around about Oliver Bullfinch, in case I could find a tidbit to bring to the police and worm my way into the investigation. I heard about ancient and deep office *ressentiments*, classic misogyny, garden-variety racism, and no sexual intrigue at all. He must have been one of the few old men, gay or straight, who had never laid a paw, even lightly, on an undergraduate in all Yale's history. He was largely retired, with a dead wife, no kids—and however terrible his feuds may have been, most of the people who might have killed him were already dead and those who were alive were pretty firmly in the life of the mind, not the body. The *New Haven Register* stayed on it, sharing every police crumb with me. People's alibis were intact. For two days, there was some steam over the Vietnamese woman on the cleaning staff who found his body, but once the police (and then the *Register*) had interviewed her 4'10" self and were persuaded that she had had no personal contact with Oliver Bullfinch, ever, things settled down.

I had no mouse to lay at the feet of New Haven's finest.

"Hi. Here you go." Allison bumped into me, spilling the latte she was trying to hand me. She dropped her scone and I caught it. "How's the private-eye biz? Any suspects?"

"It's not my case. Of course. But it is interesting."

"That's a little cold, considering an actual person is dead." She lowered her voice. "I went to the funeral. You know who wasn't there? Seriously?"

I asked who, seriously, and she got coy and I got persuasive and, after pulling apart her scone, she sighed and said, "It probably doesn't even mean anything, but . . . Daniel Markham."

She told me all about Daniel Markham, rising star in the English department. She couldn't stop telling me. Her face went into a spasm when she said his name. I told her that every woman had one man like that, the one who makes us look crazy, and I told her an edited version of mine. She blushed for me and laughed. We ate three scones and we had two lattes and I thought, there is nothing like a good talk with a good woman to make you not miss men so much.

"He had a nasty temper and they had huge fights in the department meetings. You could investigate," she said. "The police'll probably bungle it. Years ago, there was that poor girl who got stabbed to death in the middle of Edgehill Road. They never found *her* killer." She stretched in the chair, her arms grabbing the edge of her seat. Strong, defined arms and short, muscular legs.

"You are in *great* shape. Yoga? Pilates?"

She couldn't be a dancer; no one could go through years of dance class and still move like a puppet with tangled strings.

"I do Krav Maga."

"Really?"

She jumped up and jabbed her right hand toward my face, then moved to my chest and swung another fist to my face, stopping short. I tried not to flinch when she whipped her right leg up and out and rested her heel on my sternum. She smiled a real and satisfied smile.

"It's all about threat neutralization. All women should take it. I love it. I go to class six days a week. My teacher says I've made great progress. I'm taking the test for my black belt in two weeks."

Her phone beeped again and she ran to her bike, waving.

"Be careful," I called out to her.

I put my feet up in my office, also lately, sadly, my home. A shitbox room in a shitbox building at the ass end of Whalley Avenue, between Big Betty's Bar-B-Q and Ahmed and Paula's Groceries. Allison texted me: *Dinner with English Dept tonight. Wanna be my date & investigate?* I appreciated the offer. I didn't have any plans. Nothing in my bank account. One frozen waffle in the freezer. I texted back: *Ready to go. Pick me up where?* She texted back: *I know where you live. Hehe.*

I didn't want her to see my office home. I liked how she thought of me. I ran down when she leaned on the horn, before Betty could tell her to pipe down or lose her windshield. Allison went into drive with a painful crunch and we jerked forward and stalled. A bottle of cheap white wine rolled out under my feet. Other drivers yelled at us, the nicest remark being, "Learn to drive, ya fucking blind snowflake!"

"That's for the Freemans. Our hosts."

"Great. I didn't bring anything. I hope this isn't too much out of your way." I didn't want to upset her. She was gripping the wheel so tightly, little drops of water slid down the steering wheel.

We made our way up Whalley, toward Yale. She was an unusual and terrifying driver: slow, blind, and anxious. At twenty-two miles per hour, we rolled through stop signs and red lights, brushed against sidewalks, and straddled the double yellow line all the way to Freemans' house.

Since she couldn't take her eyes off the road, and I couldn't bear to watch our near misses, I studied Allison. She looked the way she did when we first met: Not glamorous. Purplish-brown circles under the eyes, premature creases on her eyelids, a little eczema in front of the ear closest to me. She wore a baggy dark-brown dress, with little gray and yellow flowers, which was too big for her, as well as being fugly. The neckline kept slipping, revealing sensible white bra straps and knobby yellow shoulders. How could anyone stand to go through life with all their waifish vulnerability hanging out, for all the world to see and step on? I resisted the urge to fix her dress.

"So, is their house far?"

"St. Ronan's. We're almost . . ." The effort of answering distracted her and she swerved toward a parked car.

Without thinking, I put my hand on the wheel and whirled it in the other direction. "I'm sorry," I said. "That was presumptuous. It was just a reflex."

She smiled tightly. "It's okay. I'm not a very confident driver. Daniel taught me to drive last fall. I grew up in Manhattan."

Her driving steadied a little bit and I took my hand off the oh-shit strap. Maybe everything would work out, maybe we'd get to and from the dinner party intact, maybe I'd find the murderer and get more work and a place to live, maybe Allison would calm the fuck down and we'd go to Tanger Outlets and redo her wardrobe. Maybe.

Allison took a deep breath. "Freeman's a Shakespearean. He got tenure as a wunderkind a thousand years ago and hasn't published much since. He's always talking about his *new* project. He's going to do a valorium edition of *The Merry Wives of Windsor*. He says that he's just an old-fashioned scholar, which means he thinks everything after 1780 is trendy garbage. And he calls women *wenches*. And he drinks too much. But, you know, he's seventy."

"Is there a Mrs. Freeman?"

"Oh, yeah. Lois." So much for feminism. "I guess she's younger. I think she was his student. She helps out in the alumni office. She's, uh, very nice. Well, I mean, classic faculty wife."

Huh.

"He's not so bad, really. It's surprising that he's interested in Gertrude Stein."

Old age had defused Freeman and he'd been clever enough to stroke Marx a little. For all her criticism, if there were a departmental conflict, she'd be in his camp.

"I'm leaving in two weeks to go to Paris, to work on a new project. I got a grant from the Omni Foundation—it's on Gertrude Stein, her theater projects. The radical inconsistencies are fabulous."

"Sure. Omni Foundation, that's a big deal. Your letters must have been stellar."

She clenched the steering wheel. "We're here." She slammed on the brakes.

"And so we are. Maybe we can have coffee tomorrow," I said.

She shrugged and then softened. "I hate seeing Daniel. It makes me tense. He makes me tense."

I patted her shoulder. We walked, arm in arm, right through the neighboring sprinklers, all working well and making things verdant in front of the stately homes.

The house was classic East Rock, circa 1927: a big two-story home with two wings off the center, both needing repair. Ghosts of live-in help fluttered by. The slightly warped black shutters framed big leaded windows and a chipped slate walkway led to a slate front porch, with two unnecessary columns and exactly enough room for two guests and the big Japanese urn with hopeful pink geraniums in it. Dusty panes of stained glass marked the second- and third-floor landings. There was the general air of past grandeur (and current deep, cossetted comfort and protection, which I wanted even more than I wanted grand). And lovely, blameless mountains of late roses and banks of hydrangeas, in full blooming white, pink, and lavender. I rang the doorbell and smiled reassuringly at poor Allison, who was holding onto her neckline.

"You look fine," I lied. "Fuck him."

A leprechaun opened the door.

Professor Freeman was as bald and red as an apple, just about 5'6", wearing the standard-issue hairy Harris Tweed jacket in a novel shade of avocado. His baggy brown corduroys drooped under his round belly and his tie was emerald green with brown and beige diamonds. I expected his socks to be green argyle and the toes of his wee boots to curl upward—and I was right about the socks. There was something irresistible about his delight in being such a snappy dresser at his age. He twinkled.

He ducked his head in a professorial half-bow and attempted to make eye contact with my breasts. "Artemis . . ." he murmured.

A lot of people find this kind of thing annoying, but I don't mind it so much, nearing forty. "Professor Freeman," I responded, grinning. "We brought wine!"

A faded pink wraith appeared next to my host. Mr. Freeman had used up their collective allotment of vitality and color. A little taller than he and ash-blond, she looked like a gladiolus at the end of the season. She tottered toward me on scuffed pink silk sandals and clutched her husband's shoulder. *My God*, I thought, *she must have muscular dystrophy or something*. Then I examined her face and saw those wet, bluish-red eyes and knew she must have been downing vodka since lunch, if she'd had lunch. Mrs. Freeman stared at me, damply, for a long minute; we all stood very still while she tried to get into gear.

"Come in, come in," she finally barked. "Don't just gawk, Albert. Make them drinks." She wasn't able to do the hostess routine very well anymore, but she knew the basics and did what she absolutely had to do. "Dumb as a bucket of worms," she mumbled, kicking their fat gray cat out of her path. I didn't ask to whom she was referring.

The living room was cheerful, in its way. There was a shabby beige velvet couch (covered with gray cat hairs) and four matching armchairs, their nap rubbed off at all the corners. And everywhere there were bits of Ireland. Shillelaghs on the walls, four-leaf clovers in amber cubes, ceramic mugs with John Kennedy's face, sepia prints of lasses and laddies kissing in the back streets of fair Dublin. The floor-to-ceiling curtains were green linen. It was a shrine to Irish kitsch and you knew that Albert Freeman had lovingly collected and arranged every bit of it. (*Freeman*, I thought. *Irish?*)

I sat down and jumped again. Underneath me was a horsehair cushion depicting the saint with embroidered snakes, 3-D style. I settled back in with the white wine Freeman handed me. I would have gone for a real drink or three, but then I would have gotten friendly, and then I would have gotten nasty.

If I've learned nothing else in my thirties, it's that I have to drink the way Allison has to drive—slow and worried. Allison, the party animal in question, drank apple juice. Mrs. Freeman continued to sip from a tall clear glass, with not so much as an ice cube or lemon slice for camouflage. Freeman (who was starting to seem more like "poor old Albert") drank Connemara whiskey and discoursed about its pedigree as he gulped. There was no food on the table, except one small bowl of fuzzy cashews. I sniffed for a reassuring scent of cooking, but I couldn't pick up anything. My stomach growled.

The doorbell rang and a man burst through the door. Apollo in white jeans, white cotton shirt, and blue blazer. No socks. No little tiny wings on his ankles. He hugged Mrs. Freeman, who smiled and said, "Daniel!" Daniel Markham focused a dazzling smile on me and gave the tail end of it to Allison, who started to perk up, then wilted back into her chair.

"Great to be here. Great whiskey, Al. How about on the rocks, with just a splash. Great."

Just as Daniel, gleaming from tip to toe, settled into one of the armchairs, the doorbell rang again as our last guest arrived. Mrs. Freeman yelled, "It's open!" and a dull mouse of a man came in.

"Hey, Jimbo," Daniel said.

Poor man with thinning brown hair worn long and floppy, a pronounced overbite, little pink mouth, small, sharp nose, and an unfortunate tendency to wear gray. But his eyes were not unfortunate. They were shiny brown and bottomless, seeing everything and thinking, clicking on all cylinders, about all he saw. At the moment, he was fastened on Allison, whose gaze was locked onto Daniel's perfect profile. Things happen in New Haven, don't think they don't.

Mrs. Freeman made the introductions in her abrupt way:

"Jim, this is . . . Jesus, who? Wait, Allison told me. Dell Chandler. She didn't make it in psych at Wesleyan, now she's like a junior lawman or something. This is Jim Fiske, he was visiting this year. Rising star but not here. Don't get attached. He'll be gone in another week or two. The rest of the department? I guess all those fuckers are out of the country."

She certainly didn't make you squirm with her desperate efforts to please.

We sat around, passing the inedible cashews back and forth, and they talked about the kinds of things academics talk about: Albert's latest bird-watching venture, the faulty transmission in Daniel's old Honda, Jim's love of all things Apple. Mrs. Freeman's eyes closed, Allison couldn't take her eyes off Daniel, and I was bored out of my mind, hoping that at any moment someone might leap up with that bloodstained bronze bust and head for the library, Colonel Mustard in tow. I thought about whiskey. I needed to focus.

Suddenly, Mrs. Freeman lurched out of her seat and headed toward the kitchen. She quickly emerged again, shouting, "Dinner!" I still didn't smell anything.

We shuffled along to the dining room and stared at the table. The Freemans didn't give us any indication of where to sit and, in any case, we were all mesmerized by the table laid with a huge platter of cold sliced corned beef, another of salami—both garnished with clumps of potato salad, with each clump topped by a big sprig of parsley (Mrs. Freeman, asserting something)—a third platter covered with slices of bologna, laid out like a mosaic, a tiny bowl of macaroni salad, a bigger bowl of coleslaw, and a breadbasket filled with sliced white bread. All in dusty Waterford glasses and Belleek plates.

"What lovely crystal," I said, and maneuvered to sit next to Mrs. Freeman, who seemed a likely informant if I could get to her before the next six ounces of vodka. Allison slouched toward Daniel while looking elsewhere. Very I'm-not-really-doing-this. I understood.

"Do you get your corned beef from Katz's? Or do you make your own?"

I wasn't sure how far gone she was. Mrs. Freeman stared at me flatly and smiled a slow, shaky, genuinely amused smile. "Right," she replied drily. "I don't make my own anything anymore. I did beef Wellington with two screaming babies, I made salmon *en papillote* when that was the thing, until it was coming out of my fucking ears. I did baklava from scratch while carpooling my brats to violin and swimming lessons, so they could become swimming violinists or some goddamn thing. Now, one's a what?—a hedge manager—and the other one, I think she *is* a swimming violinist. I don't cook a goddamn thing."

I smiled pleasantly. "That's why God made takeout. I live for Royal Palace. So what do you do now that you're no longer chained to the stove?"

"I drink, detective girl. My chains are right here."

She waved her glass around, not spilling a drop. At the other end, Albert regarded me questioningly. I smiled back. He turned to Allison.

"Albert drinks a little too much and he paws the girls. Harmless, harmless, harmless. On the other . . ." She stared at her glass.

"On the other hand . . ." I prompted.

She paused, the way they do, as though they're gathering their thoughts when all they're really doing is trying not to drool or spill the drink. If I could knock over the glass, maybe we could get somewhere. If I could have met her before whatever it was that had shriveled her, maybe we could have gotten somewhere. Mrs. Freeman took a big gulp of her drink and glared at Allison, who felt it and turned toward our end. Mrs. Freeman opened her mouth, shut her eyes, and slumped back in the chair. Her night was over. For the first time since we arrived, Allison smiled. We ignored Mrs. Freeman's little faux pas.

Albert got up to make coffee and, since the dinner partner on my right was no longer available, I turned to Jim Fiske. I have manners.

"So how do you find Yale after a year?"

The bright-penny eyes took me in with appreciation but absent the passion he had been casting at Allison. Takes all kinds. I needed to encourage the Jim-and-Allison thing.

"I find it interesting. Love Mamoun's. And squirrel fish at Taste of China. I'll miss that when I go to Iowa. I'll miss the people here: some new friends, some of my colleagues. And you, how do you find it, from your novel perspective?"

"Well, this is my hometown. Elm City. I wish I'd known Professor Bullfinch before his death. His habits, his likes and dislikes, his congeniality or lack thereof. I'm sure he was a complex person and, honestly, I just find myself wondering, why would anyone, you know . . ."

"Murder him," Jim said.

"What'd you think of him, just from faculty meetings and things like that? Did you hang out?"

Fiske snorted. I'd asked the right question. He told me about Bullfinch going all out to see that Allison was denied tenure, even undermining a summer grant to get her to Paris. That's all she wanted, he said. She admired Sandrine Boulanger, the Omni's director. He almost wept when talking about this vicious, doddering old man, vain about his reputation and indifferent to those of his junior colleagues while punishing Allison, cast in the part of Shirley Temple in *The Little Princess*—hard-done-by and plucky, brave and pure despite her shameful treatment. I looked at Allison, leaning toward Daniel, who never took his cerulean eyes off Jim and me.

"Did the police question you?"

He smiled. "Of course. Happily, I'm dull and predictable. Tuesday, I was eating a late lunch at Calhoun and meeting with students. I'm a fellow, so it's free. Then I was in the Apple store from four until about six. It was a nightmare—but a great alibi. Afterward, I had dinner at the Belgian place. The tall black girl with the dreads served me. Melisandre. She's waited on me before, and I left there before eight. Also, you probably know this but the man had no kids, no surviving relatives, and not a lot of money. If I was a PI like you, I'd be wondering about motive."

I agreed and took us back to Daniel. Fiske said, after the usual disclaimers ("I'm not saying he doesn't deserve it . . ."), that Daniel was the administration's golden boy but not so well thought of in academic circles. He said *administration* the way my father says *Internet,* with a sort of envious loathing.

Daniel and Allison were talking softly across the big mahogany table and Allison looked moist. She choked on her coffee. Daniel didn't seem worried. He put a hand on her shoulder, his long, thick fingers tucking away her bra strap. She froze, like a mouse tickled by a snake.

"Allie. Allie. Allie." Daniel's honey flowed and we watched him tranquilize her.

I couldn't stand it. I went into the kitchen to see if there was any dessert. There was a Sara Lee pound cake on the counter and a carton of Ashley's vanilla ice cream in the freezer. I went back into the dining room.

"Dessert in five minutes, everyone," I sang out, like Ina

Garten. Everyone brightened up a little, as if this were a normal dinner party. Then one of the murder suspects came in to help the detective dish out ice cream, while the hostess snored and the host brought his bottle of Connemara to the table.

I started slicing pound cake with a dull knife and putting pieces on little crystal plates. The plates were old and fragile, like dragonfly wings, probably given by someone's grandmother to the young and hopeful Freemans. I think Mrs. Freeman must have once had great charm and her life with that perfectly adorable man just sucked it right out of her. Daniel took the ice cream out of the freezer and for a few minutes we sliced and scooped.

"I don't know you," he said.

"You don't."

"Allison isn't my girlfriend."

"She's my friend," I said, pleased with myself.

Unfortunately, just then the lightbulb fizzled in the kitchen, leaving us startled and stumbling to find the switch. We were chest-to-chest in the half-dark and he put one hand on the back of my neck and the other around my waist and we kissed. We kissed like movie stars. We kissed until Albert called out, "Boys and girls! Dessert?" We carried plates through the swinging door.

Everyone gobbled their dessert. No one wanted to prolong the evening. Fiske and Allison cleared as Albert poured himself another drink, leaving his cake untouched. He lifted his wife's head and slipped a napkin under her cheek, tenderly.

Daniel turned to me and said, "Let me give you a ride home. Please."

"You're very kind." I rose quickly, thanked Albert, apologized silently to Mrs. Freeman, and went into the kitchen to say good night to Fiske and Allison and tell them I had a ride with Daniel. Fiske was thrilled. Allison frowned and dropped one of the pretty goblets. Fiske helped her pick up the tiny pieces. *That's right*, I thought. *Let him do that.*

Daniel held my arm lightly as we walked out of the house. We both sighed, standing for a moment in the warm night, breathing in the honeysuckle above the roses, and the cut grass. Other people still tended the lawns on St. Ronan's.

"This is mine," he said, pointing to a little blue MG. "I finally got rid of that old Honda I was telling everyone about."

The car was dashing and silly. It could only be driven by Bertie Wooster or a seventy-year-old geezer with a checked touring cap perched on his bald head. I would have thought a man like Daniel would drive a mud-splashed Jeep or a Maserati bought for him by a grateful old lady.

"Adorable. It's not what I would have envisioned for you."

"Nice that you envisioned me and my car. I know what you mean—I wouldn't have picked it out myself, but it's what I got and I can't complain."

I opened the passenger door and plopped in; it would have been just as easy to toss myself over the side. I wondered if he'd take me straight to my place or suggest a drive to the top of East Rock, a favorite stop for sex and suicide. If the world was run properly, all men who looked like Daniel would be wonderful human beings and all the good-for-nothings would look like Jim Fiske or worse, and women would be able to focus all of their energy on their children, their careers, and world peace.

"Dell, I want to be open with you."

Oh, that's never good. "Yes. Good, " I said.

"There's something, well, in my past which most people don't know about. I don't want people to know. But I wanted to tell you about it so you didn't hear it from someone else.

Because I like you, and . . . well, that's it, really. I just like you."

"Daniel, if there's something you want to tell me, I want to hear it. I'm not a cop; I'm barely a PI. I'm mostly just a nosy person. I'm just curious. You can tell me anything."

How do I know there's no God? Because I wasn't turned into a sizzling pile of ash right then and there.

He seemed indignant. "It doesn't have anything at all to do with Bullfinch's murder, Dell. It just doesn't reflect very well on me."

I nodded encouragingly, hoping that there'd be more excellent kissing and then he'd slip and tell me that he was Oliver Bullfinch's bastard son and that he had killed him with the bronze bust.

He glanced and turned left, away from Whitney Avenue, away from the lights. I admired his beautiful forehead with one furrow creasing it, the thick golden-red brows, smooth fox fur above the strong Scandinavian nose, down to the movie-star jaw and the constellation of dimples from cheek to chin. Ridiculous. Like dulce de leche ice cream in human form.

"Can I ask you a question?" I was trying to keep my detective brain working while my downtown party district was figuring how we could take a little break from all this tedious good behavior.

"Sure. We'll just drive. It's easier to cruise and talk."

"Did the cops question you?"

He frowned and pressed his foot down. The little blue toy took off like a kid was hurling it across the room. "Of course." He smiled and put his hand on my thigh. "And would you like it if I told you what I told them?"

"I would." And I would try really, really hard to concentrate.

"I was with Allison from two until about four. Then I went for a swim. Laps. You can check with her and with the kid at the desk at the gym. Lots of people saw me. I'm in the clear. Plus, I had no reason. I just got tenure."

He shifted and patted my knee. It seemed premature to object. I didn't want to object. I didn't want to die, but he didn't look like he was planning to kill me. Crush me, maybe, in his arms. Squeeze me where a woman wants to be squeezed. *Please*, I thought, *let him not kill me too soon.*

"I'm not like you—your professor father, your artist mother. You have a PhD of your own, is what Allison told me. You're just slumming with this private-eye shit. I grew up in Rice, Minnesota, population seven thousand. The nearest big town was St. Cloud. My father drove a truck for the Prairie Potato Company and my mother worked at Katie Ann's Country Pie. They are still there and I don't visit the way I should. I got to Amherst because Katie Ann's older brothers went there on hockey scholarships and she got them to take an interest. The MG was her brother Don's—he died in May. If it wasn't for Katie Ann and Don, I'd be the manager of Country Pie right now. When I got to Amherst, I had three pairs of pants, three shirts, one sweater, and my dad's parka. No guitar. No bike. No car, no checkbook, and no ticket home."

I felt his anger and loneliness, still hot after twenty years of practiced charm and simulated ease.

"I didn't know what a salad fork was, you know? That was okay because at that time everybody who did know pretended they didn't. But we all knew the difference between people who thought salad forks were bourgeois bullshit and people who just didn't know what the hell those little forks were for. Anyway, my roommates were three very cool guys from Grosse Pointe and Hyde Park and Long Island. They were up and coming, and they made a consortium, started a business. Of course, I had no capital, so I was the legs. We sold dope and, for the first time in my life, I had money. I bought CDs. I bought a bicycle, I bought a box spring. I was as happy as a pig in shit."

"And you got caught."

"Yup, I got caught. They couldn't expel the brains of the group since his father had just bought them a laboratory, so they just suspended all of us for a year. I waited tables." He shook his head and chewed on a thumbnail. "When we got back to school the following year, the other guys moved into an apartment off campus. I couldn't afford it. I was pretty upset. I did some damage to their apartment. And their car. And to the guys. They didn't press charges."

He pulled to the side of the road, turned off the lights and then the engine in two quick, smooth passes.

"It's who you were a long time ago. Everybody has a past with something not so nice in it."

"Whatever. Well, that's my dirty secret—poverty and a temper. What's yours?"

"I do have a PhD."

He held onto my hand and pressed it to his lips. "I don't mind. I'm very attracted to you, Dell. You know I am."

He kissed me, warm, soft, firm, and I kissed him back.

"You're very special. You are, even *you* think you are," he whispered.

Not good. Whatever that was, that wish to demean and delight simultaneously, had made the hairs on my neck as stiff as quills. I began to think, with some urgency, about getting out of there.

"I'd like to lie in bed with you a few times—before we make love. Just lie with each other, get to know each other's bodies, enjoy each other without sex, without pressure." He was murmuring in my ear. "I want to appreciate you, watch you, I want you to teach me all about your body and I'll teach you about mine. And then, when we're ready, we'll make love."

Oh, that should have sounded good but it sounded awful. I'd have rather babysat Mrs. Freeman than listen to Daniel's erotic plans. I'd have rather sat on the stoop with a warm beer, playing Fuck, Marry, Kill with Big Betty. I did want him to touch me—but without speaking. Sometimes men get upset when you say that.

"Oh wow, Daniel. Gee, I'm a little overwhelmed. Could you take me back to my place, please? I can't even think straight."

He laughed and started the car, snaking one hand under my shirt, stroking my stomach. My adrenaline was pumping along as visions of getting mutilated alternated with visions of Daniel's golden head between my legs. I stumbled out of the car. Big Betty caught a glimpse of Daniel and gave me the thumbs-up.

What was *that*?

They arrested him for the murder of Oliver Bullfinch—bronze bust included—the next day. A big day for the *New Haven Register*. We made it to the *Times* again, which managed to cluck, in its way, that this tragedy happened at Yale, that murders of one scholar by another and that murders on Yale's campus seemed to happen all the time. The bust of Melville got a tremendous amount of play. Someone made a GIF of it falling off a shelf. The motive seemed to be mutual dislike and Daniel's hot temper. People were found all over town to re-mark on his snappishness, his unnervingly good looks (which were held against him), and his high-handed ways. Most Yale murders were committed by people described as "gentle loners" or "isolated geniuses." But Daniel was described as being like the rest of us: poor impulse control leading to kicking the shit out of a hated boss. The implication was that it was a fight gone wrong, that Bullfinch's death was an accident in the end. I turned on the local news and there was attractive, intelligent Ann Nyberg telling us that his bail was very high and the charge was criminal manslaughter. She turned over the interviews with his idiot neighbors to a reporter who was just like the neighbors, but better looking.

I wanted to cheer at justice done. I wanted to be unreservedly glad that the beautiful guy who creeped me out was getting what was coming to him. But all I could see was his alibi, Jim's alibi, a big bunch of English professors, none of whom were persons of interest—and then way over in the corner and under the radar, little Allison. To the police, Paris denied and tenure denied might not add up to murder, but I could see it. See it? Hell, I'd *felt* it.

The sequence of events leading up to the crime unrolled in my mind: Allison spent a year facing the fact that she wouldn't get tenure, a year of bitter acceptance and endless hustle. She comes to terms with it. She hustles. She stays friends with Daniel, who has sway. She doesn't completely disappoint Jim Fiske, who's admired in the department. She puts herself forward for every committee and conference in North America. None of it comes to anything but there's still the Omni Foundation, which could add a little sparkle to her CV. Maybe she speaks French. She has a shot.

Omni says no. She knows—like you know when the airline says *delayed* but means *cancelled*—what's happening. Bullfinch blocked her. She goes to his office and confronts him. He acknowledges it. He's not sorry. Like the rest of us, he underestimates her. Her crush on Daniel, and those god-awful clothes, make her look weak. She's not a weak person, in any sense. Bullfinch is infuriating. Maybe he grabs her shoulder to push her out of his office. She whips out a few Krav Maga moves, startling him the way she did me. She smashes his head on the desk. So far, not murder. He sinks to the floor. He loses consciousness. Or he doesn't. He writhes and moans. The door is already closed behind her. She wrestles with her conscience, which she sees right now as a weakness, a hypocritical rag. She is not the kind of person who can easily bludgeon a man to death. But she does. She braces herself and bashes him in the side of the head one fierce, awkward time. He groans and lurches a little, away from her. She waits until he's quiet. There are places near his body, under his shirt, where the blood is so deep, she can't see the linoleum beneath it. She edges closer to his desk, avoiding the corner which shines with blood like jam on a knife.

So far, there's nothing in the room to indicate that Allison has been a part of anything except a chat with a colleague. She carefully sidles over to the window to let in some of the humid air. It feels good, warm and scented. He has stopped making noise and his hands appear relaxed. She climbs over the furniture, avoiding the red floor. She stands behind his desk. His computer is on. His screen is open. It's nothing to get into his e-mail, which is set up just like hers.

I imagine myself in front of the laptop. What would I do? I'd write the letter of recommendation I should have had in the first place.

Back in reality, I sent an e-mail to easy-to-find Sandrine Boulanger, using my old Wesleyan e-mail address, pretending I was still on the faculty. If I was wrong, that'd be good. If I was right, that'd be gratifying. Sandrine Boulanger wrote back promptly because I'd hit just the right time for a French office—August behind us, between coffee and lunch—and because I was a polite American professor.

Dear Dr. Chandler,

Thank you for your kind words about the Omni Foundation. We appreciate your inquiry and your interest in hiring Dr. Marx for the spring semester at the estimable Wesleyan University. The reason you did not see Dr. Marx's name on the original list of grant recipients is that her application was approved a bit later.

I can share with you, as you contemplate hiring Dr. Marx, that we had an exceptionally strong letter in support of her application only recently from Professor Oliver Bullfinch of Yale University, one of the most esteemed American literature scholars in the world.

We are delighted to host Dr. Marx this summer and we hope we have been able to help you.

Sincerely,
Sandrine Boulanger

Only recently. I was sure that meant the end of August. Bingo—or whatever they say in France.

Allison had known just what Bullfinch should have said. He apologizes for his previous opposition to Allison Marx (she doesn't know if he wrote or made a call, so she doesn't say) and blames it on ill health and a misunderstanding. It would kill him—I would have written—if his flu had interfered with Dr. Allison Marx's well-deserved grant. He expresses regret that there was so much competition at Yale in her field that they could not offer her tenure. It's a wonderful letter and if the miserable old fuck had written it in the first place, he wouldn't have wound up the way he did. I would have wiped the keyboard with his old cardigan, which is always on the back of his chair. I'd wipe the window latches too, and put the cardigan back. I'd tiptoe to the door and close it behind me. It's the first of September on a college campus. There's not a soul around.

In the Harry Bosch novels, Michael Connelly often has his hero say, *Everybody counts or nobody counts.* I don't quite understand that (does Hitler's well-being have to matter?) but I appreciate the tone. I felt bad, meaning furious and stupid, that someone I knew (not just murderous thugs in other countries, or even murderous thugs in my own country) was actually getting away with murder. Allison Marx was getting away with it, I was now convinced. Her getting away with it was more upsetting to me than the snuffing-out of Oliver Bullfinch's crabby, elderly candle. And the universe was rewarding her with a trip to Paris and a crack at tenure. I hadn't killed anybody at all. I hadn't even tried, and still, there was no trip to Paris for me.

Students were arriving up and down High Street, Elm Street, Church Street. Parents double-parked like crazy and five well-dressed, upper-middle-class white men screamed at each other to *Move that fucking Volvo right now!* Boxes, bags, baskets, and books came in waves. Parents and siblings and friends in little parades from the street to the door. Twin sisters from Shanghai in Chanel suits and killer heels, each carrying one small box while a member of their father's staff lugged the large, matching suitcases. Two slim, dark boys in clean, new Yale sweatshirts, each carrying a battered suitcase and a garbage bag, exchanged looks of excitement and apprehension. Some, with experience, did a bucket brigade and let their parents take them out for lunch. A father and son opened their beers and sat on the wall while two burly uniformed men moved the kid's stuff. The other families observed them with envy and resentment and disgust. The first-year students clung to every object as if only they knew where it should go and how it should be handled.

And here I was, unarmed and unofficial, ready to chat up Allison and see what conclusions we came to. I didn't think I could stop her if she decided to Krav Maga me, but I thought a gun could. There's no martial art better than a gun, which is why I don't study karate. And it's why I wish I had gotten around to cleaning and licensing Uncle Luis's Glock.

I walked up Whitney and turned down Allison's street, my favorite in New Haven: Autumn Street. A few blocks of houses, mostly classic New England with a few crazy reminders of seventies architecture. It was quiet but lively. *Haimish*, if you speak Yiddish. *Gemütlich*, if you speak German. You would walk your dog and talk to your neighbor. People had block parties there. If you were sick, a neighbor would watch you while your mother went to the store. Our particular neighbor read me *Wind in the Willows* and brought cookies with her. For a couple of years, when I was small, we lived at 175. Allison rented 236. Slate walkway, unpolished brass mail slot, charming wrought-iron bench.

She opened the door before I could knock. It wasn't her usual hunch-and-skulk. Her clothing was a hipster hodge-podge: black-and-white gingham blouse tied above her waist, baggy olive-green corduroys, and her hair was piled on her head in a flattering Brooklyn ballerina updo.

"Come on in," she said energetically. "Poor Daniel."

Her face was different. She was shining and her rheumy, half-closed eyes were open and bright. Something was very becoming. Clothes were strewn all over the living room.

"I have to move these papers. I'm sorry, you know, I was in the middle of going to Paris and now I have an offer—associate professor at Iowa. Barbara Hill's moving to Emory, she got one of those Coca-Cola chairs and she decided, last minute, to take it. I get to go to Paris and take her place in Iowa, if I want. What a lucky break. And poor Daniel. Do you know anything about it?" She almost winked.

"Word travels fast," I said. "Iowa. Isn't that where Jim Fiske is going?"

He set up Daniel and the payoff is they get married and move to Iowa? She set up Daniel, just because he was so handsome and annoying, and the payoff is Jim helps her get a tenured position at Iowa when the time comes? They always loved each other since they were kids way back when, and they set up Daniel together because once she'd killed Bullfinch, why not rid the world of another asshole? Okay, that would be more like me.

She glanced down. "Yes, it is, as a matter of fact. It's very nice that I might end up there. Also, I FedEx-ed my manuscript to the department chair at Iowa. That helped. I was just so blocked until . . . really, just the last few weeks." She said all of this with a chuckle in her voice, while Amy Winehouse filled the room.

"Allison, look, you're out of here. What do you think about this? Do you really think he killed Bullfinch?"

"I guess so." Her voice was low and sure. "I mean, who ever really knows another person, but . . . it seems clear that's what happened. Doesn't look like the police bungled this one." She gave a small sigh and smiled in a worldly way. Apparently, murder and Paris were a cure for every single thing that had ailed her.

"Can I ask, where were you on August 26?"

"What? What difference does it make?"

"Were you alone?"

"Not at all. I was with Daniel for a few hours. It wouldn't have taken him more than ten minutes to kill poor Oliver. Then I went off to be with Jim. Oh, for heaven's sake, Dell. With Jim and with Marilyn Kozlowitz from history, and Dick Price from astronomy. Jim made dinner for us all and we played bridge until midnight . . . You know, you're not actually investigating a murder." She chuckled as if I were such a goofball. She was so much more attractive now.

"And last night?" I just wondered. She looked so *rosy*.

"I wasn't alone." She smirked. "Life goes on."

"Well, for you, yeah. Congratulations."

She grinned a little at my tone, shifted her hips to "You Know I'm No Good," and asked if there was anything else on my mind.

"I see you're packing. Exciting, going to Paris. Your first time?"

She smiled again and answered in French, which I don't speak.

"What's that?"

"I said, you don't know a fucking thing about me. All you saw was glamorous Daniel and poor klutzy me. I said, I've been to Paris more often than you've been to Pepe's. My mother's French." She held up two passports.

"I don't speak French. But the head of the Omni Foundation speaks—and writes—excellent English. I was in touch with her. Sandrine Boulanger, director of the Omni. I pretended I was a professor, looking to hire you. She wrote back. All excited about the great reference you got from the estimable Oliver Bullfinch. Shall we look at her e-mail together?"

She didn't flinch. "*Absolument.*"

We stood close together, in the position of like-minded friends checking out a restaurant review or looking up an old acquaintance on Facebook together. Her eyes slid over the sentences.

"I don't think it was right of you to lie to them, *professor*. Really. But you see what a lovely person she is. I can't wait to meet her."

"You don't have anything to say about an e-mail from Bullfinch within hours of the time he was murdered?"

"No, I don't." She sighed. "I wish I'd known. I would have thanked him. We had such a hard time with each other. That was very sweet of him."

"And odd," I insisted. "He told everyone that he was going to block you for that big grant."

"He did, I know. Maybe he changed his mind. Jim lobbied for me. I guess it worked, at the last moment." Her eyes widened playfully. "Ohhh. You think it *wasn't* Bullfinch. I mean, the time of death can't be that exact, of course. You know that, right—even though you're an amateur. But maybe you think someone wrote a recommendation from Bullfinch— meaning it wasn't *really* from Bullfinch—after he died."

I pocketed my phone. On television, people crumble when you show them evidence or an e-mail that could, conceivably, constitute evidence. "I do think that," I said.

"*Oh la la.* It could be, but it seems unlikely. It's much more probable and logical to conclude that having been pressed by me and Jim on this very subject, Oliver Bullfinch decided to do the right thing—at what turned out to be the last minute." She sighed again, prettily. "That's what I choose to remember. Or it could have been Daniel, crossing the line, like the police think. We had been very close at one time. And he killed poor

Oliver in a rage. They had so many differences. Oliver was so insulting about Daniel's work, about his intelligence, really. He may have been right. We'll never know. That's what's so difficult about all this, right? We'll never know."

She stood a few inches away from me, aglow with her own cleverness.

"So," I said. "Off to France. Great food and no extradition treaty?"

"None at all," Allison replied. "But why would I care? *Bon soir*, Dell. *D'accord, vas-y alors*. That means, do what you have to do. I'll be around for a while if you have more questions about Paris or Daniel or Iowa or the vagaries of human existence. You know, questions about shit that bothers you."

She walked me to the front door.

"You know what movie we never saw together? *China-town—Forget it, Jake. It's Chinatown.* Right? So great."

She kissed me on both cheeks.

PART II

Down and Out in Elm City

THE SECRET SOCIETIES

BY ROXANA ROBINSON

Beinecke Library

The phone rang. It was Jake.

"It's Jake," he said, though I knew that. "Alison Ricks is dead."

Jake is my editor. And Alison Ricks was very old. Had been.

"She's dead?" I said. "When?"

"Yesterday," he said. "Heart failure. At home."

"How old was she?" I asked.

"Ninety-three," he said.

"A great writer," I said. I waited for him to tell me why he'd called.

"I thought you'd want to know," he said.

"I did," I said. "Thank you."

"She was a great writer," he said in a serious, slightly hectoring way, as though he wanted to bully me into agreeing, and as though I hadn't just said the same thing.

"She was a great writer," I said.

"You know, there's no biography of her." His tone had changed to airy, as though this was a curious fact he'd just learned.

I said nothing.

"So, what would you think about writing it?"

"Me?" I asked. "I'm not a biographer."

"Still," he said.

I'm mainly a travel writer. A hack, actually. I write pretty much anything for money, though when I get around to it I'm going to write a novel. Twenty years ago I published a memoir about growing up in Maine, which got some nice reviews but didn't get me the Pulitzer. Then I published a collection of travel essays which ditto. I still have the novel in mind, but in the meantime I write to pay the rent and Jake makes suggestions. *Why don't you do a cookbook? Why not write a book about your dog? What about a garden book? Why don't you write a book about Joan of Arc?*

Jake's full of suggestions, all of them terrible. I'd shoot myself before I'd write a book about food, I know nothing about Joan of Arc, and there are already too many tearjerkers about dogs. I write for a travel magazine funded by a big company, and they send me all over the world and pay me a lot. And I write book reviews and author interviews, and I do the odd ghostwriting or technical gig for a fat check, all while I'm waiting for the big time to come along and clap me on the shoulder and say, *Sarah Tennant, this is your moment.*

"I've never written anything like that," I told Jake.

"Sarah Tennant," Jake said, "this is your moment. You'd be great. You love her work. You'd have a lot to say about it."

I do love her work.

Ricks became famous in the sixties, when she first started publishing in the *New Yorker,* and for the next twenty years she stayed famous, and then she disappeared. Her stories were witty and elegant, written in shimmering gold. The early ones were set in Italy, and were a sublime entanglement of art and history and beauty and sex. They were all beautiful, and some were funny, some devastating. The one about the mother and child standing on the cliff, in the evening—you could never forget it.

Alison Ricks fans were now legion, though for years she'd published nothing. I knew as much as anyone about her, though there was a lot no one knew. There was no biography because she'd never agreed to one. For the last thirty years she'd refused to give interviews. Now the books were being reissued and taught in college. And she had won some big awards, just for being brilliant. Lifetime achievement, that kind of thing.

I own all her books. *Distant Plain, The Winter Beast, Come toward Sunrise, Raking the Field, The Stone Caveat.* Some were set in London, some in Italy, and some in New York. She'd grown up in Connecticut and a few were set there.

I tried to visit her once in London. I'd gone to her house on a whim, knowing I'd be able to sell the interview if I could get it. She lived in a tall house on a dark street in Islington. I went there one afternoon with a note saying I'd come by the next day if it were possible that Miss Ricks was available for a few minutes of conversation. And how much I loved the work.

I rang the bell and waited. For a long time nothing happened. I rang again, and this time the door opened, just a narrow sliver. The housekeeper stood inside, peering out. She was small and old, very erect, with white hair pulled back in a bun. She had strange dark eyes, nearly black, that seemed to have no pupils.

"Hello," I said, "my name is Sarah Tennant. I have a note for Miss Ricks. Would you be kind enough to give it to her?"

The woman nodded, looking at me with those black eyes. She took the note and shut the door.

When I came back the next day she opened the door again, but only the same sliver. As soon as she saw me she shook her head.

I smiled hopefully. "I came yesterday," I said, but she was already closing the door.

"I'm sorry," she said, "it's not possible." She had leaned in toward the door to shut it, so her head was very close to me. I could see her thin silvery hair, held close to her head with a fine hairnet, and an odd nick in her earlobe. As she shut the door she lowered her gaze, refusing mine.

I stood on the step for a moment. I had the feeling that she was peering at me through the peephole, to make sure I walked away.

That had been—eight years ago? Twelve?

She was now even more famous, because last year a new book of hers had been published. It made a sensation because of all the rumors. Her old editor had died, and the new one swore that this manuscript had been discovered in a closet, but the rumors were that it was really just the original draft of her first novel, *Distant Plain*. The rumors were that Ricks had had a stroke, and didn't know what was going on. But the editor claimed that the book was new, that Ricks was fine and everything was good. I hadn't read the book. I hadn't wanted to—the reviews had been bad, and it felt disloyal.

"Jake," I said, "I'm not a biographer."

"You write about writers," he said. "You write reviews of their books. You write interviews with them. You love her work."

All this was true.

"I've never done a biography," I said, but I said it in a different tone of voice.

"Come in and let's talk it over," he said.

Jake used to be head of the trade division, but his publishing house had been taken over by an international conglomerate that was—big news—more interested in profit margins than literary merit. Jake no longer had the corner office, but a small one in the middle of a corridor. One wall was full of books, and I always checked to see that mine were there, tucked in modestly on the third shelf down, reassuring me that I existed.

I sat down across from him. Jake was tall and gangly, as though his arms and legs had outgrown him. He had a long head and sleepy eyes and a big grin.

"I think you're the right person for this," he said, "because you love her work."

"And?" I said. Lots of people loved her work.

"Because you write fast," Jake said.

"She's been around for nearly a century," I said. "Why does this have to get written fast?"

"Because there are three other people writing biographies of her," he said.

"Who?"

"A woman called Jeanetta Wareham, for Jeeves and Wooster, someone called Lafferty, for Saki and Saki—she's just a novelist, she won't do much—and I can't remember the name of the third. She's an academic, working with a university press. Wareham's the problem."

"Who is she?" I asked.

"A features writer from LA. She writes celebrity profiles. And she's having an affair with her editor, who's the head of the trade division. So her book will get a lot of support, and she'll write it fast. And it will be full of scandal."

"A celebrity journalist?" I drew my head back in distaste. "My book would be better."

"Your book will have to come out first or it won't be reviewed," he said. "That will mean that hers will stand as *the* biography."

I was holding my cup of coffee in both hands, as though it was hot, but it was cold. I looked out the window: a tall building, full of windows, reflected this one. I didn't want someone to write a scandalous biography of Ricks.

"Mine will come out first," I said.

Jake cocked his hand like a gun, his index finger pointed up into the air like the starter at a racetrack. "Go," he said.

The Alison Ricks archive is at Yale, in the Beinecke Rare Book and Manuscript Library. It's a couple of hours from New York, and on the way up the Merritt Parkway I went over what I knew.

Alison Ricks had been born in 1924, in Cornwall, Connecticut. She'd gone to college but hadn't finished. She went to Italy after the war, worked in Naples for NATO, and began writing fiction. She moved back to New York, worked for another government organization, and kept on writing fiction. At some point she left New York for London, where she'd spent the last forty years of her life. What had she done? She'd stopped writing for the *New Yorker* around 1980. What had happened after that?

I figured this would take two years to write. My agent and Jake had worked out a pretty good contract, with an advance that would be big enough to live on if I didn't eat. The commute to New Haven wasn't bad, and I figured I could get my magazine to send me on a story to London, where I could do some more research. Jake had heard that Jeanetta had gotten a huge advance, but I put that out of my head. Mine would be first and best.

I got off the highway in New Haven, and almost at once I was in quiet, tree-lined academe. The buildings were neo-Gothic, made of gray stone with small mullioned windows, as though we were suddenly in fifteenth-century England. I found the Beinecke, then began looking for a parking lot. I drove around through the maddeningly one-way streets, farther and farther from the library, until I found a small private lot on Trumbull Street.

Walking back, I passed a one-story brownstone building, massive and closed, built like a tomb. It had a flat facade with three blank arches, a Latin motto inscribed over them. There were no windows, and the door was sealed shut. I thought it was one of the student secret societies; it felt like a reminder of all the things I didn't know.

The Beinecke is a pale stone tower set back from the street by an open courtyard, and as I walked across the flagstones I could hear my footsteps echo. I wondered what secrets I would find. I wondered if Jeanetta Wareham was already there.

Inside the building, it was like a church. The walls were made of translucent alabaster, and the light glowed through them, cool and elegant. People spoke in hushed tones and moved slowly.

I went down to register as a researcher. I'd done part of this online. The young woman at the desk was Asian, with black hair in a bowl cut. I gave her my name, and when I told her who I was working on, she glanced up at me.

"Alison Ricks?"

"That's right," I said.

She said nothing more, and I wondered if she had just checked in Jeanetta Wareham. I knew what Wareham looked like; I'd found a picture online. Short black hair and big teeth—too big—and small, close-set eyes, like a wolverine's. Now I glanced around for her, but the only other person I saw was a young man walking toward the staff office. The hall was silent.

They checked my ID and took my photograph and explained how it worked, and what the rules were. Where the material is brought to you, how long you can use it, what the restrictions are. You can't bring pens or markers into the reading room, or, really, anything at all but your laptop. There are lockers, where you leave everything but your computer. These libraries don't take chances: someone must once have slipped some priceless letters into a briefcase, because now everyone is monitored and there are security guards at the doors.

I put in my requests and went in to wait in the reading room. It was a beautiful space, just below ground level, with a long wall of plate glass that looks into a sunken stone courtyard, empty and serene. In the room were eight long wooden tables. No one else was there, but on one table, on the far side of the room, was an open laptop with papers beside it.

When my material arrived, I opened the heavy cardboard box and took out the first folder. I was entering into Alison Ricks's life.

The first folder held letters between her and a friend, Colewood Atchison, who was living in New York while Alison was in Naples. Inside was a sheaf of frail papers, inscribed in faded ink. The first was dated September 8, 1947. *Dear Colewood*, it began, *How lovely to hear from you.* Colewood was working for an arts magazine, and Alison wrote him about everything—her landlady, her boss, her struggles with Italian. He wrote about his job, the art scene, how high his rent was. I sank into their world: there's little as satisfying as reading other people's mail. When I finally looked up it was nearly one o'clock, and I was hungry.

The table on the other side of the room was empty.

As the days passed, other scholars appeared, each one bent

over a folder. The light came in from the empty stone-flagged courtyard, and the only sound was the quiet clacking of our keyboards. Sometimes our eyes met as we raised our heads to ponder, or when someone stood and gathered his or her papers to leave. Our eyes met, but we did not speak.

On the fourth day Wareham was at her table when I arrived. She raised her head and we looked at each other. It was her, all right: small, with no neck and a big head and short black hair. Those close-set eyes like a wolverine. She stared at me hard. I stared back at her for a moment, then turned away. I didn't want her to know I knew who she was. I didn't want her to think we were in a competition.

I wondered what she was finding out about Alison Ricks. Every time I asked for a file I wondered if I'd be told it was unavailable—if she'd have it already, spread out on the far table, revealing its secrets.

That afternoon, when I turned my files back in to the desk, I asked, "Are there any other people here doing work on Alison Ricks?"

The woman nodded. She wore a tiny gold chain around her neck, and round gold-rimmed glasses. I waited, but she said nothing more.

"Really!" I said cheerfully. "Who else?"

She shook her head. "We're not supposed to talk about the researchers."

"Oh," I said, "of course."

Someone was crossing the hall and I looked up. It was the young man I'd seen before, walking toward the door marked *Staff*. With him was Jeanetta Wareham. He held the door for her and they went inside.

I wanted to know what was in that room, and why Wolverine got to go inside it.

* * *

An hour later I asked for some more recent files. If that was where the scandal was, I wanted to know about it. Though I didn't know what it might be. I asked for the correspondence between Alison and her editor. The Asian woman shook her head. By now I knew her name: Chelsea.

"I'm sorry, but that file is unavailable," she said.

I felt a little frisson at the word, as though I'd touched an electric wire. "Unavailable?" I said. "Because it's restricted, or because someone else is using it?"

"Someone else is using it," she said.

I nodded and asked for another file.

Later that afternoon I was in the ladies' room, inside a stall, when I heard the big outer door swish open. Someone came inside and began using a cell phone.

"It's me," she said, her voice casual and intimate. "Just checking in." I'd never heard her voice but I recognized it at once.

There was a pause.

"No, I'm here," said the Wolverine. "I've just found some *amazing* stuff." She said *amazing* as if it were edible.

Another pause.

"I know you do," she said. "But it's not like that. It's just amazing." Then her voice turned guarded: "I can't talk here. I'll tell you tonight."

The days were getting shorter, and it was dark now when I walked back through the streets to the car. I used different lots, but wherever I parked it seemed that I had to pass one of those forbidding secret societies with their closed, enigmatic facades. On High Street I saw what looked like a rose-brown stone tomb, two small but massive buildings linked by a tall doorway. There was no sign there, and no street number, no information, no words. It was utterly closed to the world. Every time I passed by, it reminded me that there were secrets I couldn't learn.

What were those secrets? What had the Wolverine found out?

I drove up to the town of Cornwall, which is a tiny, sleepy village up in the northwestern hills. Its claim to fame is a wooden bridge, which doesn't really make it famous. I went to the town hall, the historical society, the library, and the only restaurant in town, The Wandering Moose. The Moose knew nothing about her, and the historical society was closed, but at the town hall I learned that the Ricks family had bought their house in the twenties, around the time Alison was born. At the library a gray-haired woman wearing blue-rimmed glasses told me where to find the place.

"No one's left in that family," she said. "She was an only child. Her parents died years ago. They were summer people, not locals. The house is closed up now. I don't know who owns it. She came back for a while in the summers, during the sixties and seventies, but when she moved to London she stopped."

"And was she popular here?" I asked. "Did people like her? Did you know her?"

The woman looked at me. "People liked her," she said, shutting her mouth like a purse with a snap. She'd been friendly before, but now something had changed.

"Did you know her?" I repeated.

The woman nodded frugally.

"After she left?"

The woman said, "I went to see her in London once."

But that's all she would say. She shook her head at all my other questions.

"Closing time," she told me finally.

I drove out to see the house, up a long open hill with hayfields on either side. It was a white farmhouse, set on the edge of a stone retaining wall. I got out and walked around, but it was closed and locked. The shutters were crooked, and the lawn was tall grass. I looked out over the view that Alison Ricks had grown up with and wondered why she hadn't come back. What had happened in London?

I was working my way through the letters. I'd finished with Naples, and moved to New York. The letters between her and Coleman had stopped because they were then living in the same city. She wrote to another friend from college, though, and there were some letters to her editor. They were fun to read. Ricks was smart and engaging. She seemed to be part of a big group of friends that did everything together. She talked about what she did and who she saw, but she said nothing about her love life, which was a little odd for a lively woman in her twenties. I wondered if she were gay, and concealing it.

I'd already begun writing the book at night, and by Christmas I'd done the first few chapters. They weren't genius—they certainly weren't Alison Ricks—but they weren't bad. I sent them to Jake and he called.

"They're good," he said, "I like them." I had the feeling he hadn't actually read them.

"What do you hear about Wareham?" I asked.

"Nothing yet," he said, which reminded me that at any moment he might find that her book was about to come out. "Have you made any discoveries? Any secrets?"

"There's some great correspondence," I said. "She writes a great letter."

"Yeah," Jake said. "That'll win you the Pulitzer."

"I think she might have been gay," I said.

Jake sighed. "Not a shocker. Would have been a shocker in the sixties, but not now."

"I know. But there's something going on." I told him about Wareham walking into the staff room. And searching through the files online I'd found there was some material that was restricted, not to be seen until twenty-five years after her death. It was only referred to by file numbers: *Alison Ricks, Files X–XIV* were not available.

"I don't know how she gets into that room," I said. "They don't give me any hint of it."

"Maybe she got special access through her editor," Jake said. "Didn't he go to Yale?" He thinks everything is determined by where you went to college. He's sort of right, but not the way he thinks.

"That wouldn't do it," I said. "It would be some other way. I think she's been buttering someone up, but who? Some big donor, maybe."

"Ask the staff," Jake said. "Butter them up." Then he changed the subject: "I did hear something about London."

"What?"

"Some rumor about the woman she lived with."

"What woman?"

"That's all I know," he said. I could hear him shrug.

The next day the Wolverine was at her desk again. She sat hunched down over her laptop as if she were about to pick it apart and eat it. She was wearing her rodent expression, squinting at the letters, ticking at her computer. Which ones was she looking at? And what had she been doing with that young man heading for the staff room?

I was buddies by now with Chelsea, and one day I asked her about the forbidden files.

She nodded pleasantly. "That's right. Not available."

"Is there any chance of just seeing them?" I asked. "Not taking notes, just reading them?"

Chelsea shook her head. "Absolutely not. They aren't even kept with the other files, so they can never be taken out by accident."

I raised my eyebrows. "By accident! Does that ever happen?"

"It has," she said, frowning. "It won't with these. They're kept in the staff office."

I nodded.

"But I've seen other researchers go into that room," I said.

"Not to look at the files," Chelsea told me. "It would be for some administrative thing. Like checking the chronology of the listings."

"Could I do that?" I asked. "Check the chronology?" I had no idea what that meant, which was so obvious that Chelsea didn't answer, only frowned and shook her head.

What was in the sealed files? I tried to deduce the content from their place among the rest, but there didn't seem to be a chronological gap.

At lunchtime each day the Wolverine would fold up her laptop and speed off, as though she were meeting someone. Of course we didn't speak to each other in the research room, where the only sound was the quiet clack of keyboards, and we also didn't speak to each other anywhere else. When we met in the hall we nodded as we passed.

One day she was there with another woman. This one was also short, but blond, with that slick streaked-hair-gold-earrings-fuck-you look, like she's too good to bother letting you cross her retina. The two of them sat side by side at the table. The Wolverine was showing her things, and talking quietly.

The next day the new woman appeared alone. I saw her at lunchtime, walking up and down outside, talking on her cell phone, and I realized, with a horrid thrill, that she was a hired assistant. I wondered again how much the Wolverine had gotten for an advance.

The letters to Ricks's editor, William Jens, in the beginning of the seventies, were entertaining. Ricks hadn't been part of the hippie crowd, but she'd been amused by it. She wrote to Jens about whatever she was working on, and talked generally about the literary world. It suddenly dawned on me that Coleman was a woman, not a man; it seemed more and more likely that Ricks had been gay. Toward the end of the decade I noticed that she began to seem uncomfortable talking about her work. When Jens asked her how things were going, instead of answering she'd deflect the question. At first she was breezy: *I wish I knew!* but then as time went on she sounded more serious: *I don't know. I don't know when the next will appear.*

The Wolverine and I continued to nod casually to each other in the halls. One day, in the ladies' room, I came out of the stall to see her standing with her back to me at the sink. She was examining her chin in the mirror. I looked directly at her, but she didn't meet my eyes, and I had the feeling she was deliberately ignoring me, she was consciously denying my existence in the world, as though I was invisible. I felt affronted, in a way that had nothing to do with our competition, and I think that in that moment, when she picked sordidly at her chin, her eyes nearly crossed in her effort to focus, our relationship turned.

That night I called Jake.

"How's it going?" he asked.

"Well," I said. "I think I have a lead." This was not strictly true, but now I was surer about Ricks being gay.

"You find out about London?" he asked, which was the question I didn't want to hear. I didn't want to leave the Beinecke, with its echoing stone courtyard and the secret societies standing guard around it. I didn't want to leave the Wolverine panting over her laptop and slipping illicitly into the staff room. I didn't want to leave her weaselly assistant. I had the feeling that if I left, something would go wrong.

"Not yet," I said.

"When?" Jake asked.

"I'll book a flight," I said.

Two weeks later I was on the plane.

During the flight I finally read Ricks's last book. I hadn't wanted to read it before, but now I had to. I read it high over the Atlantic, turning the pages faster and faster out of distaste: it was awful. The story was about a young woman in an abusive relationship, but the insights were puerile and simplistic, and the writing was utterly clumsy and dead. *The next day she woke up and sighed. It was time for some hard thinking . . . Billy gave her a heavy look, like a bulldozer.* It was painful to see the name *Alison Ricks* on the cover. Where were those golden sentences, where was that shimmering light-filled prose? I wondered if this had been her first attempt at a novel, or something written at the end, when her mind was wandering. I put it away with distaste, and also with sorrow.

I'd gotten in touch with her estate, and they'd given me permission to come to the house. There was a housekeeper in residence, and I wondered if it was the same one I'd seen twelve years earlier. Twelve or eight?

At that same tall house in Islington I knocked on the door and stood waiting on the sidewalk. For a long time I heard nothing. The street was oddly empty, and lined with high dark trees. Finally I knocked again.

The door opened suddenly. An elderly woman stood inside. I'd never seen her before. She was my height, with wide shoulders and a big bosom. Her frizzy gray hair was cut short.

"Hello. Are you the writer?" She had a loud, wheezy voice, and a slightly cockney twang.

I said yes, and she smiled and stepped back.

"Welcome!" she said theatrically.

She took me back to the kitchen, where we sat at a small wooden table. She made us tea and I asked her about Alison Ricks. I started with the basics: her name, and how long she'd worked there. I like to ask simple, factual questions first. People are sure of the answers, which gives them confidence, and then, with any luck, they open up.

"My name is Eleanor Harkwood," she said, "and I worked for Miss Ricks for thirty years. No, I lie, it's a bit longer, really, as I worked part-time here before I worked full-time."

I asked lots of questions: when had Miss Ricks moved here (1980, just before her time), how did she spend her days (working at her desk, reading, working in the garden), who were her friends?

"She had many friends," said Miss Harkwood. "Many, many friends. All writer types, I think. Very intelligent people, they were."

"And did she go out often? Or entertain?"

"She went out often, she loved it. She liked entertaining, they both did, but it was Miss Ricks who organized it. Miss Mays liked parties, but she didn't do the organizing."

"Miss Mays?" I said, my head down over my pad.

"Miss Pauline Mays," replied Miss Harkwood. "Her friend." The word "friend" seemed to be in quotes, and I looked up. She was gazing at me intently, as though hoping I was receiving some sort of signal.

"Oh, Miss Mays," I said, as though I knew who she was. "And did she live here too?"

"Oh, yes," Miss Harkwood said, nodding. "It was her house."

The estate had told me it was Ricks's house. "And is Miss Mays still living here?" I asked.

"She died ten years ago. No, I lie, it was twelve."

I tried to date my last visit to the house. Was it eight years ago? Ten? Twelve? And who had opened the door? I remembered the dark, pupilless eyes. What story had I been writing? Why was I there?

"Could you tell me a bit about Miss Mays?" I asked. "Where did she come from?"

Miss Mays came from a very grand family in Ireland, Miss Harkwood said proudly, and grew up in a very grand house. She had no family now, her parents had died when she was a child.

I asked if there any photographs of her, and Miss Harkwood got up and led me into the library.

It was a high-ceilinged room, with tall bookcases and bottle-green curtains at the windows. Against the wall stood a mahogany partner's desk, and along the back of it were framed photographs. Miss Harkwood stood beside me while I picked these up. Here was Alison as a toddler, smiling sunnily, standing by a little lake somewhere in Cornwall. Here was Alison sitting on a huge-wheeled bicycle, wearing a hat that tied under her chin.

"Miss Ricks was ever so much fun," said Miss Harkwood with satisfaction. She was a heavy woman, and she stood with her feet spread apart, supporting her weight.

I was surprised to hear that Ricks had been the party organizer, the one who was so much fun. Miss Harkwood talked more and more about them, how they all laughed. How they hated dogs and loved cats. How they had gone to Spain for Christmas every year, it was very odd, but it was what they did, said Miss Harkwood, reminiscing happily.

"And then what happened as they got old?" I asked. "Did Miss Mays die here? Was she ill?"

"Oh, Miss Mays faded away, really." Miss Harkwood's eyes took on a sentimental look. "She got a bit furry in the head. You know," she said, and I nodded. "Finally she didn't know where she was, poor thing, and she just sat in a chair all day. After that she lay in bed, and then she died."

"Poor Miss Mays," I said facilely, writing it all down. Actually, it sounded like a pretty easy way to go. "And Miss Ricks? What happened to her?"

Miss Harkwood folded her arms over her big bosoms as though she'd been waiting for this. "Pneumonia. My fahver called it the old people's friend, and so it proved to her. She was ninety-three, did you know that?" She nodded her head. "She slipped away too."

I wanted to know if the two had shared a bedroom, but it was a nosy question and I didn't want to scare her off. "Could you show me the upstairs?" I asked. "I'd love to see the rest of the house."

By now Harkwood was full of pride and information, and she hadn't had anyone to talk to for days. She took me all over the house: every bedroom (they each had their own, each with a big double bed, which didn't tell me much), and the spare rooms, and the sewing room, and even the linen closet, which Harkwood informed me was very large for a London house. I took notes on everything. We ended up in the kitchen again, and I was beginning to hear the stories for the second time.

"Could I look again at the photographs?" I asked. "I'd like to take pictures of them with my camera."

We went back in and this time I picked up each one and asked about it. One showed a pretty, laughing woman with dark eyes, wearing a full-skirted dress, with a hat and gloves.

"Is that Miss Mays?" I asked.

"Miss Ricks," said Miss Harkwood.

"I thought she had blue eyes." Surely the jacket photographs showed her with blue eyes?

Miss Harkwood shook her head. "Miss Ricks had very dark eyes, nearly black," she said. "They were strange, they looked as though they were solid black. No student."

"Pupil," I said, trying to process this. Suddenly I remembered the story I'd been writing when I'd come to the house: it was on the Chelsea Flower Show, and that was 2008. Mays had died by then, so the woman who had answered the door must had been Alison Ricks herself. But I'd have recognized her, even thirty years older than the photographs I'd seen. I'd memorized her features, I knew them from poring over those books.

"Are Miss Ricks's books here?" I asked, glancing around the room.

Miss Harkwood shook her head virtuously. "Miss Mays said it was poor form to keep your own books on the shelf. She wouldn't have a single one on the premises."

I turned back to the table again, thinking of the woman who had opened the door to me. Those black eyes, the thin white hair. The nick from the earlobe. I picked up another photograph, this one a close-up from the sixties. The same smiling, black-eyed woman, with a flirty smile. This was a three-quarters view, and it showed her right ear. There was no nick in it. Surely this was the same woman: maybe she'd gotten the nick later on?

"This is Miss Mays," I said, to see if she'd agree.

Miss Harkwood shook her head again, smiling. "No, Miss Ricks. Here's Miss Mays."

She held up another picture from the sixties, a woman with her hand over her forehead against the sun, smiling into it, at the camera. It was the picture I knew from the dust jacket of *Stone Caveat*, and I felt that electric jolt.

"I see," I said. "Is there another close-up of Miss Ricks?"

Miss Harkwood picked up another. This was taken from the other side, and the nick in the lobe was visible: I'd seen her in real life, but the camera had reversed the image. The nick was on her left ear.

"Thank you," I said, closing up my notebook. "You have been very kind."

Back in New York, jetlagged and exhausted, I called Jake. "I got it," I said. "You won't believe what happened. I'll come in and tell you."

We sat on either side of his desk and I held the cup of cold coffee again as I explained what had happened.

"I'm pretty certain she was gay," I began. "Which is why people were so closemouthed about her, and why those files were sealed."

He waved his hand.

"Wait," I said. "That's just the beginning. She moved to London so she could live with her girlfriend. But once she was there they switched identities. She stopped publishing, and she never gave interviews or allowed photographs, even when she won prizes. She had no copies of her books in her house, and over the years the new identity became real."

Jake stared at me, leaning back in his chair, his long arms sticking out at angles. "Switched? But what about Mays? She was English. People would have known her. How could she change her identity?"

"I found out more about her. She wasn't English but Irish. She must have arrived in London with Ricks and the two of them did it together."

"But why?"

"Ricks did it because she had dried up as a writer. You can see it in the letters to her editor at the end of the decade. She couldn't write, and it was painful to be asked about her work, and what she was doing, when she knew she couldn't do it anymore. Remember poor Hemingway, trying to walk into the airplane propeller because he couldn't write? I think she wanted to put that part of her life behind her, not be that person anymore."

Jake nodded slowly. "I like it," he said. "And then what about the new book?"

"Mays wrote it. I don't know when. It's probably in those secret X-files in the staff room. Then after Ricks died she got up her nerve and published it."

Jake whistled. "Zowie. And then of course she kept the house that had been Ricks's."

"It had gone on for thirty years," I said. "Kind of genius. All their London friends knew them as each other."

Jake nodded. "I like it," he said again. "But how fast can you get it down? Because I have some news for you." I waited. "It's not good. Wareham's book is on her publisher's spring list. Next year."

"*What?*" How could she be done? I'd been writing as I was researching, but I was only halfway through. How could she be finished? Well, I knew how. She'd been writing all day while the Weasel was reading the letters, then calling her to tell her what she'd found. It would be trash, pure trash, and full of clichés. And also, what was the secret she had mentioned on the phone? Was there something else I didn't know about? What had she discovered that was so amazing?

"It's going to be the lead nonfiction book," Jake said.

"I can't believe it."

"Believe it," Jake said. "Yours has to come out in the next six months or we're lost."

The next day I was back at the Beinecke. The Wolverine wasn't there, but the Weasel was, wearing a cream silk blouse and a gold bracelet, sitting at their table. In the middle of the afternoon the Wolverine appeared. She very ostentatiously did not see me, and she walked over to the Weasel and whispered something. The Weasel stood and the two of them started for the door.

I spent the afternoon going over the latest files I could get, letters from the seventies. I saw plenty of evidence of what I was looking for. When Jens asked about her next book, or even her next story, she resisted more and more. *Don't ask*, she said finally.

It killed me that I didn't have another six months to work all this together properly.

When I got up for a break, out in the hall I saw the Wolverine again. She was headed toward the staff room, though this time alone. In her clothes and style she tried to imitate the Weasel, but because she was squat and dark she couldn't. She was one of those women who throws a big scarf around her neck to appear rakish, but since she has no neck she looks as though she's drowning in textile. Today she was wearing one of those scarves, and it came up to her ears and nearly down to her waist.

She was walking away from me, down the hall, and on an impulse I followed her. I moved silently, keeping my heels from hitting the floor. I wanted to see what was behind that door. She pulled it open fast and slipped inside, but I could see through a narrow slit: several long tables, chairs standing messily about. High metal shelves against the wall held a hodgepodge of file boxes. Then the door shut and I was left out in the hall, standing on my tiptoes, wondering what she was looking at.

I had the feeling that those X-files held the fact that she was gay—which would have been a big deal decades ago, when she gave her papers to Yale, but a small deal now. So what had the Wolverine learned that was so amazing? Was it Ricks's confession, during the eighties, that she couldn't write anymore? Was it the secret of the switched identities? Or was it the secret that Pauline Mays had written the idiotic book which had been on the best-seller list for forty-eight weeks now, and which might—who knew?—mean a claim of fraud, if the publisher had presented the work of a clumsy amateur under the golden name of Alison Ricks?

The thought of Wolverine learning this made me angry. And worse, it seemed unfair that she had chewed in her horrible rodent-like way through the barrier Ricks had chosen to erect. She'd done it just by buttering up some rich donor, whereas I had done real research and found it out on my own.

There was no way I could finish my book in time to compete with the Wolverine. She had finished it in a year and a half, so it would be a quickie, superficial and trashy. Even worse, she was a terrible writer.

I'd looked up some of her stuff. I could imagine the sentences: *Alison* (she'd call her Alison, as though they were friends) *and her lesbian girlfriend, the elegant socialite Pauline May, led a scandalous life of partying and debaucheries.*

Did she even know what *debaucheries* meant? It made me angry just thinking of her using it.

Their big London town house was a party pad, full of wild times and bohemian revels. Drugs, sex, and liquor were rife.

Did she even know what *rife* meant? Could she write a single sentence without a cliché? She would write, *She must have thought* . . . a sentence that should never appear in a biography. She would call Ricks an *acclaimed author* and her work *luminous* and *provocative* and *compelling,* and say that her writing was *haunting* and her style was *deft.*

I doubted that she had even read Ricks's work, or had any idea why it was great. Whereas I had not only read every book, I also owned them all, and I had bought them years ago, as they came out.

The more I thought about the Wolverine's terrible writing the angrier I became, standing in the hall as I thought about her cliché-ridden style, and her big fucking advance, and her trashy, splashy, successful book that was going to be the lead nonfiction book on the spring list. Across from me Chelsea was standing at her desk. She looked up, her eyebrows raised interrogatively. I was motionless, doing nothing.

"Do you need something?" Chelsea called over. "Or are you just thinking?"

"Thinking," I said. "Trying to decide what angle to follow next."

Just then the door to the staff room opened and the Wolverine came out. She peered up and down the hall, then walked quickly toward us. She didn't look at either Chelsea or me, but stared straight toward the exit. She was wearing thick stacked heels and a skirt, with one of her big drowning shawls over her neck and shoulders. There was something odd about her posture: her shoulders were even more hunched than usual. They were drawn up high under her shawl, making her even more neckless.

As she walked past me, steaming along on her short thick legs, her rodent-like profile jutting out ahead of her, I thought again of her terrible writing and something came into my mind, out of nowhere. I stepped forward and stuck out my foot.

The Wolverine tripped, staggered, lurched, and fell head-long. She landed on her knees, putting her left hand out to break her fall. With her right hand she was clutching at her chest. Out from beneath the shawl fell a file folder. When it hit the stone floor it spilled its contents: a sheaf of handwritten letters.

There was a silence. No one moved.

Chelsea said, "Miss Wareham."

Then we heard the sound of the alarm, loud and metallic against the alabaster walls.

It was the first time I'd heard a loud noise in the library, and the first time I'd seen speed and confusion there, people running, hard shoes on stone floors, raised voices, the static of walkie-talkies, the complicated metallic synchrony of doors locking.

I liked the library when it was silent and light-filled, suffused with that alabaster glow. I liked it when it was like a church, where people moved slowly and reverentially, and spoke in hushed, respectful voices. I liked the library when it echoed the secrecy of the closed, forbidding buildings studding the narrow streets, with their sealed windows and locked doors. I liked the idea of closed archives, inaccessible information, facts that were not available to the public. I liked mysteries that were only to be shared with those dedicated initiates who had earned the right to be inducted into the world of secret knowledge. I liked the Beinecke when it held those secrets within its silent realm.

But I liked it like this even more.

THE BOY

BY KAREN E. OLSON

Fair Haven

While they wait, she gives the boy a glass of milk. His hand shakes, almost spilling it, and she indicates he should sit. So he does. His eyes flitter around the room, and she positions herself between him and the back door. She knows what he's considering, and she'll have none of it. He drinks the milk in three gulps without breathing in between, and she marvels at that. It's as though his thirst is unquenchable. She wonders when he last had milk. His lanky build is almost anorexic, but it could just be that he is at that age where he is growing into himself. She remembers that, how awkward and uncomfortable it is as your body molds and stretches into what it will eventually become. He is a good-looking boy, maybe twelve, thirteen. His face is long, his cheekbones high, his nose wide, his skin swarthy. His ears stick out a little from beneath the close-cropped hair. His eyes are full of fear.

She puts a cannoli from Rocco's on a plate and shoves it across the table. He gives her a wary look before scooping it up and putting half of it in his mouth at once, seemingly swallowing it whole. She hands him another glass of milk.

Taking a cannoli herself, she nibbles it slowly. Her tea went cold awhile ago, but she drinks it anyway. This was her after-dinner treat, the one that reminds her of her mother and how they'd pick out their Sunday pastries together, her mother wistfully reminding her that they would never be as good as the ones back home in Italy.

He drums his fingers nervously on the top of his leg, almost as though he is playing it like a piano. She glances toward the living room, where the baby grand sits. No one has played it in years, not since Frank died. Christmases were full of soft candlelight and the scent of pine needles and music. She wants to ask the boy if he can play, but it might embarrass him if he doesn't.

She is pretty sure it was him she saw last week downtown with a group of boys on bicycles that were from another decade, small with long seats and high handlebars. Her son used to call it a banana bike, because of the seat, and he pinned playing cards to the spokes of the back wheel and it made a *flip-flip-flip* sound as he pedaled. Those boys downtown, though, didn't want to make any noise. They pedaled past a woman with a large handbag slung over her shoulder; she was talking animatedly into her cell phone, not paying attention. It was easy for one of the boys—was it this one?—to pull the bag off the woman's shoulder as he rode past. She marveled at his swift, smooth movement, not even hesitating. It was almost as if she were watching a dance, like that show on TV with the celebrities and the judges, what was the name of it? She can't remember things anymore, not like she used to. She used to dance herself, gliding along the floor in Frank's arms, her skirt fluttering around her calves, her thin heels barely making a sound against the wood, the music swirling around them. It used to be like magic.

The boy shifts a little, his eyes taking in the kitchen. For a moment, she sees what he sees: dark wooden cabinets full of nicks, worn laminate countertops, a bright red cookie jar shaped like an apple with a broken green stem, delicate china teacups on the shelf over the table, the cross over the small calendar where she writes all her appointments. It's probably better than what he's used to.

She doesn't know what she's going to do with him until they come. She's already fed and watered him; he hasn't spoken, just stares at her with those large dark eyes. He hasn't tried to leave; it's almost as though he's relieved that it ended this way. Maybe she reminds him of his own grandmother. Maybe he was brought up right and just got in with the wrong crowd. She knows what can happen with that. She's known her share of boys who went bad.

Those boys from her past grew up over near James, off Grand. When they started their families, they moved to the other side of Blatchley near Ferry, a better area, even though they weren't but a few blocks from where they started. Grand Avenue was their Main Street; they were separate from the rest of the city on their patch of land: a peninsula surrounded by the East and Quinnipiac rivers and a swamp on the other side.

She doesn't like what Grand has become, all those shops and restaurants with Spanish signs owned by the Mexicans. Or are they Ecuadoreans? It doesn't really matter, because they don't speak English and she's willing to bet that most of them are illegal anyway. When her people came, when Frank's came, they were all legal. They were proud to become Americans and live in tidy houses and take advantage of the opportunities. Now she passes the old wooden houses in decline, three or four families living inside, maybe more, piles of junk in the backyards: rusted cars and bikes, dirty plastic toys, stained mattresses, old furniture. Does this boy live like that? Is that how he grew up?

The boy is fidgety. She doesn't have any more cannoli,

and he's finished up the last of the milk. She's only got a little half-and-half left, and she wants that for her morning coffee. She's got to keep something for herself. There might be a little bread in the box, it's from Apicella's, which is still on Grand after all these years. When she's out doing her shopping, she always stops in for a loaf of bread, the scent bringing her back to her childhood. She walks all the way to Ferraro's for everything else; she won't set foot into that C-Town ever since that one time when she saw those kids with the knife. It's cheap, though, and sometimes she's tempted because she always likes a bargain.

It's not as though she doesn't have money. She's got enough to live on, what with the Social Security and Frank's insurance. She doesn't need much. The house was paid off a long time ago. Her son wants her to move to East Haven, near him. She and Frank decided to stay here in Fair Haven back when everyone else was going to East Haven or the East Shore, and she thinks if she moves now it would be a betrayal of Frank. Her son doesn't understand, tells her how unsafe the neighborhood is now, it's not like in the old days when everyone had protection. He wants to take care of her. She told him maybe she'd consider one of those new condos along the river, but it was really only to keep him quiet. If she lived there, she wouldn't be able to have her vegetable garden anymore. It's not what it used to be, only a few tomatoes, some green beans, zucchini, garlic, and onions, but she likes to work the small plot, get her hands dirty. What would she do without it? She doesn't want to plant in the community garden, that sad little patch of land that's overgrown, showing how no one really cares.

She worries, however, that her son will put her in the Mary Wade Home over on Clinton at some point if her memory keeps failing. Agnes and Emelia ended up there, forced to leave their homes by their children, and they didn't last long. Once you go to a place like that, it's over pretty quick because you know it's the last stop and who wants to keep living with the smell of urine and disinfectant in the air all the time?

The boy shifts in his seat, and she holds up her hand. He catches his breath, stops moving, obedient. She wants to ask him about himself, where does he live, how did he end up here like that, but she isn't sure she should invest that much in him. One of the things about getting older is that you suddenly stop caring what people think or what other people's lives might be like. She lives with her memories, wraps them around her while she sips her sherry, watching the world go by from her front window.

There's the young woman who jogs in the early evenings with those wires in her ears and the young families who walk on weekends with their strollers and designer coffees as though the neighborhood is gentrifying rather than deteriorating. It's just less expensive than anywhere else, which is how they can afford to live here, making it easier to pretend that it will turn around. They close their eyes to the little ones, their eyes wide, their bellies growling with hunger, only half dressed even in the winter, leaning against the rickety railings on the decrepit front porches.

She wonders if this boy was one of those little ones, then admonishes herself. Of course he was. He wouldn't be here right now if he wasn't. He looks familiar. He looks a little like those boys she grew up with. No, that's not it. She is certain she has seen him, but she can't remember where.

She doesn't understand why he's still here. Oh, that's right. She reaches for the phone, then remembers that she's already called, that they are waiting. She opens the Frigidaire and looks for milk, but the carton isn't there. *Where did it go?* she wonders, then spots the empty glass next to the boy on the table. He drank all of it, didn't he?

She takes the bottle of sherry out of the cupboard and pours herself a small glass. The boy's eyebrows rise, and she makes a face at him. It's like with her son, always nagging her about things. Doesn't he know she can take care of herself? She's been here a long time. She's survived it all. Survived all of them. No one is left. They're not even in prison anymore. They're dead. Midge disappeared to who knows where back in the seventies. They say he's at the bottom of Bridgeport Harbor. She's always thought he might be in someone's backyard, here in town, right under their noses. Serves him right. He should have known better from the get-go. He was no stranger to the life. Holding up that card game was a mistake. It was the first time they sent him away. He might not have been a dashing fellow, that Midge, but he was always charming.

Billy was a different story. He scared her. Scared her father and Frank too. Scared everyone. Like Whitey. The two of them were the same. Cold-blooded. It was no surprise they ended up the way they did. They deserved it.

She wonders about the boy: does he deserve it?

He's looking at the door again. She reaches over and puts her hand on his forearm. He stiffens; she can feel the tension. He doesn't know what's going to happen now. He's not as tough as he thinks he is; he's not like Midge or Billy. She can see the softness in his eyes, behind the fear. Maybe this is his first time. Maybe it's like the bomb. The one that killed that child.

She pulls her hand away and sits back farther in her chair, farther away from him. She doesn't see him anymore as she pictures the shattered windows, the blood splatter on the sidewalk. Why is it that she has such trouble remembering what she needs at the grocery store, but the bus stop is as if it happened only moments ago? Every detail is etched in her memory and won't let go: Frank in the basement, heading out through the cellar door; two hours later, they were having dinner and the sound of the blast echoed through the house, making it shake like an earthquake. She rushed down the few blocks, along with everyone else, to see the charred remains of the car, the mother kneeling on the pavement next to the child with a piece of the car's fender sticking out of his chest, her screams almost inhuman, Frank whispering over and over to himself that it wasn't supposed to happen that way.

She touches the short gray curls near her ears, patting them down, pretending that she doesn't hear the low roar. She knows it's not real, that it's all in her head, but she can't make it go away, no matter what she does. Her son keeps taking her to the doctor to adjust her hearing aids, but she can't tell him that's not the problem. She can't tell him about that day. About what his father did for a living because he was a part of something that always ended in a violent death.

The equipment and tools are still in the basement. They're in a locked trunk. Her son asks what's in it, and she tells him she doesn't know, that the key is long gone. He has not pushed it, but she's often wondered if he really does know what his father used to do down there. If that's not the real reason why he wants her out of here, so he can get rid of the evidence. As long as she's living here, she won't let him get rid of anything.

What's not locked is the cabinet in the den. She reaches into her apron pocket and fingers the iron key. The boy sees her movement and flinches. She frowns at him. Doesn't he know that he's safe now? That the danger is gone? She opens her mouth to say so, but the words don't come. The ringing in her ears is worse; she wouldn't be able to hear herself anyway. So she merely shakes her head, as befits the situation.

He doesn't belong here, but he is here. How did he get here anyway? She hates it that her memory does this. Moments are lost, some forever, some come back. She has no control over which. And then as quickly as she forgets, she remembers. She was watching the news, like she does every night after supper, when the doorbell rang. Her plate with the chicken bone and potato skin is still on the counter. She usually washes up after the news.

She wasn't going to open the door tonight. She never opened the door after dinner or when it got dark—she knew better than that—but the banging started and wouldn't stop. Rage filled her—how could they interrupt her evening like this?—and she turned the knob and yanked it open, ready to give them a piece of her mind.

The boys charged into the house, shouting about something.

All she could see was the gun.

The one with the gun raised his hand, and she felt the blow against the side of her head. She spun around and watched her hearing aid skitter across the floor. She was so busy focusing on it that she didn't see him come at her from the other side. He grabbed her arm, pulling her off balance, and she stumbled, her ankle bending unnaturally. She had the crazy thought that she couldn't fall on her hip, that would be the death of her, and then the hand tightened around her wrist and yanked it. She did fall, but on her knees, which had been filled with pain for years and now it was excruciating. He dragged her across the floor and into the den. Her glasses were half off her face; everything was blurry and her ears weren't working right, sounds were muffled.

Where was the other one? She frowned. He was saying something; his lips were moving, but she couldn't make it out. He was shouting now, looking up toward the stairs, shouting more, finally dropping her arm, and she pulled it underneath her like a bird with a broken wing. The wood floor was cool against her cheek.

For a moment, he peered down at her, his lips opening, baring his teeth, and she was reminded of a pit bull she'd encountered a few months ago, but it was on the other side of a fence and this boy was leaning closer and closer until—

He was gone.

She lay on the floor, feeling the vibrations. He was heading upstairs. That's where the other one had gone. What would they find there? Her jewelry, her mother's pearls, her father's watch, Frank's cuff links. None of it is worth a thing; she'd sold the good stuff years ago to pay for Frank's care. She doesn't have any money up there; it's in the freezer, in the coffee can, an old trick that these kids probably wouldn't think of. There are some drugs, her aspirin, her blood pressure medication, the Valium—but that's so old it probably wouldn't work anymore.

It was only a matter of time before they found out she had nothing worth taking.

Frank was in her head then, telling her to get up. She couldn't die like this; she'd rather go to the Mary Wade Home and continue to lose her mind. It wasn't gone yet, though, and she knew what she had to do.

She ignored the pain in her knees and crawled across the floor. The cabinet loomed overhead, and she pulled herself up by grabbing onto the arm of the chair next to the desk. She glanced back for a second, saw nothing, fished the key out of the desk drawer, and unlocked the cabinet.

When they came back downstairs and burst into the room, she fired.

The first one fell, a blossom of red spreading across his chest.

The other one let out a shriek. He was just a boy. Her hand, no, her entire arm, was shaking, but his eyes were focused on the gun.

She waved it in front of him, stepping over the boy on the floor, ignoring the blood. It would come back, like the blood on that sidewalk so many years ago, but for the first time in a long while, her head was clear and the ringing in her ears was gone. She could even hear the siren in the distance.

Her hand steadied, and a sense of calm spread through her.

She pointed the gun at him like Frank taught her.

"Do you want something to drink?" she asked.

EVENING PRAYER

BY STEPHEN L. CARTER

Dixwell Avenue

The boy hated Mondays most. He used to hate Sundays most, but that was before Yale happened to his father.

The reason the boy hated Sundays was that church took half the morning and he had trouble keeping still that long. His mother was in the choir and his father in his black suit sat up front with the deacons, so the boy was stuck in a pew with Mrs. Percy and her girls. Mrs. Percy was very strict. Her girls could sit for three hours and never move once. The boy knew he was wicked because he couldn't sit still like they did, and Mrs. Percy was always shaking him by the arm and hissing at him to stop fidgeting. The boy understood. He had realized years ago that he was going to hell. Every week Pastor Harrigan talked about the flames that awaited the unrepentant sinners and, from the looks Mrs. Percy and the other church ladies gave him when he squirmed or dropped the hymnal or yawned, the boy knew he was one of them.

Mrs. Percy was a big, dark, round lady who wore a white hat and a veil to church. She and her son Christopher ran the candy store. Mr. Percy was dead. Christopher only had one leg. He was crippled from the war. Christopher was even meaner than his mother. If you spent too much time looking at the comic books in their spinning rack, he would yell at you to get out and then roll up a newspaper and swat you unless you were quick. But in church he liked to get up and tell the congregation about everything the Lord had done for him. Sometimes he would tell the story of how he got his leg blown off in the war by a mine and should have bled to death but Jesus saved him. The boy thought a mine was a cave where you dug for gold and he couldn't figure out how a cave could explode. One day after church, Christopher and another man got in a fight about who would be better for the Negroes, Truman or Dewey. The boy's father had to break them up. Truman was the president. The boy was not sure who Dewey was. For a while the boy was not even sure exactly what a Negro was.

Then he found out, and that was when he started hating Mondays.

After church was Sunday dinner. The boy's mother would make sausage and eggs and ham and greens and grits and sweet rolls. The family would sit at the dining room table with its pressed white cloth, the boy and his mother and his father and Nana, who was his father's mother and had the room next to the boy's. Sometimes they would have guests from the church or out of town. Before dinner his father would say a long prayer. After dinner he would say another long prayer. He was always correcting the boy's table manners. He liked to say that your manners were your passport to the world. He worked at one of the big hotels down by Yale. All around the neighborhood, people nodded when the boy's father passed by. Everyone said good morning. No one ever called him by his Christian name. Everyone called him Deacon or Mister. When he took the boy to the soda fountain the man would say, No charge, Deacon. Even Christopher, Mrs. Percy's mean son, would come out from behind the counter and shake his father's hand. People were always coming to the house with problems, and the boy's father would listen and nod and listen and nod until he had the whole story. He would give them advice, and they would say thank you. Days later, on the street, they would come up to him and say it again, Thank you, Deacon. If the boy's father was on his way home and saw kids acting up, he would tell them to stop and they would do what he said. The boy was secretly proud that his father was so important, and this secret pride was another reason he was sure he was going to hell.

The church was a small brick building on Dixwell Avenue just up from Munson Street. That was how he always heard people describing things, *just up from.* Their house was just up from the church. The doctor was just up from their house. The school was just up from the doctor. But the stores where his mother liked to shop were down, not up. They were down by Yale. The boy liked to go with her. He would watch her try on dresses and she would smile at him over her shoulder. Sometimes she would stand on the sidewalk and look in the window and say, I sure would love to try that dress, but then she would not go in the store. The boy would ask why and his mother would say, Hush, sweetie pie, don't worry about it. But the white women would walk right past her and go into the store and come out with big boxes and bags. He asked an older kid at church who told him that some of the stores down by Yale did not serve Negroes.

One afternoon his mother took him downtown to Malley's to buy shoes. There were lots of department stores on Chapel Street but Malley's, with its colorful awnings and big picture windows, was his favorite. Today the windows featured a display about the store's history. The boy looked at the mannequins in their costumes from the olden days. Each diorama moved forward a few years. The styles kept changing. One window said, *Bride of Today and Her Attendants.* The bride and her attendants were all white. The last window showed the bride and groom boarding a shiny new train on the New Haven line. The groom was white too. The boy stared. His mother told him to stop gawking and hurry up. She thought he was looking at the train.

Children's shoes were on the second floor, and that was where the birdcage was too. The boy loved the cage. He ran over. The cage was taller than his father. There were parakeets chirping and singing. They jumped and fluttered from branch to branch. A blue one flapped broad-feathered wings and looked at him. The boy looked back. A sign said not to feed the birds. The boy stood there with his nose against the wire, waiting for the parakeets to start talking, but they never did.

The boy wanted red shoes but the man said red was for girls. The man said he should try blue. The boy said no. His mother said his dress shoes were always blue. She said, You love blue. The boy said, I don't love blue. I hate it. His mother said, God doesn't want us to hate. You shouldn't say things like that. So the boy said he was sorry. He tried on the blue and said he liked them. This was a lie but it wouldn't make any difference because he was going to hell anyway. When they got in line to pay for the shoes, two of the big kids who went to Yale were standing behind them. The big kids who went to Yale all seemed to wear blue scarves or white sweaters with big blue Ys on them. One of the big kids who went to Yale asked the other why the line was taking so long, and the other big kid made a joke about Darktown ladies. At least the boy thought it must be a joke because the first one laughed. But his mother blushed and grabbed the boy's hand and hurried him out of the store, and that was the day the boy decided that Yale had happened to his mother.

The boy thought his mother was very pretty. She had big brown eyes and smooth brown skin. She loved to play the piano. She loved to dress up. People called her elegant. The boy was not sure what elegant meant but he liked hearing people call his mother that. When his parents went out on Saturday night his father would always wait downstairs in the foyer in a gray suit, and when his mother came down in one of her fancy outfits he would say things like, The most beautiful woman in the world has arrived! or, Look, it's the Queen of Sheba! Then he would hold out his hand and she would take his arm and they would walk out the door.

The rest of the week his mother did not put on a fancy outfit. She worked at Yale. She wore a gray uniform with a white ruffled collar. She left for work very early, before the boy was awake. She had to take care of the offices before the professors got there. That was what she called it, taking care of the offices. She was not supposed to bother the professors, not ever. The boy did not know what a professor was, but in his mind he saw a big scaly blue monster, because of those blue scarves the big kids who went to Yale liked to wear.

The boy liked when his parents went out. Nana would take care of him. Her hair was thin and gray. She wore very thick glasses. She loved to sit in the kitchen eating snickerdoodles and reading her magazines. The magazines had funny names. *The League for the Freedom of Darker Peoples and All Oppressed* or *The Ethiopian World Federation*. When his parents went out, Nana would feed him his supper and make sure he said his prayers. The boy knew the words to "Now I Lay Me down to Sleep" and one or two others, but his father told him it was better to come up with his own bedtime prayer, a different one every night. The boy found this hard, which was another reason that he was sure he was going to hell.

Nana didn't seem to care which prayers the boy said. If he wanted to say "Now I Lay Me down to Sleep," that was fine with her. Then she would tuck him in and sit on his bed and tell him stories about how her own father had escaped from Virginia and how they sent a man to make him go back and her father had shot and killed him. Or about how when her brother went to France in what she called the First War, he was treated better there than back home. Or about how the Negroes of New Haven tried to build a college of their own a hundred years ago but the white folks wouldn't let them. Or about how Marcus Garvey would have saved the whole darker nation except that the white folks wouldn't let him. One night he asked her if the man her father had shot went to heaven. She laughed and said, He was a wicked man, but th' Lord's mercy don't know no bounds. After the day his mother bought him the blue shoes at Malley's, the boy asked Nana if maybe he could go to Europe one day. Nana laughed and said he could do pretty much anything he wanted.

The boy decided that Yale had never happened to his Nana.

On Tuesdays through Saturdays the boy went to Vacation Bible School in the basement of the church. The boy liked Vacation Bible School. It was summer and the days were very hot. There were ten big signs around the walls, one for each of the Commandments. The kids would sit there in the basement sweating in the heat and Miss Deveaux would lead them in prayer. Miss Deveaux never sweated. She was very strict, but the boy liked her. She also had the best job in the whole wide world. She worked for the A.C. Glibert Company, painting the American Flyer trains. She was surrounded all day long by black engines and green Pullman cars and red cabooses. The boy wished he had her job. So he was going to hell for envy too.

After prayers the class would sing a hymn and then one of the kids would read a psalm and then Miss Deveaux would read them a story from a thick brown book. One morning the story was about a boy named Dick who was trying to win the prize for never missing a day of third grade. Dick was so proud of never missing. Then one day he saw an old man who needed help with his apple cart. Dick helped the man and missed a day of school. The moral of the story was that helping the old man was better than winning the prize. The boy didn't know if that was right. What if Dick really needed that prize? What if Dick was a Negro and the prize was a trip to France? What if the prize was an American Flyer train set? But the boy never asked questions like that. Just thinking those questions was probably enough to send him to hell.

After story time, the class would sing another hymn and then Miss Deveaux would read them another story, like about why Jesus came and how he died for them, or about how Hannah wanted a baby and prayed until God gave her one. Then they would stand up and make a circle and join hands and sing some more, and then it was time for lunch and school would be over for the day. Usually the boy had to stay late, because his mother could not pick him up until three o'clock. Miss Deveaux or Mrs. Percy would look after him and a few of the others whose mothers had to work. Mrs. Percy would shake her head and say how terrible it was that a woman should have to work. Supporting the family was the husband's job, she would say. The boy wondered whether that meant it was sinful for Mrs. Percy to run the candy store.

On Saturday mornings the boy's father would come to Vacation Bible School. He wore the same black suit he wore for Sunday services. Miss Deveaux would warn the kids to be on their best behavior while the senior deacon was talking. Then she would fold her hands and sit quietly, just like the kids. The boy's father would stand in the front of the room. He would talk about why it was important to listen to their elders and do what they were told. He would tell them how God had put them on this earth not to do what they wanted but to do what was right. He would tell them how the only way to know what was right was to listen to their parents and their teachers and go to church and also read the Bible with their families. Sometimes he would go around the room and ask each of the kids their favorite Bible verse. Some of the kids would say things like John 14:6 or Matthew 8:27, and some would say things like the story about the loaves and the fishes. His father would nod and go on to the next kid. But if one of them didn't have an answer, his father would write a note to the parents, and the kid would have to bring it back the next day signed. And the kids who didn't know any Bible verses were always so embarrassed that they knew five by the next time the boy's father came. The fact that the kids were all scared of his father was another reason the boy was so proud of him, even if he was scared of him too.

After Vacation Bible School on Saturdays, the family would climb into the big black Buick and go motoring. That was what the boy's father called it, motoring. Nana usually stayed home. Sometimes they motored to the beach. Sometimes they motored to a state park. But what the boy loved best was when they would motor up to West Rock and park by the fence and get out of the car and watch the men blasting a tunnel through the mountain. The men wore helmets with lights on them. They would go into the tunnel pushing a cart on a track and a little while later there would be a big explosion. The fence would shake. The boy would think about Christopher getting his leg blown off by a mine. But it looked like a very exciting job. All of the men digging the tunnel were white. The boy watched closely for any injuries. It's dangerous work, his father would say as they motored back home in the shiny black Buick. Let's remember to pray for them tonight. His father had been in the war too but he still had both of his legs. The boy wondered if the men digging the tunnel prayed for the Negroes.

Vacation Bible School had Mondays off, and so the boy would stay home all day with Nana. After he did his chores she would let him read comic books and sometimes even listen to the radio. When his parents were home, they usually listened to music or shows with important-sounding names like *America's Town Meeting of the Air*. But Nana liked to sit in her room with her eyes closed and her feet up and listen to the radio preachers. Or she might tune in *Aunt Jenny's Real Life Stories* and listen to the recipes and say things like, No, no, Jenny, that's wrong, you don't use paprika. Nana was always complaining about the heat, so the boy would go down to the kitchen and pour her some lemonade even though his mother did not really allow it upstairs. He would sit with Nana and rub her feet. When it was the boy's turn to pick a radio show, he chose *The Answer Man* and *Ripley's Believe It or Not!* And if he did a few extra chores, Nana might let him listen to *The All-Star Western Theatre* or *The Lone Ranger*, even though she knew his father disapproved. But there she would draw the line. The other kids were always talking about *Amos 'n' Andy* and *Baby Snooks*, but Nana would say, No, boy, you know what your father says, they are forbidden in his house.

Then she would close her eyes again. Nana's feet were big and wrinkled and knobby. Sometimes while the boy rubbed her feet she would call him by his father's name.

Then one Friday Nana could not get out of bed. The boy's mother took her to Grace–New Haven Hospital and came home that night and told the boy's father that they were keeping her in the ward while they did some tests. His father nodded his stern head and went out on the porch. The boy asked what was wrong and his mother said to leave his father alone just now. They stood by the parlor window and looked out at the dark street. After a while the boy asked his mother if having tests meant that Nana was going to die. His mother's eyes got teary and she gave him a hug and kissed him and took him upstairs to wash and say his prayers and get tucked in.

On Sunday the pastor asked everybody to pray for Nana. He called her Our Sister. After church his parents took him to the hospital. It was a big brick building with dark hallways. It smelled. There was a new wing that was brighter but Nana was in the old part. There were twelve beds in her ward and there was a woman in every one of them. A lot of them had bandages, and a lot of the bandages were dirty. There wasn't much light because the windows were mostly blocked by the building next door. There were liquids spilled on the floor. There seemed to be only one nurse. Nana was in the last bed, down by the wall. Screens were set up between the beds. Each bed had a wooden chair, so his mother sat next to Nana and held her hand, and his father stood on the other side and held her other hand. The boy wanted to rub Nana's feet but they were covered with a sheet. His mother and father did not pay attention to him, so he decided to go look at the other women. No one seemed to mind as he wandered along the row of beds, peering past the screens, trying not to step in any of the spills. He noticed that all of the women in the ward were Negroes. Maybe white people never got sick.

That night the family ate cold fried chicken from the Frigidaire. His mother did not believe in leftovers on Sunday but she served them anyway. She seemed sad. His father looked just as stern as he did every other day. He scolded the boy for getting crumbs on the cloth. He scolded the boy for being too slow clearing the table. After prayers, he told the boy that because Nana was in the hospital, she would not be able to take care of him tomorrow. The boy wondered if that meant he would be able to listen to *Baby Snooks*. But his father was still talking. Neither I nor your mother can take a day off just now, he said, so you will have to go with me to work tomorrow.

The boy was surprised. To the hotel? he asked.

That's where I work, his father said. Pray for Nana tonight, he said, and his voice sounded funny.

In bed that night the boy could hardly sleep. The hotel! He had never seen his father at work at the hotel. His father never talked about what he did there. But the boy was proud that his father worked at the hotel. It was taller than the church spires on the Green. It was taller than almost all of Yale. It was built out of red bricks, except the top stories, which were covered in white stone. People were always talking about the time Babe Ruth had stayed there. And Albert Einstein, although the boy only knew he was famous; he did not know exactly who he was. The president of the United States had stayed there too, although the boy had no idea which president. The other kids said the hotel had even been in a Hollywood movie, but the boy wasn't sure whether to believe them.

On Monday morning the boy's father put on a dark suit and

a white shirt and a dark tie. He carefully combed his hair. He told the boy to put on nice clothes and his new blue shoes. They boarded the trolley even though the hotel was not that far away. His father said, We can't afford to be sweaty. The boy liked the streetcar, the way it clacked along the tracks ignoring the other traffic. The engineer would blow his horn and the cars would get out of the way. Some of the drivers honked back. The boy listened to the crackle of the pantograph. He said it would be fun to drive a trolley when he grew up. His father said, I expect more than that of you. Besides, he continued, the city will be getting rid of the streetcars soon and there will only be the buses left. The boy asked why.

Money, his father said, with that stern disapproving look.

The boy gazed out the window as they passed Yale. He was watching for blue professor monsters. But he only saw the big kids who went there. All of them were white. Nana had told him that when his father was young he used to shine shoes for the Yale kids. He was not allowed to go into the buildings where the boys lived, she said, so he would stand under the window and the Yale kids would throw their shoes outside. He would take them home and shine them up and bring them back the next day. He would knock and one of the Yale kids would open the door. He would take the shoes and say, Wait here. Then he would close the door. The boy's father would wait. Ten minutes. Fifteen minutes. Sometimes half an hour. Then the same Yale kid would open the door again. He would pay the boy's father for the shoes he shined, fifteen cents a pair. That was a lot of money in those days, Nana would say. A lot of money.

The boy and his father got off the trolley at the corner of Chapel and College. The boy took his father's hand. He stared up at the hotel. He was very excited. They walked right past the big glass doors. His father did not even turn to look. The boy was surprised. Aren't we going in? he asked. His father told him to shush. They walked around the side all the way to the back where there was a wooden door that said *Staff*. Inside was a hallway. It was very crowded. People were walking this way and that. Most of them wore brown uniforms. The men had brown hats with shiny black bills. The women had little brown caps. The boy was proud of his father again because he was wearing a suit. There were a lot of doors in the hallway. One of them said *Staff Men Dressing*. His father told him to wait here. He went in. The boy waited. There was nowhere to sit so he stood up. There were notices on the wall about all the things the staff was not allowed to do while on duty. The door opened and a tall man came out. He was wearing the brown uniform and the brown hat with the shiny black bill. He walked straight toward the boy and held out his hand and at first the boy was scared until he saw that the man was his father. His father took his hand and led him to another room. The sign said *Men Staff Lounge*. The letters were faded. Inside were some old tables and chairs. A couple of men were sitting by the window with their uniform blouses open. They were smoking cigarettes. The boy's father drew him into a corner and pointed to a bench and said he had to stay here and be quiet all day. The boy could not stop staring at this stranger in his brown uniform. His father said he would have a break in three hours and he would come and take him to the bathroom. He said there was a drinking fountain in the hall. His father was starting to say more when a man walked into the room and went straight up to him like people always did on the street. The boy wondered if he needed advice. But the man did not ask the boy's father for advice or shake his hand. The man was fat and white and bald. He called the boy's father by his Christian name and told him he was late and he'd better get about it if he expected to keep this job. Then he looked down.

Oh, he said. Who's this?

He's my son, sir, said the boy's father. With his grandmother in the hospital, I'm afraid—

The fat white man interrupted him. He spoke to the boy directly. You just keep out of the way, boy, he said. We can't be having you causing any trouble now, can we?

The boy said, No sir.

The fat white man smiled and ruffled the boy's hair. Then he walked away. The boy's father had a funny look on his face, a look the boy had never seen before. He took his son's hand and sat him on the bench.

Stay right here until I get back, he said. Do you understand?

Yes sir, the boy said.

His father left.

For a while the boy sat there. He was embarrassed. He had never seen anybody talk to his father like that. He wondered who the fat man was. Other men kept walking in and out in their uniforms. One or two of them glanced his way but mostly they did not pay him any attention at all. The boy sat on the bench. He glanced down at his shiny blue shoes. He was still upset about the way the fat white man had talked to his father. The boy kept expecting his father to come back, but when he looked at the big clock only half an hour had gone by. Finally he could not stand to wait any longer. It was wrong to talk to his father that way. He would have to find somebody to tell. He slipped off the bench and walked down the hall the way his father had gone. Nobody stopped him. He opened the door. He was in a big kitchen. He smelled fried food. He smelled spices. There was a lot of yelling back and forth. He saw the people in uniform going out a little passage off to the side, so he went that way too. He wound up in some kind of room with shelves and suitcases. He went out another door. He was in the lobby. The lobby was very bright and cheerful. The floor was tiled. The ceiling was two stories high. There were chandeliers. There was music. White people in fancy clothes were coming in through the front doors. Luggage stood on shining gold carts. Black men in uniforms pushed the carts. One of the men was his father. He was walking with a young white couple, a man and a woman, pushing their luggage on a golden cart. He walked with the couple to the front desk. The man was wearing one of those Yale scarves. He turned to the boy's father and said, Thanks, boy, and gave him some money. His father said, Thank you, sir, that's very generous, and if there's anything else I can do for you, just call down and ask for me. He gave them his Christian name. The white couple was talking to the clerk behind the desk. The boy's father just stood there waiting with the cart. Then the clerk handed over the key and the boy's father and the white couple went off toward the elevator. The boy followed them. His father said, I'll meet you upstairs with the bags, sir. The white man turned around. He said, Can you shine my shoes for me and have them back in an hour? His father said, Of course I can, sir. It would be my pleasure. Shall I pick them up when we're upstairs? The white man said, Well, I can't very well give them to you now, can I? Not when they're still on my feet. His father nodded his head and smiled and said, No sir, I expect you're right. Here's the elevator now, sir. Another Negro in a uniform stood inside. His father said, Take these nice young folks to the eleventh floor. He said to the white man, I'll see you upstairs, sir.

The elevator doors closed. His father rolled the cart down

another hallway. The boy stood there staring. He had never seen his father smile before. Not like that.

When his father was gone, the boy went back into the room with the suitcases and back into the little passage and back into the kitchen and back into the hallway and back into *Men Staff Lounge.* He sat on the bench again. He sat there for two more hours. His father came in, stern and unsmiling. He took the boy to the bathroom. He gave the boy an apple and a peanut butter sandwich to eat. He said, You'll only have to sit here a few more hours, son. I'm leaving early today.

The boy sat on the bench for three more hours. Then his father came back. He asked if the boy had to go to the bathroom. The boy said no. They went out into the hall. His father went into *Staff Men Dressing.* He was out fifteen minutes later, back in his suit and crisp white shirt. He took the boy's hand and they left the hotel. Across the street was an ice cream shop. He bought the boy a cone and they walked to the trolley stop. His father hardly said a word on the ride home. They passed Yale again. The boy looked out at the stone towers with their long windows and wondered how it would feel to be one of the kids inside throwing his shoes out.

That night after dinner the boy got down on his knees to say his prayers. His mother sat on the bed. She reminded him to pray first for others. So he asked God to make Nana better. Then his mother said he should give thanks. So he said, God, thank you that Monday is over and tomorrow is Tuesday and I can go back to Vacation Bible School. Then he said, I hate Mondays, God. I really hate them. His mother was upset. Don't say things like that, she said. I told you, God doesn't want us to hate. The boy said he was sorry. But he already knew he was going to hell. Then his mother said he should say a prayer for himself. He shut his eyes tightly.

Dear God, he said, when I grow up, please, God, I will do anything you want. I will be anything you want. But please, God, please, don't let me grow up to be a Negro. Amen.

[Author's Note: For more on the origin of this story, see Chapter 1 of my novel Palace Council, *as well as the author's note at the end of the book. The Edward Malley store on Chapel Street did indeed have the window display the boy describes in 1948. In the fall of that year, New Haven did indeed retire the streetcars. The Vacation Bible School lessons are drawn from Florence M. Waterman,* Standard Vacation Bible School Courses: Primary–First Year, *published in 1922.]*

SECOND ACT

BY JESSICA SPEART

Food Terminal Plaza

I t was the way her hand hovered around the deli case that first caught his eye. It fluttered back and forth like a butterfly caught in a moment of indecision. Her palm finally came to rest between the salami and the tuna salad and her fingers lightly tap-tap-tapped on the glass window case.

"Come on, already. Pick something, will ya? I wanna order a sandwich and get back on the road," groused the trucker behind her.

Jimmy saw the heat rise in her cheeks and planted his meaty fists on the countertop. "Leave the lady alone. I'm sure McDonald's can wait a couple of extra minutes for your delivery. Take your time, miss. Don't let this bum rush you."

The trucker angrily tugged on his blue *Ferelli Sausage* cap. "Screw you, Jimmy. The taco trucks have better food than this place does, anyway."

"Sure, if you like chowing down on crappy corn cakes filled with mystery meat. Try not to choke on the truck fumes coming from I-95 while you stand there eating your lunch."

Annabelle's eyes lowered as she drifted off into thought. She didn't say a word although she knew the food trucks they were talking about. Parked on a thin strip of asphalt along the waterfront, they resembled a flock of exotic birds with their colorful array of plume-like flags and flashy yellow, green, and

red exteriors. The pulsating sounds of salsa and mariachi music blared from their speakers most of the day and into the
night. She'd been drawn to them one evening after rehearsal.
Their siren song had lured her past Ikea, under the highway
overpass, and on to Long Wharf Drive where the sun was
beginning to set. It hung in a fiery ball above a group of white
petroleum storage tanks, round as moon pies, that lay across
the Sound.

She had walked past the semitrailers and parked cars to
where a crowd had gathered. Truckers and New Haven college students stood in separate groups laughing and talking as
they ate quesadillas and burritos topped with bright green
salsa. One college boy had looked at her askance as she'd
joined the end of a line.

"I'll take two tacos, please," Annabelle said upon reaching
the front of the food truck.

"What kind do you want?" asked the young girl leaning
out its side window.

"Oh, dear. I don't know. I don't eat Mexican food all that
much." Her mind drew a blank as she studied the menu board.
What she wanted to do was turn and run.

"Try the pork loin. They're nice and juicy tonight," whispered a voice in her ear.

Spinning around, she saw a trucker standing behind her,
his T-shirt stretched tight across his chest and his nipples
erect from the wind whipping across the Sound. His gold
tooth caught the last rays of light, gleaming bright as hidden
treasure.

"Trust me. They're so moist you're going to be begging for
more. It's a good night to try things you've never had before."
He leered at her and she did as he said. "Give her a beer too,"
he added.

That was the first of many drinks Annabelle had that evening.

"My name is Tommy Corona. You know, *Corona*. Just like the beer."

It was the last thing she remembered him saying. The next morning, she woke up in a strange bed.

"The chicken salad is nice and fresh today, miss. Why don't I make a sandwich of it for you?"

The words plucked her from her thoughts and she looked up to where Jimmy stood smiling at her across the deli counter.

"Thank you. That would be nice. I'm sorry that I made you lose a customer."

"Who? That mook? Oh, hell. Don't worry about him, pardon my French."

Annabelle watched as he spread the chicken salad neatly between two slices of bread. He was portly with a sparse head of hair that was carefully combed across his scalp. The tip of his tongue, pink as a wound, grazed his upper lip as he deftly sliced the sandwich in two. This was a man who clearly enjoyed his food.

"There. I think you'll need a bag of chips to go along with that."

Annabelle quickly calculated the total in her head. "Please don't bother. Just the sandwich will be fine."

"Here, take it," he said, waving her ten-dollar bill away like a pesky fly. "Lunch is on the house today for having to deal with that jerk. I'd hate to think you wouldn't come back again."

"Of course I will. I'm rehearsing a play at Long Wharf Theater next door. So I'll be working here for a while."

He brightened and Annabelle thought he wasn't such a

bad-looking man after all. He'd be quite handsome if he were only thirty pounds lighter.

"I thought you looked like a movie star! What's your name? Have I seen you in anything?"

Annabelle cringed inside, although her smile remained in place. She always sensed the disappointment that usually followed her answer. "Probably not. Most of my work is on the stage. I'm Annabelle Rogers. I'm sure you've never heard of me before."

"Annabelle Rogers," he repeated. The name tingled on his lips like a fine sparkling wine. "Well, if you're not a movie star yet, you should be. You're as pretty as one and you've got a good name. Pleased to meet you, Annabelle Rogers. I'm Jimmy Carbonara. You know, *Carbonara*. Like the spaghetti sauce."

Annabelle shivered at the memory of Tommy Corona.

"You're cold! Here, take a cup of coffee with you. Let me know if you like the sandwich and I'll make something special for you next time."

He couldn't take his eyes off her as she smiled. Annabelle Rogers was no twenty-year-old, but still totally doable. Tall and slim, she was stacked in all the right places. She was an absolute babe and completely out of his league. He'd never thought about going to the theater before. Maybe it was time he got some culture. He was already dreaming what to make her for lunch tomorrow as she waved goodbye and walked out the door.

Refrigerated trailers hummed where they sat in their bays and hand trucks groaned under the weight of crates loaded with sausages and boned chickens. Annabelle hurried past the meatpacking plants and walked through a parking lot the length of three football fields. Close to the docks, the theater was located in the heart of New Haven's food terminal.

She hadn't performed at Long Wharf Theater before and was grateful for the job. People always assumed an actor's life was filled with glamour and glitz, but the profession wasn't all it was cracked up to be. At least it hadn't been for her, so far.

It had been nearly a year since her last acting gig, and the ones she tended to land paid very little. Some of them paid nothing at all. Unemployment checks gradually kicked in, but they eventually ran out and then she was left to scramble. Annabelle usually managed to find work waiting tables, temping as a phone-sex operator or a lowly telemarketer dialing for dollars. There were days when she felt as if her life had become nothing more than a walking cliché.

People always said that talent and hard work would eventually pay off. Annabelle had believed that to be true when she'd left Kansas and moved to New York City. She'd relentlessly studied her craft and gone on endless auditions and cattle calls. But years later she remained just another pretty face, one in a long line of hopefuls who were still pounding the pavement. Only now, at forty-six years old, she was no longer so young and her beauty was on the wane. It wasn't the same for men. Show business could be cruel that way. George Clooney was box-office gold at fifty-four while Anne Hathaway felt washed up at thirty-two. A woman of Annabelle's age was considered ancient.

She had vowed to give up acting any number of times but couldn't get off the merry-go-round. A small role always seemed to come along that was just enough to keep her going. She found herself trapped in a perpetual game of trying to grab hold of the brass ring. What Annabelle needed was a decent break but she'd begun to think it would never come. Not until a few weeks ago.

Thank God for the casting director who'd seen her perform in some half-assed play at a run-down warehouse in Brooklyn. Her prayers were answered when he'd called and offered her the lead in a new production at Long Wharf Theater the very next day.

All those years of heartache and scrimping to get by might finally be over. A plum role and good reviews would help to launch her career. With any luck, the play would move to Broadway and movie roles would begin to roll in. Maybe she'd no longer be plagued by nightmares of being a bag lady. Instead, Ryan Seacrest would ask to interview her as she walked down the red carpet of her dreams.

She had worked hard for this and paid her dues. Success was now within her reach. Annabelle Rogers was bound and determined not to let anything stop her.

Jimmy Carbonara's heart skipped a beat as she entered his store the next afternoon.

"So you must have liked the sandwich, huh?"

Annabelle smiled and he had to remind himself to breathe as the rest of the customers melted into the background.

"It was delicious, Jimmy. The best I've ever had."

Just the way she said his name made his testosterone level soar. "That's 'cause I put a little extra love into it. What can I get you today?"

"Surprise me, Jimmy. Make me something special."

Annabelle couldn't have been feeling better. She was beginning to remember her lines and the director seemed to be happy, even if rehearsals were still a bit bumpy. Then there was Jimmy. A man hadn't looked at her this way in years.

He thrust a round to-go tin into her hands. "Here, I made it for you this morning in case you showed up. How about I take you out to dinner tonight? Nothing fancy, just some good food. We can go to the Italian place next door."

She hesitated. "Thank you, Jimmy. That's very nice, but—"

"Aw, come on. Give a guy a break. This way I can say I once went out with a famous actress."

She took a peek inside the tin. A mound of egg salad had been molded in the shape of a heart.

"Hey, I know I'm not Sylvester Stallone, but I'm no Pee-wee Herman either."

Annabelle was surprised to hear herself laugh. "No, you're not. You're my charming gentleman caller."

"Oh yeah? Who's that?"

"He's a wonderful character from *The Glass Menagerie.* It's a play by Tennessee Williams that I was once in."

"So, what do you say? Can I take you to dinner tonight or what?"

Annabelle considered the invitation. What harm could it do? She'd been working hard and was tired of living on canned tuna and pizza. Besides, an evening out might help her relax.

"All right," she agreed. "I'll meet you here at seven o'clock."

Jimmy gave her a wink. "I'll be waiting with bells and whistles on."

He kept an eye on the time for the rest of the day. At six forty-five, he opened a bottle of wine, poured two glasses, and slipped some mood music into the boom box. When she hadn't arrived by seven fifteen, his stomach started to churn. He began to anxiously pace the floor when the clock hit seven thirty.

What in the hell's going on? Is this bitch standing me up?

He was cursing every woman he'd ever known by seven

forty-five when she finally opened the door. He'd never seen such a vision before. Annabelle Rogers was decked out in a gauzy formfitting red dress. B.B. King wailed the blues as she walked into his store. Now *this* had been something worth waiting for.

Her body tingled as she saw him checking her up and down. "Is one of those glasses of wine for me or do you plan on drinking them both yourself?"

His pulse throbbed as he handed one to her. There was something different about her tonight. Annabelle's hips swayed to the music as she took a deep sip. His hormones morphed into fireworks while he stood and watched, mesmerized. Jimmy wouldn't be able to keep his hands off her if they stayed here any longer.

"What say we finish our drink and split this joint? I reserved us a table next door and we're already late."

Annabelle thrust out her lips in a playful pout. "It's such a beautiful evening, I'd much rather be outside. Why don't we go and eat at the food trucks? I can hear music playing there and we'll be able to dance."

Her hips swiveled as B.B. King crooned "I Put a Spell on You." She twirled and wine from her glass spilled onto the floor like tiny drops of blood. How could he deny her anything?

"It's a pretty rough place for a lady. Especially with the way you're dressed tonight. Have you ever been over there?"

No," she lied. "But I feel perfectly safe with you."

His eyes remained glued to her hips. "Okay. If that's what you really want to do."

"It is, Jimmy. It's what I want more than anything," she whispered in his ear, setting his body aflame.

She needed to drown herself in music after what had happened that day. Rehearsal had started off all right but had gone quickly downhill from there. She'd kept forgetting her lines and been told that the director was looking for a replacement.

Jimmy put an arm around her waist and guided her across the street, past the highway, over to the food trucks. He placed his jacket over her shoulders to shield her from the wind.

"Buy me a beer, Jimmy. I'd like a Corona," she said, and immediately started to dance.

He considered himself a lucky man as every eye in the truck lot turned toward her. By his fourth beer, Jimmy had to admit that the food trucks weren't half bad. Even better, Annabelle pressed herself tightly against him. The air crackled with sexual tension as they danced, her body moving sinuously with his. It seemed to mold itself to the part of him that was growing. Jimmy was fantasizing how the night might end when a trucker came up and stood closely behind her.

"Hey, mama, remember me? I'm your big daddy from the other night."

Annabelle turned her head and her heart leaped into her throat. It was Tommy Corona, the trucker she'd gone home with. "I'm sorry, but you must have me confused with someone else."

"No way, mama. I'd know those hips of yours anywhere. I've been thinking about you and was wondering when you would come back again."

Jimmy's temper flared when the man brazenly placed both of his hands on Annabelle's hips. "The lady said she doesn't know you, buddy. Comprende? So do yourself a favor and back off."

The trucker's gold tooth shone bright as a star in the dark. "She knows me all right. She enjoyed nine inches of me the other night. Didn't you, sweetheart?"

"That's enough, you goddamn son of a bitch." Pushing Annabelle aside, Jimmy began to beat the man. He didn't stop until the trucker looked like a piece of raw veal.

"Come on, Jimmy. Let's go before the police get here," Annabelle urged. She began to reach for his hands before realizing they were covered with blood. "Oh, dear. Are your hands all right? Are they hurt?"

He quickly pulled them away. "Don't worry. I'm fine. I've dealt with tougher guys before. Your friend got the worst of it. I think he's going to be needing another gold tooth."

Annabelle grew quiet but she'd never been so turned on in her life. Jimmy Carbonara was a lethal weapon and he was all hers.

"Is what that guy said about you back there true? Did you sleep with him?" he angrily demanded as they headed for his store.

Annabelle's eyes welled up with tears. "No, of course not. How can you even ask that? I've never seen him before in my life."

Jimmy felt like dirt for having questioned her.

"You're my hero, Jimmy," she said while straddling him in bed later that night. "You're my big, strong protector."

He cupped her buttocks in his hands and gazed at the swell of her breasts in the moonlight. Jimmy wished she hadn't made him turn off the lamps. She was probably self-conscious but she'd have to get over that. Annabelle had a terrific body from what he could tell, and he wanted to see every inch of it. So what if she was no spring chicken? Neither was he. How had he gotten so lucky? "I'd do anything for you, Annabelle. You know that."

"Would you? Would you really? I've been hurt so many

times, Jimmy. Promise you'll always protect me and won't let anyone hurt me anymore." Leaning over, she kissed him lightly on the lips.

"I swear it," he said, and meant it.

Annabelle didn't show up at his store the next day or the day after that and Jimmy started to worry. What had happened? Had he done something wrong? He stopped by the theater and was shown to her dressing room, where a woman could be heard crying inside.

"Annabelle, is that you? Is everything all right?"

Her eyes were red and swollen when she opened the door.

"What's wrong?" he asked. Stepping inside, he closed the door behind him.

Annabelle's bottom lip quivered and her breath caught sharp. "Oh, Jimmy. It's the director. He's firing me."

"What do you mean he's firing you? What's he doing that for?"

She placed her head on his chest and he thought for sure that his heart would break.

"Another actress wants the role. She's a friend of his so he's letting me go and giving the part to her."

Lisa Larson was to be her replacement. The woman was the bane of her existence. She'd been making Annabelle's life a living hell for years. Every role that Annabelle lost seemed to go to her.

"Can he really do that to you?"

Annabelle nodded. "The director can do whatever he wants. This role was supposed to be my big break. What's going to happen to me now?"

"Don't worry about that. I'll take care of you, but it still doesn't seem right. How about I speak to him for you?" The guy needed to be taught a lesson. Jimmy's sore knuckles throbbed at the thought. "Maybe I can talk some sense into him. You know, make him see things my way."

Annabelle's head lolled on her neck, seeming as weak as a baby bird's. "No, that wouldn't end well for either of us. It might even get me blackballed. Besides, Lisa Larson is the real problem. If only there was some way to get rid of her. She's coming by the theater later tonight. She wants to talk to me about the role." Annabelle dropped her head in her hands and began to sob harder.

Jimmy couldn't bear to see her cry. Something had to be done. Hadn't he taken a solemn vow not to let anyone hurt her? "How about if I put a little scare into her? I bet then she wouldn't want to stay and you'd get to keep your job."

Annabelle raised her head and smiled wanly. "Would you really do that for me?"

He gently wiped away her tears. "You're my girl, aren't you?"

She pressed herself against him until he could feel every muscle inside her move. "You know that I am, Jimmy."

"Then stop your crying. I'll take care of this for you."

Annabelle plucked a tissue from its box and blew her nose. "How? What are you going to do?"

"You leave that part to me. Just make sure you bring her out the back door of the theater tonight. Say you want to take her for a drink or something. It'll be dark. I'll wear a mask and rough her up a little bit. Just enough to put the fear of death in her."

"And what about me? What do I do?"

"You don't do anything except maybe pretend to be afraid and run away. Just don't attract attention or scream."

* * *

Annabelle spent the rest of the day preparing for her role that night. She wanted to be ready when her rival arrived and the proverbial curtain went up. She was seething by the time the actress swept into the dressing room.

Lisa Larson's toned body and tight skin were part and parcel of her successful career and only helped fuel Annabelle's rage. The woman could afford to hire a personal trainer and plastic surgeon with all the money she made. Even so, the wrinkles around her neck were like the rings on a tree. They gave away her age. The bitch had to be at least fifty years old.

"Oh, poor Annabelle. I feel so bad for you. But you know how Billy can be when it comes to this sort of thing. He prefers to work with actors who he already knows."

Annabelle wasn't fooled by Lisa Larson's sad face. She saw the scorn flickering beneath her mask of concern and, for once, she remembered her lines perfectly.

"Don't worry, Lisa. There are no hard feelings. I know it isn't your fault. That's why I came here tonight. Can we go discuss it over drinks?"

Lisa Larson breathed an audible sigh of relief. "That's a wonderful idea. Maybe I can get them to hire you as my understudy. Let's keep our fingers crossed."

She cast a questioning glance as Annabelle slipped on a man's jacket and a pair of large gloves. A rubber band around each wrist held them in place. "I'm not used to this weather and my fingers get cold," she explained.

She had rehearsed the next step at least a dozen times in her mind. Everything would be fine as long as Jimmy was on time and didn't miss his cue. Annabelle made sure no one was around as she led Lisa Larson through the bowels of the theater and out the rear door.

"Why don't we go back inside and use the front entrance?" Lisa said nervously when a man in a ski mask appeared.

Annabelle didn't respond but pulled a blackjack from her pocket and mustered all her strength. The club slammed into Lisa Larson's skull with a resounding thud. Had it been a baseball, she would have hit a home run. Lisa Larson's legs folded beneath her and she fell to the ground like an unstrung marionette.

Jimmy stared in disbelief as the woman's head bounced twice on the pavement. "What in the hell did you do that for?" A puddle of fluid formed at his feet.

"I was afraid she was going to scream."

Jimmy kneeled beside the body and felt for a pulse. "Jesus Christ! You bashed in her skull. She's dead!"

"I was only thinking of you, Jimmy. I didn't want you to get caught."

She dropped the weapon into a plastic bag as Jimmy headed over to his car to collect an old tarp. Carefully wrapping Lisa Larson in it, he placed her body inside the trunk.

"What do we do now?" Annabelle asked. She peeled off the gloves and slipped them in with the weapon and shoved the bag in her pocket.

"Quit talking so much and let me think," he snapped.

Annabelle was shocked at his response. Jimmy was clearly panicked. If he was going to treat her this way, he could fend for himself. She was beginning to think maybe he couldn't be trusted.

"There's a processing plant at the end of terminal. The security guard there owes me a favor. Stay here until I get back."

She watched silently as he drove over to a cyclone fence, opened the gate, and went through.

* * *

Jimmy's nerves were shot to hell. What in God's name had just happened? Things weren't supposed to go down this way. He'd talked about scaring the woman, not committing murder. The bitter taste of acid filled his mouth and his stomach was starting to burn. Damn it! He'd kill for a swig of Mylanta right about now.

He parked near the back of the plant and killed the headlights.

"Hey, pops," he said, poking the security guard who sat fast asleep on the job.

The old man woke with a start and began pecking at the night like a hungry chicken. "Who is it? I don't have any money. What do you want?"

Jimmy glanced around cautiously. "You know that favor you owe me? Well, it's time. I'm calling it in. How about you take a cigarette break and I'll keep watch for a while."

"Sure thing, Jimmy. Whatever you say." The old man's bones creaked as he stood up, stretched, and hobbled off in the dark.

Jimmy took a deep breath and opened the trunk of his car. The remaining heat fled Lisa Larson's body as he pulled out the tarp and dragged her down the steps of the processing plant.

Jimmy had worked as a butcher before. He'd carved plenty of animals and knew what had to be done. After cutting her up, he threw the body parts into the chopper where a lethal line of sharp blades went to work. From there, the flesh was blended in a large vat and fed through a funnel and came out the other end looking like a meat smoothie.

He swore he'd never eat another hot dog again. But there had been no choice. It had to be done to protect Annabelle. His loins tingled at the thought of how she would repay him later tonight. Annabelle owed him big time. She'd be at his beck and call. Yet when he drove back behind the theater, she wasn't there. He scoured the area, but she was nowhere in sight.

There had been no time to think about things before. Now that he did, the images that came at him were fast and furious. Annabelle had been wearing the jacket he'd loaned her the other night. His gloves had been shoved in the pockets. As for the blackjack, she must have found it hidden in his desk drawer. Jesus Christ. Had she been setting him up all along?

Jimmy rushed back to his store. Annabelle wasn't there either. But a note had been slipped under the door. He unfolded the scrap of paper with trembling fingers.

Sorry, Jimmy. It was fun while it lasted. But all good things must come to an end. Think of me whenever you go to the food trucks. It's time that I begin my second act.

THE GAUNTLET

BY JONATHAN STONE

Edgewood Avenue

In my junior year of college, I lived off campus with several roommates—Larry from Rye, New York, Roger from Brentwood, California, Bruce from Chagrin Falls, Ohio, and Lionel from Lincoln, Nebraska. We rented the basement apartment and the open-plan, skylighted second floor of a blue clapboard house whose first-floor apartment was occupied by Keneisha—a sometime prostitute and drug dealer—and her six-year-old son Marcus. (We bought dime bags from her—probably the only genuine convenience of off-campus living, as it turned out.) Keneisha wore a gold necklace with a gold phallus pendant, which nestled in permanent thrall deep in her cleavage. I got the sense that Keneisha at some point had put out the word to leave the Yale boys alone, but her word apparently went only so far. Because while we were never burglarized or attacked inside the house, on the walk from the house to campus we were, it seemed, fair game. Hell, we were more than fair game. We were sport.

This was Edgewood Avenue. Edge*wood*—accent on the second syllable for the proper local pronunciation. We'd say it like that in jest to each other—out of the locals' earshot, of course. My Smith girlfriend was in France for the semester. So this was my semester abroad. My own cross-cultural experience.

Edgewood. Six blocks of anarchy in the shadow of Yale. At that time, New Haven, 1976, a lot of the blocks around Yale were seas of, and lessons in, anarchy. Say "New Haven, 1976" to Old Blues of a certain vintage and we shake our heads in mournful recognition. Just the name of the city coupled to the year calls up tensions, hostility, urban America at its worst.

Our Edgewood education started even before the semester officially began. The windshield of my Volvo was smashed on our first night in the house, when I left the car out after moving my stuff in.

Oh, you have to garage it.

Our shiny bikes—stolen from right off the front porch.

Oh, you have to bring them inside with you.

Our dreams of a little freedom from the constraints of Yale. A little liberation for five boys who had followed all the rules all their lives to get here. Looking for a little independence, a little adventure, a modest little divergence from the constrictions of academia and convention and expectation.

Oh, freedom *is* just another word for nothing left to lose.

As fate would have it, for the galloping hormones of a nineteen-year-old Yalie, my basement bedroom was contiguous to where Keneisha "partied" with her gentlemen callers, and the thumping of music—KC and the Sunshine Band, "That's the Way (I Like It)"; Ohio Players, "Love Rollercoaster"; Vicki Sue Robinson, "Turn the Beat Around"; Donna Summer, "Love to Love You Baby"—drowned out whatever other audible accompaniment there might be, though the music did not purge it from my imagination.

My bedroom had a sliding door onto a small junk-cluttered backyard. Metal bars held the slider closed, but I would hear the door jiggle occasionally while I was working at my desk. That's when I would grab the five iron I slept with under my bed.

A five iron. The comfort of its familiar shaft in my hand. That should tell you a lot about Yalies on Edgewood: a five iron for protection.

I did not stroll down Edgewood with a five iron, though. I walked only in daylight. One walk to campus in the morning, one walk back before dark. There was no consistent theme or look to those six blocks—a tiny Ukrainian bakery, a locksmith, a few empty storefronts, some residential "projects" whose crazy pink, purple, and tangerine pastel doors were comically bright spots—some developer's idea for a little accent of cheerfulness—that only highlighted the slapdash, thoughtless, halfhearted attempt to dress up the drab brown brick around them. And even those doors were quickly faded and besieged by graffiti.

In New Haven in 1976, it was essentially running a gauntlet, walking those six blocks. Day was risky. Night was lawless.

I walked focused, intent, staying alert, watching around me every step, probably not a good target. If I was going to a party on campus, I'd stay in a friend's room. I lived my life around timing the Edgewood walk right.

Lionel Patton did not. Lionel ambled, strolled, looked around casually, curiously, taking it all in.

Lionel, from Lincoln, Nebraska. Big-boned, loose-limbed, ambling down the sidewalk oblivious—a creamy-skinned, bright-eyed, howdy-there-how-ya-doin' friendly Midwesterner. Black-framed glasses on an open face. Big, outgoing, cheerful. Carrying his French horn everywhere. It was practically attached to him, and he was here because of it. Recruited by all the Ivies for his French horn prowess.

The world had always been his oyster, you could tell. His family were rich corn and soybean farmers. Farmers with thousands of acres. The kind of farmers who took frequent trips to Europe and the Far East. Life an ongoing project in growth and learning.

He was the kind of Yalie who comes east to school and maybe finds a pretty wife (prime breeding stock), and after graduation heads to Europe for more cultural education, maybe finds a European wife instead, returns to the Midwest eventually to take over the family holdings and tend them for the next generation. Lionel let drop once that his family had loaned some money to a bright young fellow, name of Warren Buffett, and had gotten some stock shares in return. In short, the kind of Yalie you can't make up. And I'm sure that when he told his folks, *I'm going to live off campus, Ma and Pa*, they had a certain bon-vivant vision of it that did not match the reality of New Haven, 1976.

Lionel was, in short, a target.

Might as well have painted a bull's-eye on his French horn case.

Although they never took the French horn. They didn't want a French horn. They didn't even know what a French horn was. They wanted his wallet. They wanted his new sneakers. They wanted his suede jacket.

It was a certain group of kids. I'd seen them, and managed to avoid them. They swarmed out of nowhere on their bikes, in their hooded sweatshirts, yelling and laughing and posturing for each other, intimidating girls and the elderly, and then disappearing into the housing projects or alleys just as quickly. Street guerrillas. A gang in its formative stage. A project for some enterprising Yale anthropology major with a suicide wish.

Lionel, unlike the rest of us, insisted on reporting it every time. That was the proper thing to do. So the weary cops would come out, hold their pads in front of them, and dutifully take down the information, looking at Lionel like he was from another planet, which he clearly was.

Beyond the insult of being intimidated by skinny, arrogant, undernourished fifteen-year-olds, privileged Yalies could of course absorb the forfeiture of a few material goods. Part of me thinks those little Edgewood hoodlums knew that, and it peeved them to see Lionel with new sneakers and a nice new jacket a few days later, and that's why they upped their game.

And in a way, this is where this story really begins:

With Lionel coming in our front door one evening, left ear and head bleeding profusely, shirt collar and right sleeve ripped, scratches on his face and hands.

As soon as he was safely inside, he slid down the wall in the front hall in relief, and we gathered around him as soon as we saw what had happened.

"Jesus, Lionel, what the hell!"

"Whoa."

"Oh man."

Roger hustled to the kitchen and brought back a couple of wet towels to start cleaning up the wounds, to get the blood off and see what we were dealing with.

Lionel said nothing in response. Smiled up at us dumbly, vacantly, probably a little in shock. Then shook his head in annoyance, embarrassed in that Midwestern way to be drawing so much attention.

The cops got there pretty quickly.

Lionel did his best to describe the kids. "Three of them, officer. About fifteen years old." He described their sweatshirts. Gray. Baggy jeans. He didn't remember much more. "A lot was happening, officer."

I noticed that Lionel didn't mention their race. But for cops in that neighborhood at that time, you didn't have to. In that Edgewood section of New Haven, 1976, you'd only mention if they *weren't* black.

"How'd you get the head wound?"

"The one karate-kicked me."

Wow.

"Kung fu kind of thing. I was not expecting it," said Lionel, formally.

Jesus. Trying it out on you. Like kicking an inflatable clown.

The problem was, we learned, the cops couldn't do much. "Look, if you're right and they're fifteen, then it's juvenile. They're not yet sixteen. Thing is, they didn't pull any weapons, they know what they're doin', these kids, they've already learned what they can and can't get away with as far as the law. That's why he karate-kicked you. That's why they punched you. 'Cause that's not gonna land 'em in anything too serious."

Officer Perez, I remember. Stocky, bushy mustache, alert black eyes. A messenger, a repository of street knowledge. Translating it all for us.

"See, their parents don't trust us, think we're the enemy, so they instruct the kids to lie to us, and they defend the kids, accuse us of exaggerating the events and even fabricating the charges, and as juveniles they and their parents retain a lot of rights, so a lot of times we can't even get to square one with kids like this. We'll go look for them, Mr. Patton, and we might even find them, and might even get them into the juvie system, with your testimony and if you're willing to skip a lot of class time, but I do want to point out to you that when they learn it was you who brought charges, and they go back home as they eventually will, they're only gonna have it in for you more."

I find this line of logic infuriating, of course, but Lionel has a completely different reaction, which trumps my fury.

Lionel adjusts his glasses. "Well, look, they're not bad kids, really."

What?! Kids who just karate-kicked you in the head? Punched you in the face?

Perez stops writing for a moment. Clearly distracted by what he's just heard.

"I mean, look what they're faced with. The deck is stacked against them," says Lionel, who looks at the cops, at us, and then reveals the rest: "I asked them why they were doing this."

The second cop—Landry, tall, freckled—is genuinely confused. He blinks twice, trying to understand. "Wait. You asked them . . . why?"

"Yes. *Why are you doing this, fellas?* I wanted them to explain themselves."

Fellas. I could hear him saying it. Good God.

"I mean, you know, beyond the sneakers and the jacket," says Lionel. "In a larger sense. Why?"

Wanting three fifteen-year-old thugs, apparently, to stop and examine their own motives. To look into their own souls.

Perez taps his pencil against his chin a couple of times. "During the attack, you asked them *why?*"

I see the cops exchange glances with one another, and then Perez glances at me.

"My questions only seemed to make them angrier," Lionel acknowledges.

Making philosophical inquiries of fifteen-year thugs on Edgewood Avenue.

"Why did they do this, officer? Why do they behave this way?"

Now turning the philosophical inquiry to the New Haven Police Department.

Perez looks at me. Asks wordlessly: *What planet is your roommate from?*

Nebraska, officer. The planet of Nebraska.

"I'd like to help those kids somehow, officer." Blood still running down the side of his head. It hasn't fully coagulated yet. "I'd like to change things for them somehow. Clearly they need help."

Perez has had as much as he can handle. He takes a breath. "I think the most helpful thing you can do, Lionel, is stay out of their way. Be alert. Avoid them. I think that might be the most helpful behavior right now."

When I close the door behind the cops as they leave, Perez turns back toward me and says, somewhere between annoyance and alarm, "Tell your pal to cut out the humanitarian relief effort." He peers at me warningly. "Gonna get his ass killed."

Lionel Patton. With black-framed glasses off, pretty good looking. Naturally modest in a way that hard-nosed Eastern Yale women liked. Khakis, white shirt. High school class president and valedictorian and captain of his high school tennis team. (I kid you not.) Skating lessons. Flying lessons. Chess lessons. Golf lessons. Lessons in everything. The well-bred, high-achieving Midwesterner—very much a Yale tradition. (A tradition that helps keeps Yale's coffers full and flowing, generation after generation.)

Here at Yale, a music major. (Because he could. Because he was going back to inherit and oversee four thousand highly profitable acres of soybeans and corn, so he could major in any damn thing he wanted.)

And by the peculiar chain of circumstance that produced Lionel Patton, by the coincidences and alignments of his particular existence, he had never known anything but brightness, cheerfulness, good fortune. Not a moment of doubt or deprivation. By the concatenations of luck and privilege and advantage and happenstance, he had never confronted the forces of darkness. He went whistling down Edgewood Avenue. Literally. (I knew it because I had heard him—whistling the same French horn part in Mahler or Mozart that I heard him practicing at the house.) And when the forces of darkness swarmed around him, it was unexpected, inexplicable, and he was ill-prepared. It was an ambush, in a way, that went beyond the literal. Beyond Edgewood.

Once the cops were gone and Lionel was cleaned up, and he sat down with us (the bong on the wooden shipping-crate-cum-coffee-table between us—Lionel did not typically partake, though the rest of us felt that his encounter certainly merited a fresh bowlful), I felt the occasion called for a little bit of philosophical discussion from safely within our walls.

"Lionel, you can't discuss motives and ethics and right and wrong with fifteen-year-old black kids on Edgewood Avenue."

"I just want to understand why they would do this . . ."

"Why? 'Cause they wanted your sneakers," said Roger.

"Why? 'Cause this is what they know. 'Cause this is what they see. 'Cause this is their world," Larry said.

"Then we have to try to change it. We have to try to make things better for them." He looked at us with bright resolution. "I'm gonna reach out to them."

Oh Jesus.

"No you're not."

"Listen," I said. "Marcus, Keneisha's little boy? Six years old. He tried to hold me up with a sharpened pencil."

"Serious?"

"That's the world he knows. That's what he aspires to. And you and I are not changing that in a semester."

"But what if they see that I care about them? I'll bring them a dozen donuts. We'll get started on better footing, they'll see I'm a nice guy."

Donuts!

"Lionel, they *know* you're a nice guy. That's why they're doing this to you."

You have success, happiness, joy, privilege written so loudly on you, Lionel, they can't take it. They can't take you ambling up Edgewood, whistling. Whistling classical music at that.

The quest for understanding. The clearly marked trail of knowledge. It had been a way of life for Lionel, a unifying theme. But here, there was no *understanding*. That was darkness's creed, the wild steed it rode, its trusty companion, part and parcel of its power. *No understanding*. Blunt irrationality. Comprehensive incomprehension.

Officer Perez was right about everything, I was sure. But he turned out to be wrong about the use of weapons.

The next time it happened to Lionel, there was a knife.

The knife changed everything.

But not in the way you think.

Not in the way any of us thought.

Same three kids. And feeling thrilled, victorious, adrenalized, invincible from the success of their previous encounter, no surprise, they were not done with Lionel.

Same cops—Landry and Perez. I'm glad they happened to be on duty that day, to come around to our Edgewood house again, to be there to experience the same disbelief that we all did. The same intersection of Yale and Edgewood. The same sobering result. The same rethinking of all our assumptions.

Because with the unfolding of that knife, the flash of its blade, something else unfolded and flashed in Lionel Patton. Some new edge was suddenly exposed.

The appearance of that knife, gleaming there in the afternoon sunlight—an expression of Edgewood itself? . . . of accelerating events? . . . bringing them literally and figuratively to a point?—the appearance of the knife changed the calculus. As it always does.

Held there, inches from his chest, arrogantly—creating pure power, pure powerlessness. Generating in Lionel a sudden complex math of threat, insult, terror, instinct, rage, memory, confusion, the formula's coefficients arranging and rearranging themselves in milliseconds.

If you've ever had a knife held at you (and at that moment in time, New Haven, 1976, many of us had), then you know how it alters the moment.

And oh, it altered the moment for Lionel.

His French horn—his trusty French horn—unexpectedly, from stage right—swung into action. Twenty mighty, unexpected, highly effective pounds of defense—and offense, as it turned out.

He knew his weapon intimately, after all. He'd swung it onto buses, under desks, into car backseats, balanced it on bicycles, lugged it since the age of seven. He had total control of it. He could wield it. Hefting twenty pounds for over twelve years, your carrying arm and hand get strong. Unexpectedly, acutely strong. Uncannily precise. He was at one with it.

He punched the French horn case at the knife and knocked it out of the first kid's fist with such force, and to such stunned surprise, that the knife tumbled to the sidewalk.

Clearly, three armed teenage thugs on Edgewood Avenue were not expecting the attack of a French horn.

And when the kid bent down to retrieve it, the instrument swung with equal force and violence at his head. He was literally dumbstruck.

And when the other two kids came at Lionel in blind, unthinking retaliation, he karate-kicked the first one—perfectly, effectively, in the gut—then swung the horn at the second, its twenty pounds catching him solidly in the lower back, sending him to the sidewalk doubled up in pain.

Like I said: French horn, All-Ivy.

Amid all the music and golf and chess and skating lessons back in Lincoln, Nebraska, Lionel had years of martial arts lessons as well, and had been sternly and repeatedly instructed never to deploy what he had learned; it was an art and a discipline, and such stern instruction it must have been, because his teachers could not imagine a circumstance in which Lionel Patton, bright-eyed, cheerful, upbeat, friendly Nebraska farmer's son, would ever have to actually use it. But fortunately, into that meticulously developed cerebral cortex of his at that moment came a neural signal that perhaps this *was* the appropriate deployment of those long-honed martial skills. And maybe in the end that was fortuitous. Because it added the element of surprise—for Lionel himself, and therefore for his adversaries.

Like I said: lessons in everything.

A symphony of violence, with a French horn solo. You can hear the solo, can't you? Heraldic sounding—but only in our imaginations. In reality, a solo of thumps and thuds.

And then, a final flourish, and a predictable one, as it turned out.

As the kids backed away, stunned—holding their heads, doubled up in pain, unsure what to do next—Lionel grabbed the knife off the sidewalk.

Did he hold it to their chests? To their throats? Turn the tables on them? Show them how it feels to have a knife held inches from you?

No, Lionel reverted suddenly to Lionel.

"I told them they should not be carrying something like this around and threatening people. I told them it's wrong. And I confiscated it."

Confiscated it. Good Christ.

And knife in one hand and French horn in the other, Lionel continued up Edgewood Avenue.

Those are the details of that afternoon, related first to us, and shortly thereafter to the astonished cops. With one notable difference.

"So what happened to the knife?" Perez asked him.

"I don't know," said Lionel.

That straightforward, honest Midwestern face. That do-gooder Boy Scout demeanor. "Things were happening so fast, I didn't notice."

"Too bad. It would make prosecuting this a slam dunk."

"My testimony's not enough?"

Perez looked at that big, honest face. A Midwestern French horn–playing Yalie. Assaulted by three black kids. And there were no actual stab wounds, anyway, thank God, so the knife was not crucial evidence anyway.

"Yeah, your testimony is probably enough."

* * *

And it was.

Two of the three kids went straight into juvie. Their first port of call, their entry at last, into the criminal justice system. Where they no doubt turned from rambunctious, chaotic, delinquent fifteen-year-olds to angry, hate-filled, avenging adults. Where, as the overwhelming odds and statistics predict, they learned more violence. Committed more crimes. Graduated from menace to full-fledged criminals. Edgewood started them on their path. But Lionel Patton hurried them along it. Pushed them into the system, started their formal criminal educations.

The French horn case was permanently dented. The horn inside survived unscathed. I went to see Lionel performing Mahler's Fifth.

It's got a French horn solo.

The solo he'd been practicing incessantly. The solo he'd been whistling.

Lionel performed it with passion. With beauty.

He had walked to the performance. Walked Edgewood.

So I knew he had the knife onstage with him in magnificent Woolsey Hall.

A few weeks later, in the process of buying another dime bag, Roger and I were surprised to be invited into Keneisha's apartment.

It was quiet, warm, a refuge from Edgewood Avenue, and a heartbreaking display of middle-class aspiration. Comfy couch. Big TV. Big stereo speakers. A song of consumerism. Not knowing anything else. Not aspiring to anything else. A living room filled with objects. Filled with want.

And amid our straightforward transaction, out of nowhere, with no preamble, but clearly because she wanted us to know, she confirmed my original deduction: "I tol' them to leave you alls alone, you know. And they did too, mostly. But they couldn't leave that one boy, they said. They tol' me they just couldn't leave that one boy. And I can't control them." She shrugged. "Ain't nobody can."

There is no understanding.

Knife in one hand. French horn in the other.

That is how he continued to walk Edgewood for the rest of the semester.

Not quite the same happy, cheerful Midwesterner. Never again.

Now taking that knife, a little bit of the streets of Edgewood, with him everywhere he walked. Just like his French horn.

Don't mess with Lionel.

PART III

DEATH OR GLORY

INNOVATIVE METHODS

BY ALICE MATTISON

Lighthouse Point Park

A cloud obscured the sun as we rode down the shadowed driveway into the park. The staff ushered the kids off the bus, watching to make sure nobody strayed. Wind blew across Long Island Sound. The kids looked smaller here than inside the residence, though some were almost adults. The jagged line of teenagers moved toward the massive old stone lighthouse above the rocky beach, the restored carousel, and the pavilion with its picnic tables.

We let them hang out on the stony shore before lunch, waving them off the battered wooden fishing pier, which was posted with *Danger* signs. It was too cold for swimming. The water was gray, its surface broken by wind. Some kids didn't go near the water, but others tried to see how close they could get without wetting their shoes, and ran back as the water slid forward.

I zipped up my windbreaker and pulled the sleeves over my hands. I'd been working as a clinician at the residence for a little less than a year, and this was my first picnic. I usually saw the kids one at a time for psychological testing and counseling, and some didn't recognize me here. Maybe I looked different—they certainly did. I hadn't known that Luis owned a Yankees jacket, that laconic Tiffany had a loud voice and spoke in obscenities.

We distributed lunch in the pavilion. Gulls wheeled and

descended. Above the woods beyond the parking lot, two hawks circled.

Next the kids would ride the carousel, and after that, I'd been told, Dr. Frank always offered boat rides. The kids couldn't learn Frank Gillingshurst's last name, and by analogy some called me Dr. Jennifer, though I'm an MSW. Dr. Frank had driven his black pickup, with his boat on a trailer, and parked in a lot near the water. A staff member would go along on each boat ride, and others would keep an eye on those waiting on land. Years ago, a fifteen-year-old had run away from the picnic and was picked up by the police after hitch-hiking halfway across Connecticut.

As I ate my apple, Dr. Frank strode toward the trash can and opened his big, muscular hand above it, releasing the remains of his lunch. He walked away without looking back; a napkin floated to the ground. He was a well-built white man with thick eyebrows. He was somewhat famous: Frank Gillingshurst, early in his career, had become a leading practitioner of an innovative form of child therapy involving unusual informality between therapist and client, and sometimes bluntness on the part of the therapist. He'd published a book, which I'd read. It made me uncomfortable, though I couldn't quite say why.

Dr. Frank climbed into his truck. The black pickup with the boat trailer rolled out of the lot, the slim white speedboat large and anomalous on land. The truck descended a sloping gravel road to the boat launch below, then turned and backed slowly toward the water. Dr. Frank got out and did something to the white boat. He returned to the truck, backed up a little farther, then climbed out again. A girl said she needed the bathroom, and I accompanied her. When I returned, Dr. Frank had eased the boat into the water, where it rocked slightly.

The anchor, a coffee can filled with concrete, lay on the shore, and the truck was on its way back to the parking lot. So far that day, he had not acknowledged my presence.

Dr. Frank was the only member of our party, resident or staff member, who didn't ride the carousel. We had full use of it for an hour. Apart from one or two other supervised groups, the park was empty.

I rode a black horse that went up and down. The happy, tinny music was—paradoxically—sad. As a child, I loved and feared carousels. This one exhilarated me, and it made me forget what was going on in my life. Frank stood staring, and each time I circled I saw his gaze, his thick pale eyebrows. When I stepped off the platform, I stumbled.

He looked at me at last. Okay, Jen?

A little dizzy, I said. Your turn.

I'm good, he said. The yearning music started up once more. The horses rose up and plunged down, their graceful legs bent forever, seeming taut with ungratified desire as they circled within the wooden shell, which looked as if a strong wind might blow it down.

We shouldn't have let him come, Frank said.

Who? I said, though I knew.

Gavin. He hasn't earned a picnic.

The picnic isn't something they earn, I said.

Oh, he would have understood. Then he said, Diane overruled me.

Diane was the director, now circling and waving, rising and descending on a white horse with brown spots. She smiled broadly, her big square glasses glittering. Her straightened hair held its shape, and she wore a ruffled blouse under her pantsuit.

I tried to pick Gavin out of the group revolving past me. We didn't fill much of the carousel, and the kids were lonely figures here and there. Gavin was a stocky, moody, light-skinned boy with a big forehead, now astride a brown horse that didn't go up and down. I wasn't his therapist but I knew him—a boy with a serious diagnosis who'd been thrown out of several schools for fighting, a couple of times with a knife. The first time I saw him was at a staff meeting at which Frank explained some of his theories. Then Gavin was invited in, and he spoke in a loud, clear voice about an abusive father, about trouble with the police, about anger he couldn't control—until now, because Dr. Frank helped him.

Gavin was not one of those who came forward when boat rides were offered. There was a little shoving, as half a dozen vied to be in the first group. The wind had picked up. I managed not to be the assisting adult on any of the rides. Some children wandered off down the beach, throwing rocks into the sea, pretending to throw them at each other. Some circled the locked lighthouse.

Only two kids fit into the boat along with Frank and a staff member, so even though some didn't go, the rides took time. The motor was loud, and the boat leaned on its side and swung in reckless—or seemingly reckless—arcs through the gray water, beyond which West Haven and the taller buildings of New Haven were visible in the distance under the gray sky. The kids screamed as spray pelted them, and the wake started up curls of foam that broke on the shore with a bit of a crash. The first ride made some waiting kids decide not to try it, but others stepped forward.

So there was some confusion about who had been in the boat and who had not, how many kids had wandered off along the shore with the shift supervisor and her assistant. I was annoyed at how long it all took. I wanted coffee, but the concession stand at some distance along the beach was closed for the season. It started to rain. Diane—her hair now slightly less neat—climbed out of the boat, waved an arm, and called, Okay, enough! Everybody back to the bus!

It wasn't until we were all seated inside that the shift supervisor counted us and we realized someone was missing. Gavin, the kids said, before the adults figured out who it was. Diane and I hurried off the bus. Now the park seemed vast—there was a playground I hadn't noticed before; the beach wrapped around meadows and parking lots. In the other direction was the woods.

Frank was walking toward his truck, about to load his boat, when Diane called to him sharply and waved him over. He didn't get upset. This kid's not like the other one, he said. Then he added, in a voice that made Diane frown at him, Gavin's a coward at heart. He won't find his way out of the park. Frank spoke slowly, as if he were reading lines he couldn't quite make out in dim light. Or as if he'd been caught unawares—well, of course he had been, just like the rest of us; but he was claiming that he *wasn't* surprised, that this was almost ordinary.

I told myself that he was right, and that Gavin's disappearance probably had nothing to do with other things that had happened. Downtown New Haven is at the bottom of a U-shaped curve in the shoreline, and the park is at one tip of the U, separated from the rest of the city by a narrow residential area next to the water, and then the mouth of a river that's crossed by a highway bridge. This was unfamiliar territory to our kids.

Nothing to worry about, Frank continued. I'll drive him

back. Then I'll return to load the boat. No, wait—Gavin will help me load the boat. It'll do him good.

But we don't even know where that child is! Diane said.

He's behind a nearby tree, Frank said, patting her on the arm. I know Gavin, he continued. All the trouble is bluster. He wants to be found—just not in front of his friends.

We'll keep the kids on the bus, I said. We can wait.

I didn't think all Gavin's trouble was bluster, and I knew Frank didn't think that either.

Absolutely not, Frank said. They know I take him places. Tell them I'm driving him back to the house.

I hesitated. Frank, I said, at least I should stay. I'll help you look.

Nonsense, he said, and all but pushed Diane and me onto the bus.

I've asked myself many times why I allowed myself to get on the bus. There was no reason why two searchers would be any less effective than one—obviously they would be more effective, no matter who they were. The truck was big enough that all three of us could have ridden back to the house together. I think Diane didn't chime in and encourage me to stay because she was desperate to pretend things were normal—and Frank alone with one of his own clients would be very normal. He'd taken two girls hiking in a different park a few weeks earlier. Diane was arguing with herself, I found out later, about whether it was essential to call the police immediately. Gavin was sixteen. If the police were alerted it would be terrible for the residence, terrible for Diane. It might also be terrible for Gavin if he were found by the police: he was a known juvenile offender; he was a black teenager. It would be much better if we could consider his disappearance something that concerned no one but us, a problem we could solve easily.

My immediate response when Frank sent me off was shame, as if I'd proposed a sexual encounter and he'd said he didn't find me attractive. Or attractive any longer.

One afternoon a few weeks after I was hired, I stepped out of my office and observed Frank, whom I scarcely knew, peering through a corridor window. Something about the way he stood, or his amused expression, drew me in. He seemed as if he were about to say something outrageous: I was detecting that he wasn't a docile follower, but a skeptical observer. I was not happy in the job, which would lead nowhere. The administrators were competent but unimaginative. I needed a friend who'd raise an eyebrow—and Frank had such grand eyebrows.

Out the window, sitting on the front steps—though it was winter—were two girls. They're deciding whether to sneak out, Frank said.

The kids were allowed on the porch, but no farther.

How do you know? I said.

Nobody sits on the steps in this weather. They're making sure nobody sees them, but they're not too bright—they haven't thought of windows.

Will you stop them?

No. He shook his big blond head.

They could get into trouble, I said.

Girls get into trouble by getting pregnant, he said, but they won't want to miss supper, and they can't get pregnant between now and supper. They'll just walk to the convenience store and buy cigarettes.

They'll get lung cancer, I said.

That I can't prevent, Frank said. He turned from the window. He was outrageous but not too outrageous, I decided. He took an emphatic step or two, then called over his shoulder, I hear you're from Philly.

So I caught up to him.

Me too, he said. We should get coffee.

I'd like that, I said.

The first time we had dinner, we ended up at my apartment. I'd never slept with a man who had such big bones, such vigorous arms and legs. Frank was on all sides of me: we were Leda and the Swan. His arms glowed—his arm hair was golden too. When eventually he got out of bed that first night, he clutched his lower back and then pulled a vial from his pants pocket, swallowing a handful of pills without water.

What's wrong?

Sciatica.

I'd have brought you a glass of water! I said.

He said, I can find the faucet. I don't need water.

He took many pills and never with water. You're addicted to prescription painkillers, I said a few weeks later, and he shrugged, which startled me: I had intended hyperbole. By then I was dependent on the sex, maybe a little in love, or, at least, more vulnerable than I liked. Frank would stick his head into my office and say Tonight? or Dinner? without bothering with conventional greetings and inquiries. That felt thrillingly intimate. He couldn't get enough of me—but then he might become impatient and resentful, as if we were only in the same room at the same time because I'd tricked him. My stories about my middle-class, ethnically mixed family (I'm half Korean, half Jewish) bored him, and he said so. His cynicism about the job went beyond my irreverent jokes about Diane's love of rules or her assistant's fussiness about paperwork. He dismissed the administrators from his mind, as if of no consequence.

When Frank talked about himself, he generally began with ambition, though I sometimes learned about something else as well. Hearing about a prestigious conference in Vancouver at which he'd been invited to speak, I learned that he was afraid of airplanes, though he flew often. I learned about the conference in bed, when he took a call after we'd finished.

I've been hoping for this, he said. I know what I want to do.

What do you want to do?

His talk, he explained, would include videos of him working with Gavin. He said, One of my students is taping us. And after I show the videos—then I introduce Gavin himself! He paused, then added, I'd better bring a chaperone. He has an uncle. My research money will pay for their plane tickets.

Frank had some kind of university appointment.

Videos? I said. What about confidentiality?

No last name, Frank said. He stood up, rubbed his back, and went to the bathroom.

But still, I said when he returned.

Still what? I just wish I didn't have to fly!

Confidentiality.

No last name, he said again. I have his permission, of course. And he's being photographed from behind.

Why bring him? I said. If you've got him on video . . .

Q&A, he said. They'll eat it up. It all has to do with teenagers getting past anger—not letting it get them into trouble.

What do you do that's so different? I said. I too spent hours every week with angry teenagers, and I knew that any of them might get into trouble at any minute.

He was silent. Gavin's going to be the subject of my next book, he said then. I'm writing a proposal. There's interest.

From the people who brought out your last book?

From agents. That was a university press. Now I'm going big time.

Soon, I calculated, Frank would be offered a more lucrative job in a bigger city.

One night at the beginning of summer, Frank and I met at a restaurant. He was late, and came in looking rushed, whipping his napkin from the place setting. Did you order for us? he said.

I wouldn't have dared order for him. When we were finally eating, he said, I just confiscated a gun.

From who?

He shrugged. That's why I was late.

From Gavin?

Gavin? Of course not. Gavin doesn't have a gun!

Who, then? How did you find out?

I'd rather not say.

But don't you have to turn him in? I said. A gun was serious. The client might be sent to a more restrictive facility.

I'm not turning him in, Frank said.

You're not? What then?

I'll keep it. When he's ready, he and I will take it to the buyback program. They'll pay me, and I'll give him the money.

Won't he just buy another gun?

By then he won't want one.

I suppose he'll spend the money on books, I said drily.

In Latin, Frank said. Greek.

We ate. Where is it now? I said.

Frank shook his head.

It's not in your pocket, is it?

Forget it, he said.

I'd intended to work on reports that evening, but had

decided to postpone them when Frank suggested dinner. I expected that he'd come home with me. But at the end of the meal, which he paid for, I thanked him, mentioned the reports, and left while he was pulling out his credit card.

After that Frank was less interested in me. I was sure he blamed me for timidity. I blamed myself. Obviously Frank wasn't dangerous! I liked him for his outrageousness, I scolded myself—but apparently I couldn't handle someone who went beyond making lame jokes about the administration and actually tried innovative methods—risky ones, yes, but taking risks led to progress.

Then, one evening, he phoned: a quick, impersonal call. Can I come over now? When he arrived he accepted some Scotch and sat down on my sofa. I have a proposal for you, he said. I don't mean I'm going to propose!

I didn't think you did, I said. You're not down on one knee.

I felt flustered, unable to be at my best—too needy.

The organizers of the conference in Vancouver, he told me, were so pleased by his plan to bring Gavin, and by the video Frank had sent, that they had offered to make him one of the main speakers in the plenary session. They'd pay him a good sum, as well as expenses. The only problem, his contact had said, was the unfortunate, unspoken message conveyed by the fact that Frank was a white man and Gavin a black boy. The pairing—and the absence of a speaker of color, or a woman, in what would now be a longer part of the program— might seem insensitive.

That's *all* that troubles them? I said, but Frank kept talking. The organization, he explained, prided itself on its diversity, and on making clear to the public (Frank's segment would be filmed and offered to news organizations) that all clients aren't black, all therapists aren't white. So they'd made Frank's featured participation contingent on his bringing along a non-white colleague, preferably female. Would I be willing to join him?

You're not in the videos, of course, he said, but you can interview Gavin before the Q&A—bring up concepts the videos don't get to. Or accuse me of invading his privacy! You'd like that. A little controversy will be perfect.

I'm not black, I said. I wanted to do it, and I knew I shouldn't. I said, Isn't the idea that you should have someone *black* with you?

They said *nonwhite*, he said.

I'm mixed, I said. Maybe ask Diane? But I didn't want him to ask Diane.

Frank turned his head quickly. Diane can't hear about any of this! he said sharply. Diane thinks I'm a show-off. Then he said, And at this point in your career, the exposure will be fabulous for you.

I had thought of that. I'd never been to Vancouver. Frank and I would have hours together on the plane and in the hotel. Gavin and his uncle would be present much of the time, but even so . . . I wondered how much money I'd get. I began to think about what I might ask Gavin in our public conversation that would make the whole thing ethical after all.

It would be easy not to tell Diane, whom I respected: I didn't want to know her opinion.

I didn't say yes, but Frank talked as if it were settled, and I didn't argue. From his chair he reached to stroke my arm with one finger, then put down his drink, stood, and took me in his arms.

When I awoke in the night he was asleep beside me—naked, sprawled, the blanket twisted around one leg. I got out of bed and crossed the room to the chair where he'd laid his clothes.

In his left pants pocket I could see the outline of his bottle of pills. I put my hand into his right pants pocket and felt the flat leather billfold he carried, and something made of metal. I snatched my fingers back, then let the tips graze the edges of the object: the barrel, trigger, and grip of a small handgun.

A few weeks later I heard shouts from the lunchroom while I ate a sandwich at my desk. My next client told me Gavin had gotten into a fight.

Really? I said. I didn't think I should ask who started it, but the girl told me anyway. Gavin had claimed that another boy shoved him while he ate. He jumped up, punching.

My client said, That boy *touched* Gavin. She reached out a finger to show me.

There were a couple of other fights.

Frank and I didn't spend time together during those weeks. Late one afternoon, I stuck my head into his office. How can you claim he isn't angry? I said. I couldn't begin to say whether I was asking a legitimate professional question, trying to find out the status of my participation in the conference, arguing with him, or looking for a way to go to bed with him.

Oh, that's part of the story, Frank said.

He didn't ask me to sit down but I took the client's chair. He was at his desk. Backsliding, he said, but accepting appropriate punishment—it makes it more convincing. He's lost some privileges—he gets that. You worry too much.

That was all, and I soon left. Embarrassed to be caught worrying again, I bought my ticket. Frank had explained that we'd be reimbursed after the conference. But the next time we talked—outside the facility, a week or so later, as we headed to our cars—he said Gavin was refusing to go to the conference. No videos, no trip, he said. The little shit.

Oh! I said. I stopped, clutching my tote bag full of reports. Frank, I said. I was uncomfortably aware of all the fantasies of this trip I'd been allowing myself. And the ticket was expensive.

Not a big deal, he said. I'll reason with him. But I can't until he calms down.

What if he doesn't calm down? I said.

He will. He sounded stern. I wanted him to be right so we could go to the conference—but also because I wanted his theories to be true, so as to prove that my doubts were unfair: I wanted my lover to be the distinguished psychologist I had thought was seducing me, not a smooth-talking fake.

I think he misread my expression—or maybe he read it too well. Look, I know what I'm doing! he said with real anger. For the first time, there was uncertainty—desperation—in his eyes, and he didn't look as if he knew what he was doing. It was a hot, sunny afternoon in September, and we were standing on a cracked sidewalk two doors down from the residence, which had a parking lot so small we often couldn't use it. His car was parked at the curb where we stood; mine was half a block away. Brown leaves were accumulating, though the leaves on the trees were still green.

I tensed. I didn't want him angry with me. I said, No, no, of course he'll calm down. Of course you know what you're doing! My foot played with a piece of broken sidewalk.

But he stared at me, his eyebrows too dignified for failure. His blue shirt seemed to be sticking to him. I turned protective. If you can't talk about Gavin, I said, aren't there others?

He shrugged and turned away, opened his car door, and got in.

It will work out! I called lamely.

* * *

I didn't hear from him after that. At work we barely spoke.

One Friday—maybe two weeks after that conversation and a week or so before the picnic—the day was chilly, so I wore a jacket to work. When I left that evening, Frank's door was open and I called, Goodnight! as I passed, but he didn't answer. I went downstairs, left the building, and was almost at my car when I remembered the jacket. I had left it in my office. I would want it over the weekend. I turned back.

Now Frank's door was closed, and I heard voices as I neared it. The sound of crying. In a rough, sarcastic voice, Frank was saying something I couldn't quite make out. It sounded like *break*. Break, sure, the break, of course, the break! It was the tone that stopped me, a kind of wild rage. I didn't know what he actually said—still don't. Then I heard something more clearly. I guess the crying was quieter. You really are worthless, Frank said. I don't care what happens to you.

I didn't decide to open the door and walk in, I just walked in. Gavin was crying but standing up, his arms tensed, ready to strike; Frank was sitting at his desk. Gavin was small for his age, I realized, but he moved like a man as he faced Frank.

Frank looked up, startled. You don't believe in knocking?

You scared me, I said.

So knocking isn't required when you're scared? His voice was heavy with sarcasm. Sorry, I didn't know about that rule!

Gavin turned and dropped his arms. He looked embarrassed.

Gavin, I said, do you want to come with me?

He glanced from one of us to the other. No.

We can go now and tell Diane what just happened. Dr. Frank shouldn't talk to you that way. She could assign you to a different therapist.

No, Gavin said.

I think you should mind your fucking business, Frank said. You have no idea what's going on in here.

I know it's not all right, I said.

Frank said, Gavin has made it clear that he doesn't need your help. Right, Gavin?

Gavin nodded. I didn't know what to do. I went downstairs, but Diane had gone for the day. I left the building, again without my jacket, and drove home. All weekend I tried to decide what to do. Finally I phoned Frank. I'm sorry I walked in on you, I said.

No, he said. I'm the one who should apologize. I understand why you did. I sounded insane. But I wasn't—truthfully, I wasn't.

Can we get coffee? I said. What he'd told me was a relief. I wanted to hear his explanation. I wanted to get back to what we'd had before. Somehow. I wanted what had happened to go away, and maybe he could tell me why I didn't have to keep thinking about it, why I didn't have to act on it.

I pointed out to myself that I had no way of knowing what went on between Frank and his patients. Maybe this was some kind of role-play, some kind of exercise. I knew it was harmful, but surely, I told myself, it would be better to persuade Frank that what he had done was not appropriate than it would be to tell Diane what I'd heard. He'd lose his job. Anyway, I'd heard clearly only part of what he said.

We met at a coffee shop. I suppose he knew that whatever else I wanted, I still wished to go to bed with him. When he came in, he leaned over to kiss me on the lips, then bought himself coffee and pulled his chair around to the side of the table, so we were shoulder to shoulder.

Who have you told? he asked.

Nobody.

I knew it! he said. You're too smart to get upset about something you don't understand. You trusted me, on some level. I was right to sign you up for the conference—we think alike, Jen. We've got a good future.

Is the conference still on?

Well, Gavin didn't want to go downstairs and tell Diane I was yelling at him, did he?

I said slowly, He was too scared of you to be honest with me.

No, Frank said. I think I understand Gavin. Anger is ordinary to him. He knows I'll scream at him when I'm angry—he gets that. I respect him enough to tell him candidly what I think.

That he's worthless?

At that moment, when he was saying no to me? Yes, that's what I thought. I don't always think that. He knows I don't always think that.

I let myself believe him. Coffee turned into dinner and dinner turned into bed. I'm glad we're colleagues, Frank said as we headed into my apartment. I'm glad we're lovers, don't get me wrong—but I'm even gladder that we're colleagues. Which of course was the most romantic thing he could have said to me.

I phoned Frank twice in the hours after the picnic, when he and Gavin didn't return. Leaving for the day, I stopped at Diane's office. Her eyes were heavy and she seemed small and rumpled behind her desk. She said, I don't even know his cell.

I gave her Frank's number and she called him, but he didn't pick up. She left a message asking him to phone her, as I had.

I didn't tell Diane I intended to drive back to the park. It was still raining. There was traffic on the Q-Bridge and then it took me a long time to drive through the neighborhood that bordered the Sound. Everything seemed deserted when I parked in the lot where the bus had been. It wasn't dark yet. Frank's truck remained in the other parking lot, the trailer behind it, still without the boat.

I pulled up the hood of my windbreaker and set off toward the pavilion, the lighthouse, and the shore. The rain obscured the buildings across the harbor. The wind was stronger than before. As I approached the top of the slope above the water, I saw the boat rocking in the same place. I took out my phone and called Frank again, and while it was ringing, I caught sight of him. He was on the shore, at a distance, head down, in a raincoat I didn't remember. It must have been in the truck. He made slow progress. He was dragging something—something heavy—and then he bent as if to lift it. He laid it on the ground and stopped, bending his knees in a way he sometimes did; he said it relieved the pressure in his back. I didn't leave a voice mail. Instead I hung up, then used my phone to take a picture of him. But he was too far from me; nothing would show. I stepped back from the edge of the hill.

He had been struggling forward, I saw, for a long time. I didn't know if the burden he dragged was Gavin. If it was Gavin, I didn't think Frank would have shot him. Maybe he'd stuffed pills down Gavin's throat, without water, as he stuffed them down his own, and Gavin was unconscious. Was it that hard to subdue him? And why was Frank walking on the shore, not toward his truck? He stopped again to rest, then dragged whatever it was a few more feet. He was heading toward his boat.

The next time he stopped, I phoned him again, and this time he answered. Frank, I said, what's going on?

I can't find him, Frank said. I don't know why I was so sure. I feel terrible.

I took a few steps back. Should I call the police?

There's one more place I want to look, Frank said. After that, if I don't find him, I'll call the police. You're at home?

Yes, I said, glancing left and right. I'm at home.

Diane is leaving me voice mails, he said. Call her and tell her what I told you. Tell her not to call the cops.

Okay, I said. I ended the call. Then I dialed 911. I wasn't coherent but they listened.

I couldn't have said clearly what I was starting to think. Frank would row out, I guessed. A motor might be heard. He would slide Gavin into the water, and call the police after rowing back to shore. The book Frank would write—Gavin lost forever, just as his doctor's theories had begun to help him—would be devastating, with details no one could deny about moments in Frank's office. Throughout the book there would be difficult moments, like the scene I'd witnessed, and the therapist would bravely confront his own limitations. It would end with a sad chapter about the psychologist's fruitless search, his new understanding—as days passed and the boy was not found: not in the park, not in the surrounding city, nowhere—that life for kids like Gavin is even harder and more unpredictable than he had imagined. A much more exciting book than one about Gavin's resistance and Frank's anger.

I hurried toward the park entrance. The rain was heavier now, and I was soaked through, freezing—but I wished I were even more uncomfortable, so as to have something simple to think about, something that could be remedied. The police car came quickly, but it felt as if I waited for a long time. I pointed the way down the gravel drive toward the water.

SPRING BREAK

BY JOHN CROWLEY

Yale University

S o the last proj I did junior year at Spectrum Cumulus
College was with my bud Seymour Chin, who was in
Singapore—I was in Podunk, OH. It was a proj in Equal-
ity Engineering, required, tough but not *so*. We picked Toiletry
and had scads fun and then did the CGIs, and we thought if the
world had these johns and janes it would be equal more, definitely. Remembering now the probs we thought up. "Trans-
gen women can't go in the women's jane, hey," Seymour said.
"They're men actually, they might abuse."

"Nah," I said. "They got no interest, yah? What you got
to do is keep the lesbians out. *They* could abuse. They got an
interest."

"Obvi."

"Ident," I said. "Run a kit. Ten thousand self-ID'd lesbians amalgamed in half-length pix. Surveillance cams can scan
and match in .9 seconds. Match, they get sent to the john."

"Harsh."

"Gentle it. Just a few words." I flashed him words: *Please
use the adjoining facility.*

"I see a problem."

"Yah?"

"Yah. No one in the john knows you're a les."

I pondered. "So if they go in the john men could abuse."

"Yah."

So all that was actually utter dumb and from old, but I was on propranolol and Seymour was drooping, four a.m. Singapore, which is five p.m. mytime the day before. Next meet we switched the thinking to unigender, made progress. Can't remember how we scaled it, but we got PASS on it and that's what counts.

Then: Spring Break! My first Spring Break, because costs. Fam decided this time to go in on it for me, because PASS. Max lucks!

All over the world, Spring Break time.

Received welcome package in gmail, unzipped it. Nice oldtime fonts. *Heyjoe! Great year, yah? Now's for rest-n-rec, yah? As a fulltime student of Spectrum Cumulus you hereby receive a special invitation to Spring Break at our Grandparent College, "Yale"!*

Went on a bit about Yale, this place, the oldness, the motto—*Luxe y Vanitas*, same as ours—and the many years that SCU.edu/sg and Yale had worked together, and-cetera. Pix and vids, leafy, stony, grassy. This was to be so fun.

Then Seymour Chin checked in. Seymour hates-*hates* to type like words, so what I got back was a string of emojoes to express. I got the meaning right away.

"Heyjoe, we not on?" I flash.

Seymour has affluenza—nose running, coughing, sick like a dog. (Do dogs get specially sick? Don't know. Never had one.) Not going to make it, not on day one anyway.

I'm on my own at Yale.

So it used to be I guess that Spring Break was in the you know spring, like March. Everybody left Campus and went to crazy-hot places to party—not like now. But who wants to go to New Haven in March? If not snow, rain, ice, and-cetera.

So they do it in June, which was when back then a student would get their diploma. And since there's nothing else going on there then these days, good time. But they still call it "Spring" Break. Know what? You can actually get a train ride (*take a train*, they say) from New York up to New Haven, get off. There's a Shuffle that meets this train and takes you to Campus. Town is wastrel, but then you drive through this stone portal—like in a fantasy RPG—and there you like are.

Wow. The place *is* old. The buildings look like castles. Old corroding I guess granite. Pointy windows. Pointy tops. Pointy everything. And what happened just as we drove in and down this avenue? *Bells started ringing.* They were playing songs, but with bells, somewhere up in a tower. Ancient songs I remember from as a kid. I sort of teared up a little it was so amazing.

We were led through another portal into this big square of lawn, a *quad* it was called—four sides, get it?—where there were long tables and these young guys and women were waiting to hand us stuff, all of them waving and saying Welcome and Hi and Get in Any Line. The spring-breakers were some of them zonkered with sleeplessness, come from around the world like Seymour Chin did or actually didn't, others up for it and giving high fives and whatnot. The woman I came up to checked my name/pic on their pad, and started piling things in front of me, calling out the names as they did it. Sheets and stuff! Orientation materials! One six-pack beer! One swechirt (with huge white *Y* on it)! Goodie bag! Hat!

It was a blue flat cap—blue for Yale, Old Blue—and it had a number on the front, *2017*. "What's that?" I asked them.

"What's what?" they said.

"The number."

"Heyjoe, that's *your class*!" They took it and put it on my head and tugged it down, laughing, really white teeth. "Class of twenty-seventeen!" they said, and shook my hand. "Welcome to Yale, Yalie!"

So the hat and the number were for the old-time scenics too. I laughed with them—they were sort of actually quite hot. "2017!" I told them. "That's like my *dad's* year!"

"Yeah!" they said.

Actually my dad didn't go. Because army. But if he had.

I loaded all this stuff up plus my kit and started off. A whole bunch were headed for the dorm we were assigned, only it wasn't called a dorm, it was called a college, which they said in this special way, a College. Why a college in a college? Who knew. My orientation pack explained, probs. And *it* was a castle too. It had a fucking coat of arms over the archway. All of us pouring in through the iron gate yelling, like overthrowing peasants, minus torches.

I have seen actually a lot of dorms, the boys and women in their little rooms, bunk beds, the stuff that happens. Squeeing and flaming on, the micro cutoffs and docked Ts, pizza boxes, selfies. Actually, now I think of, a lot of that was in porn. Vintage porn, but it gave you the scenics. The room I actually got was *not* like a dorm room. It was more fantasy RPG. The monk's lair or hmmever. A *marble fireplace.* Like *wood walls made of oak.* Dropped my stuff and sat down on a futon couch and felt a little—you know—I don't know.

But you know what? The john/jane was also like from another age. *Urinals?* Yes. Had to try one. Everything we designed out in our Toiletry proj. Flashed Seymour Chin but no emojoes in response. Then seven guys and a woman came in and it was sorting out the rooms and the beds (the wood room with the vampire-castle fireplace was just to hang in) and we cracked the comp six-packs and the night began. Hoo-hooting and woo-wooing from all around the quad.

I put on my droops and the gimme swechirt and 2017 cap, went out with my class into the quad. There was plenty of light there but most of the buildings, classrooms, and such were all dark inside. Way up far-off on a hill was a regular-type building, part of the Science Center I think we got told, lit up normally but looking so far away. These old parts had been left behind years ago.

I'm not that great in crowds—always have this impulse to say things, right, like actual things and not just tags. The Meaning of Life. Sometimes I guess I put people off. Anyway thinking like this I got away from the quads where the spring-breakers were. Thinking of all these buildings being full long ago, now when it's all collabs across the world, actually better for sure, but still there was a kind of sadness to feel, just wondering what it would have been to go to classes in those buildings and throng around the quad all day hugging books, talking to professors like f2f. Maybe I was born too late.

Tomorrow was going to be utter. We go to *class*. We hear a lecture by some heyjoe about some subject. Like we walk all together into one of these lecture halls with seats that have these paddle arms where you put your *notebook* and take *notes* with a pencil. I got a pencil in my goodie bag. No paper. Maybe the note stuff was like for kidding.

By now I was somewhere that was pretty empty of spring-breakers. The buildings felt like they were sort of looking down on me, like looming. Up in the corners of buildings and on the edges and gutters were these faces—little heads of monsters or like demons. Staring, grinning, showing teeth. Not for kidding: they were there.

Freaking out a bit. What happened to everybody? Was this still Yale? I went past a building that was like a giant white cube, with squares on each face, sort of like a ginormous Rubik's Cube without the colors. *Not* old. Not old but cold. And then when I hooked a left and a right there was the most, the tallest, the most looking-at-me building ever. It had to be a church. I've seen churches. This was the churchiest church I'd ever seen. The steps that led up to the churchy-pointy door were worn away, by a million feet going up and down a million times. I stood in sort of shock. Ancientness.

Then I saw that the door was open. A little. I could tell that if you went up and pushed on it, it would open more.

So I did.

See, what I learned: that you can be born too late, and really old things can seem, like, familiar to you. There's a sadness. What it is, it's more of an entrancement. Which is on the whole *not* a good thing, because you can just wander on and never come back. Not that knowing this was any help, as it turned out.

The church was just like in this VR tour of somewhere I did once. It was huge and empty and gray. The pillars of it ran together into arches high up. There were little windows made of colored glass, pictures in glass made long ago, or looking like it. What wasn't there were all the rows of seats to sit in and like worship. It was empty, it was the emptiest place I've ever been in. It made you gulp. The VR tour not so much.

I went over to one of the pillars and put my hand on it, the stone, worn by the ages. Cold and rough. Not even VR can give you feels. I was liking this when a weird feeling came over me, like somebody was nearby.

Somebody was. I don't know how he came up to me that close without making a sound, but when I turned I saw him and I did the *guh-guh-guh* thing.

"Looking for something?" he said. I didn't know then how

long I was going to be listening to that voice, or how much I would want to not hear it. He was a little guy with a round head, almost bald, with this farcey mustache. Smiling.

"Is this," I said, "a church?"

"No indeed," he said. "Or in a way, yes, a church. A Cathedral of Thought. It is in fact a Library."

"Wow."

"Yes."

"And who are you?"

"I am," he said, "the Librarian."

"Wow, so a Library." I took a few steps farther in, and he kept close to me. "And you're a Librarian."

"I am *the* Librarian. There are no others. Not anymore."

What's that ancient movie, Seymour sent me snips once, a Cathedral, and this ugly messed-up heyjoe who loves the bells and climbs up the tower to ring them? For some reason I thought of it now.

"Why," he asked, "does your hat have the number two thousand seventeen on it?"

"Oh, 'cause I'm a student, and that's my class." I could tell he didn't quite get it. "I don't really know why I'm here, I just . . ."

"Oh, I know why you've come here," he said, getting a little too close.

"You do?"

"Because you're a Student. You're drawn to books."

"Actually not so much."

"You love books."

"Um." I made that look—eyes sort of closed, shoulders up, hands out to show they're empty. Like hmmever.

"You don't. You don't. Like books. You hate them."

I laughed. "Well they're sort of *heavy*, you know? A whole lot of them together especially."

He laughed at that, kind of wildly, which made me think I was making a like good impression. Poor guy. His eyes were sort of bulge-y, that condition, you know? And they sort of vibrated. Not his fault, but.

"So books?" I said. "Where are they?"

"In the stacks."

"Stacks? You mean all piled up?"

"Well, 'stacks,'" he said with the double-finger-waggle. "*Called* stacks. All neatly placed on shelves. You went up, up . . ."—he pointed up, like to heaven, to the ceiling—"and got the one you wanted. If you were allowed."

"Uh," I said. "Who's not allowed?"

"Students," he said. "Haha, too bad for you. Haha, not true, you could, but long ago, no."

"So . . ."

"We-ell," he said, as though I was little kid, "what you did was, you looked up the book in the card catalog. You see those cabinets over there? They're all that's left of the system, and they're now actually empty. But once there were hundreds of cabinets, and each drawer in each cabinet held hundreds of cards, all in *alphabetical order*"—here he stared at me with his goggle eyes vibrating, like to make sure I understood what that is, which I do, sort of—"and the card told you what the book's *call number* was, and then you looked at that sign over there, which told you where in the Library that range of numbers was."

"You called the number?" I dialed with a finger, another finger to my ear, like in oldtime cartoons means *call me*.

"No no. You'd write it on a paper. And ask a clerk to go find it."

"Every book had a different number?"

"Every book. Every. Single. Book."

"Of like how many?"

He bent over so close to me, with this creepy suspishy smile, that now I was thinking that he, or well they, was maybe gay or bi. "Millions," he said.

That sort of staggered, yah? *Millions?*

"You want to see them," he said. It wasn't a question.

"Don't know," I said. "Do I?" I looked away and up and around, the darkness was like solid, there was no sound. Place was entirely soundproof, with all these books—like a million pounds of insulation.

"Jeez. They must be unbelievably valuable. I mean worth a *lot*."

"Not really so much," the Librarian said coldly. "Not one by one. All the really valuable ones—they've been taken out, they've been put with all the *most* valuable ones in that big marble cube—you saw it, right?—the Beinecke. And locked up so no one can steal them or handle them or even *see* them except the big shots, who don't care much anymore anyway."

He looked up to the spaces overhead, as though he could see the books up there, in stacks. "What's here are the ones they don't care about. Oh, *they* aren't valuable, no. They're just here. Abandoned. This building's kept safe and locked and a few lights on until they can decide what to do with them. Ha. Pretty clear what they'll *decide*."

I thought: place had not been locked when I arrived.

"Listen to me," he said. "I'll tell you something no one knows but me. There is one book in this library that is *unique*. If they knew it was here they'd take it and put it in with the Audubon Elephant Folio and the Gutenberg Bible and all the rest over *there*. Because you know why?"

"Why."

"Because there is *only one copy of this book in all the world*."

His nose was almost touching mine, far back as I pulled, and he whispered, like somebody might hear, "It's one thousand years old. It's covered in gems. The pages are made of the skin of goats, pounded so thin you can almost see through it." He smiled this mad smile. "Only one copy. It's never been kindled. It's not on the Internet Archive. It can't be accessed online. It is *fabulously valuable*." He goggled at me. "This book is *mine*."

"Okay," I said. Mostly I was trying to picture jewels stuck on a goat's skin, and getting nowhere.

"You want to see it?"

"Yes. Maybe. Sure."

He let out this strange sigh, as though deflating, like after you've held tension a long time. "Yes," he said. "You do." He jumped up, dusted off his core-droys, and set off, wagging his hand for me to follow.

I followed.

He took me down the hall to this place that would have been an altar, if it was a church, and then around and through a little door.

"Up," he said.

This was a different space, narrow not big, closed not open, low-ceilinged, tight.

"The stacks," he said. Slowly by slowly we went up the zigzag stairs. They made this ringing noise in all that silence. His steps, my steps. Now and then we go through a padded door and then up again. There was an elevator, but a lock bar bolted over it. He'd look back at me grinning, like a dad taking a kid for a treat.

There were so many books. Endless. Lonely. Fearsome. Looking at me, like those demon faces. Thinking their words, reading themselves to themselves.

I knew we were high up now, but it didn't feel like it; it felt like being down in a mine. There was only a light now and then, and it was just an emergency or like a nite-lite. "What's that smell?"

"Books."

It was a strange smell, musty or mildewy but dry and not ick, sort of appealing actually, like I don't know what, a nice cave or a grandma's bedroom or. It smelled . . . *old*.

He turned down a narrow passage and ran his hand gently across some books, looking no different to me than the others. "Poe," he said. "You've read Poe, of course."

This suspishy look in his eye made it clear I was supposed to say *Of course*, but of course I couldn't. "A little, maybe," I said. "I think I played the game a few times."

He took one out, opened it, and spoke words, not like he was reading them, like he was remembering them or making them up. "There was a discordant hum of human voices!" he whisper-yelled. "There was a loud blast as of many trumpets! There was a harsh grating as of a thousand thunders! The fiery walls rushed back! An outstretched arm caught my own as I fell, fainting, into the abyss. It was that of General Lasalle. The French army had entered Toledo. The Inquisition was in the hands of its enemies."

The Pit and the Pendulum. Didn't know that then. Sure do now.

He closed the book gently, like it might be hurt if he smacked it shut, and put it in its place like putting a baby to bed. Patted it.

"Up," he said. He pushed me along to the next stair up.

Then another smell, almost not there at first, then more. Not nice, bad. Something dead, dead rat like we once had in the basement.

"Books," he said.

"Not books," I said.

"Up," he said. "It's up this way." He pushed me ahead of him through another padded door and up another metal stair. It was starting to feel a little close-to-phobic. "Where's this book?" I said. "I gotta go. There's a party. There's a class."

"Here!"

There was an empty space in the ranks of shelves, where they'd been sort of dismantled somehow. He grabbed my shoulders and turned me toward it. I was done here, hey, I wanted out, and wondered if I knew how to *get* out. "Okay," I said, "just a peek, then we go, yah?"

"Shut up," he said. He gave me a shove in the back, he growl-shrieked, and then that's all I knew. I guess a minute or two, or seconds, and things appeared again, like coming into focus. I'd got hit on the head. *Hit on my fucking head with something by this fucking heyjoe.*

I reached out to smack him, and I couldn't. Fucker laughed. I was stuck to the metal shelving. With zipties.

"What the fuck," I said, calmly. I even tried a little laugh.

"What indeed," he said.

"Heyjoe," I said. "Come undo. I can't."

"I see that you can't."

Getting so weird. He was looking at me like I was a big goodie bar.

Then. This happened. No shit. He turned and from the shelves across the walkway he started pulling out handfuls of books and plopping them down around me. Then more. "You'll be happy here," he said. "Right here with the other book lovers, haha. Yes. One on each side of you. Kyra I think was the name. And Ira. Or something. Tweedledum and Tweedledee. You'll be right in the middle, like Alice."

"Shut up," I said. "Get me out."

"You won't have much," he said. "And soon you won't need much. Oh, but you'll have what no one else does. You'll have books!"

He was piling up the books any which way, pressing them against me. Working like a madman. I almost couldn't see over them now. I could hear the Librarian breathing, almost panting, like—well, like panting.

"For shit's sake!" I cried. "For the love of Mike!"

"Yes," said the Librarian, calm-cold, still piling books. "*For the love of Mike*."

There was no more light now. I was behind the wall of books. It was black dark. I couldn't even read the titles. I started yelling. I knew it was no good, but I did it anyway. Actually it wasn't a plan. I just did it.

"Calling for help?" the Librarian said, and I could hear the sneer. "Who do you think will come to your rescue here? Pip? Holmes? Allan Quatermain?"

I didn't know those guys. Or any guys. My wrists were bleeding from fighting with the zipties, you can't break a zip-tie, this I knew but still.

"If you need me," he whispered into the cracks in the book-pile, "I will be downstairs. In Reference." And he laughed like a maniac, which he actually was. I could hear his feet go down the metal stairs. "No!" I yelled. "I love books! *Books!* BOOKS!"

Nothing. No sound. Probs I gave another scream. I don't actually remember. *In a Library no one can hear you scream.*

How long was I in there, behind the books? A day? Days? I blacked out, then came back, and there were books. I believe I peed my pants. When I was alert I could only see books; also when I was passed out. Once I thought I'd got free and was reading one, but that wasn't factual. It seemed all the time that the books were actually *coming closer to me*, like pressing in, the stacks squirmishing forward to crush me. He came back once. I heard his feet. I thought he'd had a change of heart. I sort of moaned-pleaded, I could hardly speak; he nosed around like some rat sniffing for what he could get.

"Help," I whispered. "Oh help." Then I wandered away again into nowheres and when I came to he was gone again.

I was done for. Like Kyra and Ira. I could see them in my mind, skeletons hung up with zipties like corpse pirates, behind their books. I was just in the act of passing out again, for good this time, the books smothering me in revenge—and at that exact second I heard footsteps, foot-dings, on the stairs, not one person's but two or three's, coming up from below. Then came this wild kungfu yell and the books were pushed away, this side, that side, and a little light came in. An outstretched hand caught my arm.

It was the hand of Seymour Chin. The Singaporean had reached New Haven. The Library was in the hands of its enemies.

What I remember after that is not much. Seymour Chin looking at me like his face was going to pop—I'd never seen the man in the body. Behind him this very large diversity person in body armor, Yale blue, their hand on their gun, looking like they'd seen a well you know.

Then I fainted.

So what it was that happened, which I learned later in the Yale hospital where they checked me out: Seymour'd followed a thumbnail microtag we worked on freshman year—our first proj! I installed it on myself way then and forgot! Amazing he could trace his way up through the stacks, but that was what the tag was supposed to do, and damn it did.

Seymour explained about the rumors. Hadn't I heard them? The Old Campus Vampire. No I hadn't. Heyjoe, everybody tells them for giggles, just. But some people really had disappeared over the years, maybe just wandering in the empty buildings or like looter-ish. Never found. Seymour was very into stories like that in gaming and such. But not kidding? Not one kid, he said. The Library Ghoul. The Book Fiend. We had to laugh, but it wasn't actually funny. Because it wasn't just Kyra and Ira. It was others. They're still looking.

"Heyjoe," he said to me when we'd left the hospital and got out from around the media collected there. "Still time. Let's go to the College, get a beer. Wet T contest! So I heard. Rock out!"

Seymour too loves old things.

"Not for me, Seymour, sorry to say." I checked my watch, saw messages and-cetera. Relief. "Love you, heyjoe, but you know what?" I said. "Spring Break's over. I need to get back to the real world."

Then I see it's the Library Fiend. Like looking at me out of my watch. Startled, very. Then I see it's like Foxnews, it's his what, arraignment? In this dim New Haven courtroom. He seemed so *small.* When the public defender person said something about a psych-eval he piped right up, and his weird eyes started revolving. "True!—nervous—very, very dreadfully nervous I had been and am; but why will you say that I am mad?" He tried to get to his feet but a cop shoved him back. "The disease had sharpened my senses—not destroyed—not dulled them. Above all was the sense of hearing acute. I heard all things in the heaven and in the earth. I heard many things in hell. How, then, am I mad?"

Well fuck yes you are, heyjoe.

"Poe," I said. "I bet."

"Hmmever," Seymour said. He was guiding me along the street through the crowd. They were going in and out of the tech stores and the clothes and shoes and such. But not into one store, on a corner, that seemed closed. We got closer and it looked closeder. But it wasn't. There were lights on inside, and on the window was written *BOOKS*.

I stopped.

"I wonder," I said. "Poe."

"Oh no, heyjoe. Step away from the door."

"Just books, Seymour."

"Heyjoe," he said, tugging. "You can't be too careful."

SILHOUETTES

BY CHANDRA PRASAD

Wooster Square

"It's not the same one."

The shopkeeper tried to hide his disappointment and annoyance. He was clutching a copy of H.G. Wells's *The Time Machine*. It was a small miracle that he had the book at all. "Look—good shape," he insisted, gesturing to the gold-embossed cover. He flipped through the pages, revealing mostly crisp, stainless paper.

"It's not the one I used to have," the customer, a young man, replied. "Mine had a sphinx—with wings—on the cover."

The shopkeeper shook his head, struggling to understand. Nearly everyone who entered his shop spoke Italian, usually infused with the southern cadence of Amalfi and Atrani. It was disconcerting to encounter a person like this, someone with no trace of the old country.

"I give you discount . . ." the shopkeeper said, beginning to despair. It had been terribly slow all week at his store, which mainly sold dry goods. Maybe he should shutter the little alcove of English and Italian books he kept in the back. He could use the additional space to sell fresh bread and his wife's homemade salami. Books were an indulgence few could afford these days.

"I don't want it. But would you keep an eye out for the one I do want? The one with the sphinx?"

The shopkeeper nodded, although he didn't quite understand. He didn't like this customer, who spoke tersely, without warmth or congeniality. Still, business was business. He would try to find another copy. One with a different cover. That much he understood. "Come back in a week," he called out as the young man left, the bells jingling on the door behind him.

The man walked slowly down Court Street. He took off his brimmed hat, trying not to perspire on what promised to be another scorching day. He was conscious of his limp, although it was subtle now, not the problem it had been when he was a child. But he was sure people noticed it: the contrast between his youthful appearance and elderly hobble.

He passed several men—metal nails in their mouths, hammers in their hands—boarding up yet another building. The economy had soured since the crash and factories around Wooster Square were folding like poker hands. Without work, people were running out of money. The row houses along the street, once grand and stately, showed a hundred signs of neglect: chipped paint, sagging porches, missing shutters, sunken roofs. Fifty years ago they'd been opulent single-family homes for the rich; now they were overcrowded rooming houses for the broke.

Still, the young man saw signs of resilience and self-sufficiency too. He passed household vegetable gardens and chicken coops. He passed bakeries, meat markets, and pastry shops still holding on. The unemployed were turning their houses into makeshift shops, leaving their windows open so that the delicious smells of their cooking would lure passersby. More than once, the man had stopped impulsively to buy tomato pies or rich, sweet pastiera. If his mother were still alive, she would be shocked. Her Irish son eating Italian food.

A few minutes later he reached his workplace, a hulking brick building called Strouse Adler—one of the few factories in Wooster Square that was still turning a profit. He went in the front entrance, noting a drunk loitering near the door. No doubt he was there to leer at the female workers who flooded the main entrance at 8:15 every morning. Mr. Russo, the boss, was strict about punctuality. He threw on the power switch at exactly 8:30, and God help anyone who was late.

The man maneuvered through the corridors, nodding curtly at passing seamstresses and bundle girls. His room was on the second floor. A year ago he'd been hired by Mr. Russo to be the company's chief advertising artist. He drew portraits of girls modeling Strouse Adler's products: corsets, mostly. His drawings were published in newspaper advertisements throughout the country, although he was never credited. Mr. Russo was a stickler for discretion too.

The man put a sketchbook on his easel and sharpened the dull ends of his lead pencils. Today he would be drawing a model wearing a "Smoothie," one of Strouse Adler's most popular corsets. It was constructed with a newfangled material, latex, which was nothing like the thick, coarse cloth of the past. Modern women seemed to love the flaw-disguising stretchiness of latex. Mr. Russo loved it too, because of the savings. Only a little material was needed for each corset, compared to the eight yards of yesteryear.

After the metal sewing machines whirred to life on the floor below, his first model sashayed in. Antonia Colavolpe. She and her younger sister Cecilia were frequent subjects in Strouse Adler's advertising. Although both girls were beautiful, they were not the kind of models Mr. Russo typically employed. As a rule, he didn't hire local girls.

"Italian fathers can be a nightmare," he'd once confided. "And none of them want their daughters posing in underwear."

Even so, the Colavolpe sisters, with their natural eighteen-inch waists, had been too good to pass up.

Antonia shut the door behind her. "Good morning," she said cheerfully, tossing back dark, pin-curled hair. Behind a partition in the corner of the room, she took off her clothes and put on the corset that awaited her. "Will you be finished by noon, Lewis? I have to be somewhere." She poked out her head and winked at him. "Secret rendezvous."

Lewis knew most fellas would find her irresistible: her boldness and bright red lipstick. But he bristled when she used his first name. It breached a professional distance he tried to maintain. "We should be done by then," he replied.

"Thanks. Oh gracious—this one's divine."

She stepped out from behind the screen and ran her fingers along silky paneling and lacy, beribboned trim. The corset fit her like a second skin.

"Hands at your sides, please," he instructed. "Tilt your head a little and cock your right hip. Just a couple inches."

He sketched her for about twenty minutes as she chatted merrily about the possibility of seeing a double feature on Friday night. Or maybe finding a new beau. She was too blithe and animated for his taste, but at least she kept her body still. That was all Lewis really cared about.

"Any plans for this weekend?" she asked.

He didn't answer her right away. "Nothing very interesting, I'm afraid."

"Really, you can be such a wet blanket, Lewis."

He ignored that and began to draw the contours of a face. Not Antonia's face, though. He never drew the real faces of his models. Because Mr. Russo demanded absolute discretion, yes, but also because Lewis preferred his drawings to be anonymous. He liked to imagine the heads separate from the bodies. That way, when he sketched a sweet, wholesome face, he didn't have to worry about it contradicting the bombshell body to which it was attached.

"I'd let you take me out," she said coyly. "So that when someone asks you what you did on Saturday night, you'd have something to say. Would you like that, Lewis?"

He stared at the paper and licked the tip of his pencil. "Miss Colavolpe, I'd like it if you stopped talking."

After Antonia had gone, he headed for the kitchenette, a room of sea-green walls and checkerboard floor tiles that was reserved for management. But being a favorite of Mrs. Russo, he was allowed access.

Lewis couldn't quite remember when or how their routine had started. At some point, Mrs. Russo had decided to pack him a lunch. Now she did it every day. The two always met at noon—sharp—and ate together.

Today the plate that awaited him was spaghetti with anchovies and fennel. Mrs. Russo always cooked Italian food, although she—like Lewis—was not Italian. She'd learned the recipes, she said, to satisfy her husband.

She smiled warmly when Lewis joined her at the table.

"Thank you, Mrs. Russo," he said. "This looks divine."

"I've told you a thousand times to call me Doris."

"Thank you, Doris."

Mrs. Russo's own meal remained untouched. She was too busy sewing to eat. In her fingers were pattern pieces for a new corset. She liked to make original designs with unusual fabrics and hardware. Sometimes her work even made it into production. Out of everyone at Strouse Adler, Mrs. Russo probably knew the most about corsets, which was ironic since Lewis had never seen her wear one. She was a big-boned woman, thick in the rear and middle in particular. Yet she moved about self-confidently, unbothered by the fleshy rolls that Strouse Adler deemed the enemy.

"What's this one going to be like?" he asked her.

"Different. Modern," she replied. When he raised an eyebrow, she laughed. "Don't look so alarmed. It's not the second coming of the electric corset."

He laughed too. It was a running joke between them: how Strouse Adler had once deigned to manufacture Dr. Scott's electric corset, which had promised to cure everything from paralysis to impaired circulation. An electric corset: quackery at its finest.

"Who was the model this morning?" she asked as she stitched.

"Miss Colavolpe. The older one."

"You mean the greedy one. Do you know she had the nerve to ask me for more money? She makes four times what our seamstresses make—and I have to hold back their raises. Again."

"You and Mr. Russo are very generous to the models."

"Too generous. I told that Antonia, *No sirree*, and that if she doesn't stop sweeping through the front entrance like Hedy Lamarr, she won't have a job at all. She's attracting too much attention. But I think she likes that."

He nodded, and she sniffed in satisfaction. Lewis felt an ease with Mrs. Russo that he didn't feel with anyone else at work. Or anyone else in his life, really. Perhaps it had to do with the fact that he was not only the Russos' employee, but also their tenant. A few blocks away, he rented the basement apartment of their brownstone. He had a separate entrance, and thus, privacy and independence. Even so, his life felt tethered to theirs.

As Lewis dug into his meal, Mr. Russo popped his head in.

"You forgot the anchovy sauce," he said testily, staring at his wife. He was holding his plate in his hands—the same lunch Lewis was enjoying. Seeing him, Mr. Russo softened. "No matter—just remember it next time," he muttered.

"I'll be done with the *New York Times* ad by tomorrow morning," Lewis told him.

"Good man."

Mr. Russo ran his hands down the front of his slacks, which were always perfectly pressed. He was a dapper man, by any standard. Tall and elegant, he carried himself well. Lewis had observed the models try to flirt with him many times, but he was always dismissive. Lewis admired that.

"I have to eat this in accounting. Harold bungled the Chicago shipment again," Mr. Russo complained.

"Good luck, dear," his wife said, although it was Lewis he glanced at on his way out. She put the corset pieces on the table and smoothed them with her fingers.

"He acts like a baby," she said, shrugging, apologetic. "Maybe because we have no babies of our own. When I first got married, I thought we'd have half a dozen by now." She looked like she wanted to say more, but didn't. Instead, she fiddled with a thimble that was too small for her meaty thumb. "What about you? Do you plan on settling down and becoming a father?"

He didn't want to admit that the question had never occurred to him. He still felt worlds away from marrying, never mind having a child. Not that he wasn't old enough. There were plenty of fellas his age who already had children—he saw them every time he walked though Wooster Square. Fathers trying to untangle themselves from gaggles of small, cherub-cheeked children. It was a sight Lewis couldn't relate to. He'd been an only child, and he couldn't remember ever clinging to his father. Quite the opposite; he'd only ever wanted to be with his mother. *Fed you from the tit until you were five!* his father had said once. *It was unnatural!* Lewis shuddered, trying to push the memory back into whatever dark recess it had crawled out of.

"Are you feeling well, Lewis? You've gone pale. I hope I didn't upset you."

"Everything's fine," he assured her. Briefly, he patted her plump fingers, savoring their warmth.

She sighed and held up the corset, which was now loosely fitted together, and shook her head. "It always shocks me how busy these things are. When they're finished, you'd never know how much is inside of them: the busk, bones, grommets, channels, casings, and lining. When all's said and done, you don't see any of that—only the silhouette."

"It's the art of disguise," he said.

She nodded. "That's right. In more ways than one."

A week later, Cecilia walked into his workroom. In contrast to the brazen entrances Antonia made, Cecilia's meekness was refreshing. She tapped on the door first, opened it an inch, and whispered, "May I come in?"

Mr. Russo was on his way out. He'd come to request a couple changes to the *New York Times* ad. "I want a blonde, not a brunette," he'd said. "And can you make her face younger? For Pete's sake, that old mug reminds me of my grandmother." He took his hand off Lewis's shoulder, where it had been resting for quite some time, and waved off the girl as she attempted to greet him. "Get it to me by quitting time," he said to Lewis, shutting the door behind him. Lewis could hear the beat of his glossy black shoes as he walked down the corridor.

Head bent, Cecilia moved behind the partition. Lewis put

down his pencil and stretched. He was stiff from sitting so long. Nervous too. Strangely, Cecilia made him even more uncomfortable than her sister did. She was always punctual and polite, and didn't prattle on about her personal life. She struck him as a decent girl. A good girl.

When she reemerged, she avoided his eyes. The corset was cut modestly, generous and straight at the top, covering most of her bosom. It wasn't very fancy, with minimal flourishes and decoration. Lewis was grateful. He didn't want her to feel any more self-conscious than she already was.

"Hold your hands behind your back loosely, please, and stare off into the distance—as if you're admiring a sunset," he told her.

She did as instructed.

"Raise your chin a little and tilt your head to the side. That's it."

She stood motionless for a few minutes as Lewis sketched her in broad strokes.

"I've been reading that we might get involved in the war," she said, still staring toward an imaginary sun. "Do you think so, Mr. O'Connor?"

He flicked his pencil back and forth, then began to narrow one of her thighs. "I don't know. What do you think?"

"I think we will. I think we have to. It's terrible that we've abandoned Great Britain like this. And now the Soviets are joining the fight too." When he didn't reply, she went on: "I know others would disagree. They say we have to focus on ourselves—and fix the problems here in America. But I say, you should never abandon a friend in need."

Lewis decided he would use Cecilia's eyes in the drawing. He liked how wide and frank they looked. As long as he distorted the other features, he could keep them. "Sometimes it's better not to have friends," he said.

"What a strange thing to say."

He shrugged. "It's hard to know who to trust."

"Well, I know we can't trust those Nazis. And besides, isolation hasn't worked so far. The economy is still terrible. In my family, my sister and I are the only ones who have jobs. And I'm counting aunts, uncles, and cousins. The whole kit and caboodle."

"I prefer to be an outsider," he maintained. "You can see everything better from a distance. It's when you get too close that things go wrong."

"I never looked at it that way."

A silence ensued, but not an uncomfortable one. Both Lewis and Cecilia were lost in their own thoughts. He continued to sketch, shading and filling in detail.

"I like talking with you," she said suddenly. "You don't waste words. Have you noticed that most people do? Waste words, I mean."

Again, he didn't answer. She began to blush.

This is why Mr. Russo hired me, Lewis thought. *He knows I'll never take advantage of my position. He knows there's something in me—something strange—that doesn't want to.*

"I was w-wondering," she stammered, "if you'd like to take a walk with me after work sometime?"

He had to admit that she looked pretty, her pink cheeks a lovely contrast to her pale skin. He wondered if, just once, he ought to take a chance. Do something a normal man would do in a heartbeat. He wondered if maybe he ought to give Mrs. Russo's question more thought. He'd be lying if he said he wasn't lonely—that he didn't want companionship. It was hard—and exhausting—to be so different, to want things he couldn't even mention.

"It's okay if you don't," she whispered. "I didn't mean to

be presumptuous. Maybe you have someone . . . or maybe you're not interested. Oh God. I've never done this before. My mother would be horrified."

"I'd like to take a walk with you," he said finally. "How about today?"

"Today?"

"Yes. After work. Let's walk to the green."

"But all the grass is dead there—it's been so hot."

"We don't have to look at the grass."

She smiled bashfully. "Okay, Mr. O'Connor."

"You can call me Lewis."

"Okay, Lewis."

They didn't talk much at first. He was preoccupied with his limp. He hoped she wouldn't notice it, or if she did, that she wouldn't mention it. It seemed to him that she was as nervous as he was. She kept playing with her hair and smoothing the skirt of her polka-dot dress, which rustled in the warm breeze.

"At least it's not as humid as yesterday," she said.

He nodded. They were walking close, but not too close. A lot of people worked at Strouse Adler—he didn't want to give them something to gossip about.

"Lewis, have you noticed that this summer feels different?"

"What do you mean?"

"Summer is usually such a happy time. All the children are running outside. The men are playing bocce. There are parties and dancing and gelato . . ."

"I see all of that."

"Yes, but this summer there's something else. A kind of shadow. I can't explain it."

"Do you mean a dread?"

She looked at him sharply. "Yes—that's exactly what I mean! What do you think is causing it?"

"Maybe it has to do with the quilt fire."

"I think you're right, Mr. O'Connor. I mean, Lewis. It must be the quilt fire. It was terrible, wasn't it?"

The fire at the New Haven Quilt and Pad Company had indeed been terrible. Though the incident on nearby Franklin Street had happened months ago, Lewis knew it still haunted Wooster Square. Ten people had been trapped in a fire on the third floor. Rumor had it the automatic sprinkler system had been turned off and the fire doors ordered shut. These measures wouldn't have surprised Lewis. Every factory in this part of town cut corners. Savings always trumped safety.

"I lost my favorite cousin in that fire," she said.

"I'm sorry."

"Did you know anyone that worked there?"

"No."

"Really? You're the first person I've talked to in Wooster Square who's said that."

"I don't know many people. I try to keep to myself."

"Why?"

"It's part of my policy of isolation," he said, smiling at her wryly.

They had reached the green. She was right about the grass. And the elms weren't faring much better. Those few that had survived the big hurricane in '38 were beginning to look sick. He wondered if another wave of the tree disease was underway.

"I'd love to sit in the shade, but I don't think there is any," she observed.

They found a seat on a sun-soaked bench and looked around. A few young men sauntered by and one of them stole an appreciative glance at Cecilia's shapely calves. Lewis knew he ought to feel protective, even territorial, but he didn't.

"I love to watch people," she said, oblivious to the attention. My sister and I try to figure out what they're thinking. Where they're going. What their lives are like." She paused and turned to him searchingly. "Why do you prefer to be alone, Lewis? Is it because you're shy?"

"I just don't relate to most people."

"Do you think you could relate to me?"

He studied her face. She wasn't wearing any lipstick or rouge, not like her sister, who seemed to use a trowel to apply her cosmetics. Cecilia was a fresh-faced, lovely young woman. And that was the problem.

Suddenly she leaned in and tilted her head, just the way he'd asked her to do hours ago. She closed her eyes. Her lashes, thick and long, nearly rested on the ripe apples of her cheeks. He knew what she was waiting for.

"No," he said.

"What?" Discombobulated, she opened her eyes.

"I don't relate to you at all."

He offered to walk her home, but she refused. She was too embarrassed. *Mortified* was the word she'd used. Lewis felt bad. He knew he'd handled things poorly. He should have been more kind. He should have made a gentlemanly excuse. It wasn't the girl's fault, after all. Their outing had been an experiment. A failed experiment.

When he got home he soaked his feet in a bath. He looked at them side by side. The right foot was normal. The left was a disfigured, swollen, scarred clod of meat. It didn't even have toes, just oddly shaped nubs. And the skin—it didn't resemble regular skin. It was tough and rubbery and crosshatched with gleaming-pale connective tissue.

Even under the warm water, his bad foot throbbed. Sometimes it did this, especially when the weather was very hot or cold. He sighed, undressed, and slid his whole body into the water. Through the narrow basement windows, the aroma of a hundred dinners wafted in. It was getting late, he should have been hungry by now. But the walk had left a bad taste in his mouth.

He went to bed soon after, lying awake and listening to Victrolas, men singing opera, squealing children. The pain kept him up, as did the persistent feeling that he was a reject, abnormal, maybe even a monster.

It must have been two o'clock by the time he finally drifted to sleep. He awoke to a sharp rap on the front door. He sat up abruptly, thinking it was daybreak. He must be late for work. But when he opened his eyes, darkness still streamed through his windows.

More knocking.

His instincts told him that it was Cecilia. What did she want? An apology? A second chance?

"It's me," a voice called out.

"Mr. Russo?"

"Open up, Lewis."

Hurriedly, he slipped on pants and opened the door. He was sure it was an emergency; Mrs. Russo must be ill. Maybe she needed to go to the hospital.

"What is it?" he asked worriedly.

But Mr. Russo didn't appear distressed. He leaned his head against the doorframe, and then the whole of his weight. He smelled like a distillery.

"Someone said they saw you," he mumbled in a gravelly

voice. "You were with one of the Colavolpe girls." He sounded irritated, but not angry. Lewis was worried that he would slump over and fall to the ground.

"We went for a walk," he replied.

"Consorting with a model is not acceptable."

Lewis rubbed his large, pale eyes. "I'm sorry—I lost my head. It won't happen again."

Mr. Russo rubbed his eyes too; they looked bleary and bloodshot. "I didn't peg you for that type, Lewis."

"What type do you mean, sir?"

"The type that would exploit an opportunity."

"I didn't do any such thing. We just went for a walk."

"It has been my experience, Lewis, that men like yourself aren't always forthcoming about the truth."

Lewis was fully awake now, and cross. He resented Mr. Russo for showing up on his doorstep at this time of night, for causing him concern, for accusing him of something he hadn't done. Lewis had thought that Mr. Russo had a better opinion of him. He'd always believed there was a trust between them, unspoken but implicit.

"I am being truthful," he said.

Mr. Russo stared at Lewis, and as he stared, his expression softened. Tenderness, or something like it, replaced consternation. He reached out and brushed Lewis's cheek with his fingertips.

"Men like *us* aren't always forthcoming," he whispered.

Lewis has no idea what to say. Mr. Russo had taken a step closer. His foot was practically across the threshold. Lewis saw that his tie was loose, the top buttons of his shirt undone. A tuft of curly black hair peeked out from the starchy opening. He looked like a different man.

Lewis breathed deeply. He hated the whiskey smell of

Mr. Russo's breath. He knew that odor all too well. It was his first olfactory memory—forever branded on his brain. He remembered his father bending over him, hands clenching his spindly arms like vises, the whites of his eyes pink like Mr. Russo's. His father promised another thrashing with the belt. The thick brown one with the heavy metal buckle. The one Lewis feared more than anything in this world.

That memory of his father contrasted deeply with his early memories of his mother, which were visual and tactile. He recalled the scratchy straw-stuffed mattress they used to lie on. The way he would snuggle against her corpulent body, nestling deep into the warm, protective rolls of her flesh. He'd felt so safe there, as she read to him from their favorite book. She must have read it thirty times, but he never tired of listening to it.

And then one day everything ended. His father came home more drunk than usual, stumbling through the door, angry and jealous about something Lewis didn't understand. He ranted, grabbed the book, and threw it into the fire. Lewis remembered being picked up roughly, and then dangled over a large pot of boiling water, his mother screaming "Stop!" and "No!"—but it was too late. His father dipped his foot into the pot. Lewis recoiled like a wild animal fending for its life— thrashing, biting, clawing. He remembered being dropped to the floor, his mother futilely beating his father with her fists. From the ground, his view somehow magnified, Lewis watched his father strike his mother's face with the back of his hand. She toppled over, hitting her head on the sharp corner of the counter.

Lewis remembered his father's expression, anger and anguish in equal measures, as he gazed down at his wife and son, realizing the permanence of what he'd done. And then Lewis's pain became intolerable, growing with the pool of sticky, scarlet blood on the floor under his mother's head. His own wailing reached a piercing crescendo. His father fled and a neighbor entered, followed by a policeman. This was as much of the story as Lewis could dredge up, for he must have passed out.

After that, everything in his life changed. He lived somewhere else, bunking in a room with many children. He barely spoke, but drew incessantly on the paper the nuns gave him: old newspapers, magazines, wrapping paper, cut-up cardboard boxes. He grew older in a place where parents no longer existed, until he was old enough to leave.

"I understand your message," Lewis now said, meeting Mr. Russo's eyes meaningfully. "You don't need to come around again."

For a second Mr. Russo glanced down, then looked up again bitterly. Lewis quickly shut the door. After a pause, he locked it too.

The next morning, Lewis awoke with a headache. It was as if he'd been the one drinking whiskey all night. He cringed when he remembered whom he was scheduled to draw that morning: Antonia. Lewis knew there would be trouble. Women always talked to each other. And sisters—they must tell each other everything. He'd been foolish to ignore that fact.

She strutted into his workroom without a word, shoulders squared, back straight as a lightning rod. Behind the partition she noisily changed her clothes. She emerged in the day's garments: a conical brassiere, garters, stockings, high heels, and a waist-high, lace-up corset. Lewis took a deep breath. Behind his sketch pad, he felt unnerved. By contrast, Antonia appeared supremely confident.

"We'll be drawing you from the front today. Straight on. One hand on your hip, the other dangling, fingers relaxed," he said. "Look at me directly, please."

She glared at him as she assumed the position he'd requested. Under his arms, sweat stains bloomed.

"I hear you went out with my sister," she said. Lewis knew more was coming. Her voice was smug, indignant, and jealous all at once. "She said you were quite peculiar, but I could have told her that."

"Relax your hands, please. They're clenched."

"She said you didn't like her."

Lewis didn't reply.

"She said she's not your type. But I guess I'm not your type either, am I, Lewis?"

He wiped his brow. Now his whole body was perspiring, though this was one of the few rooms at Strouse Adler that was air-conditioned.

"What I want to know is—what *is* your type?"

"I don't think that's an appropriate question, Miss Cola-volpe."

"But it was appropriate to take out my sister?"

"No, that wasn't appropriate either," he conceded.

"All I want you to do is answer the question. What kind of girl do you want? My sister thinks the problem is that you don't know what to do. I think you know what to do—but *can't* do it."

Quietly, Lewis chose another pencil, licked the tip, and kept drawing. He wasn't sketching Antonia, however. The body he created was naked, lush, and fat—thick in the middle. A baby suckled on a swollen, unconstrained breast. Antonia continued to antagonize him. All the while, he wanted to argue, but he'd promised himself he wouldn't insult her.

* * *

The rest of the day passed in a blur. He picked at the meal Mrs. Russo had packed him. He still had no appetite. She fretted, asking him if he was feeling well.

"I'm fine," he replied, avoiding eye contact.

After lunch he crumpled up the picture he'd drawn. From memory, he tried to sketch how Antonia had appeared that morning, like an angry empress, but his mind was muddled. His hands kept trembling and he couldn't concentrate. Eventually, he threw his pencil on the floor and left the room to wander the halls of the factory. On the first floor he loitered outside one of the huge workrooms. Like the others, this one had a wood floor and slow-moving fans. Corsets and brassieres and other silky things spilled out of bins. Many lay scattered about on the ground. The air was thick with lint particles.

The ear-piercing cacophony of sewing machines filled his head, giving him a respite from his thoughts. From outside the room he watched row after row of tired women hunched over their machines, working in tandem. Occasionally they paused, or tried to take a smoke break. But those were discouraged, as was talking. Mainly, the women hummed or sang as their fingers busily guided fabric under sharp needles.

Young bundle girls moved the garments from station to station, for there were many stages before a product was complete: cutting, sewing, embroidering, eyeletting, boning, binding, trimming, starching, ironing, lacing, and packing. By comparison, Lewis's job was a breeze.

The noise distracted him for a time, but it also made his headache worse. He decided to leave work early—something he rarely did. With nothing to do, he walked New Haven for hours, until his legs tired. Until his left foot felt like it was on fire.

* * *

On his way home he decided to walk down Court Street, to the store that carried books. Over a week had passed; he'd counted the days. He opened the door and greeted the shop-keeper, who had a twinkle in his eye.

"I have it," the man said proudly.

Lewis was skeptical. In his heart he didn't believe he would ever find that childhood treasure again. Sometimes he wondered if he had imagined it in the first place.

The storekeeper disappeared into the back, returning a few moments later with a book in his hands. *The* book. The same version of *The Time Machine* that Lewis's mother had read to him when he was a young boy.

"It's a *sfinge?*" the shopkeeper asked, pointing to the cover. "I find it—for you."

"Yes, the sphinx," Lewis said, wide-eyed. There it was, front and center, the same mythical, lion-haunched creature he remembered.

"Hard to find. Very hard to find," the shopkeeper said, holding fast to the book. Still smiling, he sized Lewis up. "Per-fect condition. I take only ten."

"Ten dollars?"

When the man nodded, Lewis nearly lost his breath. It was an unreasonable sum, especially now. Especially here. No-body had that kind of money. But Lewis could not possibly leave without the book. He opened his wallet and gave the man what he'd asked for.

The man examined the bill carefully, then nodded again. Humming, he wrapped the book in brown paper, tied it with twine, and handed it to Lewis. "Glad you happy," he said.

Lewis tipped his hat on his way out. He thought that *happy* wasn't quite the right word. What Lewis felt was transported.

* * *

It was dusk by the time he finally returned to his apartment.

He fell asleep in a chair while reading the book, having lost himself in familiar characters from another time. Hours later, a knock on the door awakened him. He was annoyed, although it was still a reasonable hour—not the middle of the night. Readying himself for a conflict, he was shocked to see Mrs. Russo—instead of her husband. She smiled and held out a steaming plate of food.

"I brought you dinner. I was worried about you at lunchtime today. Still am. You look sick, if you don't mind my saying."

"I'm fine," he said brusquely. Now that he had the book, it was going to be harder to keep the bad thoughts at bay. "But I appreciate your kindness," he added, trying not to look at her.

"My husband's out with the boys tonight. They play cards once a week. Pinochle. Those games must be something."

"Why do you say that?"

"When my husband comes home, he always looks like a freight train hit him."

"Boys will be boys," he muttered.

"Indeed."

Lewis noted a quaver in her voice. Perhaps she understood more than she was letting on. Perhaps she needed a confidant, someone to pour her heart out to. He knew he shouldn't let her in, for her own sake, but he didn't want to disappoint her either.

"Would you like a cup of coffee?" he asked after a beat. It felt funny to ask—it was her house, after all.

"If you don't mind—that would be nice."

He'd been right: she wanted an intimate. She needed him—although not as much as he needed her. He guided her inside and motioned for her to sit in one of the wooden chairs that flanked the kitchen table. Primly, she adjusted her voluminous floral dress, her ample figure overflowing the seat. Lewis watched her intently. He had a sudden urge to sit in her lap, to feel himself engulfed in the soft, snug folds of her flesh.

When she caught him staring, Lewis turned away in embarrassment and started the coffee. He found the bottle of milk and the sugar jar, napkins, and spoons. He glanced at the stove, ashamed at how dirty it was, and at the greasy cast-iron frying pan he kept on one of the burner grates.

"The coffee will be ready in no time," he said.

"Thank you, Lewis. You're always very good to me."

"I was about to say the same thing about you, Mrs. Russo . . . Doris."

"We're like family, you and I, aren't we?"

Lewis realized that his hands were shaking again. In his fingers, the sugar jar trembled, its lid tinkling. He wished she hadn't said that. It was hard enough to distance himself without hearing that kind of talk. Now that she was here, alone with him, he couldn't stop thinking that the book might be a sign—a sign that the time had come.

"You said you thought you'd have half a dozen," he blurted, a new coat of sweat covering his body. "What if you could still have one?"

"Pardon?"

"I could give you what you want."

"What are you saying, Lewis?"

"Someone to hold," he said. "I could give that to you."

She scrutinized him, her warm eyes cooling. "You should eat your dinner, Lewis."

"Don't you see?" he said, gaining momentum, unable to stop. "Everything is coming together."

"I think I need to wish you a good night, Lewis."

She stood up quickly and clumsily, the thin fabric of her dress clinging to the thick, undulating ripples of her body. Staring at her unabashedly, he realized how close he was. Terribly close.

"Please," he begged, "don't leave."

But she turned her back and snatched her purse, like she had finally caught a whiff of his freakishness. He set down the rattling sugar jar and stared at the stove. He hadn't wanted it to come to this. But when he reached for the handle of the pan, he knew what he had to do.

Later, when the pan soaked in a sink full of sudsy red water, he realized that his foot had stopped hurting. It must be a miracle. He couldn't remember the last time he'd felt such relief.

The heat wave was still in full force, and his apartment was sweltering. Even so, when Lewis crawled into bed, he slipped under the covers. With a satisfied sigh, he nestled against the pliant, ponderous body beside him. Still warm, it yielded as he maneuvered under the shelflike bosom. That spot had always been his favorite, the place he had preferred when his mother had read to him all those years ago. She couldn't read anymore, of course, but he could tell her the story. The same book, the same pages, as close as he was ever going to get.

THE MAN IN ROOM ELEVEN

BY Michael Cunningham

Chapel Street

T he tenant in room eleven of the Hotel Duncan on Chapel Street has a lifetime lease, paid monthly, agreed to by the hotel's long-deceased original owner. No one who is currently employed by the Duncan (a rigorously plain building of dun-colored brick) has seen the man in room eleven in at least twenty years, which is the tenure of the longest-employed of the maids. That sole remaining maid does, however, remember stories told by another of the maids, long gone, who claimed to have seen the man. She described him as courteous, reserved, and perfectly manicured, though he kept his fingernails longer than was the general custom among men. He sported a mustache so thin and precise it might have been drawn on over his upper lip with a pencil, and always wore a hat, even in the upstairs halls.

That older maid (who died of a heart attack while cleaning on one of the upper floors) had said as well that he was a perfect gentleman, and a generous tipper. She was puzzled by, but grateful for, his request that his room never be cleaned. It was that much less work for her, after all, and the guests of the Duncan occasionally left their rooms in states of rather extreme, if conventional, disorder: the dark stains on the sheets, the moldy pizza slice that somehow fell behind the bureau and went undetected for weeks.

The older maid (not long before she died) did claim to

have been cleaning one of the rooms after its occupant had checked out, and to have found something too awful to describe. When pressed for details, she'd simply shaken her head, crossed herself, and said that it was gone, that she had gotten rid of it and that was the end of the story.

The Hotel Duncan is hardly luxurious. It is, however, respectable, and relatively clean. It still books rooms overnight, like any hotel, but has become more prone, over the years, to guests who stay for longer periods: weeks, months, or, occasionally, years.

They are mostly, but not exclusively, men. They often spend hours in the hotel's lobby, which, though in need of renovation, is possessed of that timeless, neither-here-nor-there quality common to certain older, less prosperous hotels: the crepuscular eternity of deep armchairs among potted palms, Persian rugs that appear to be indigo and black in the dim light, the sporadic chiming of the bell as the elevator makes its extremely slow progress from floor to floor.

The guests who frequent the lobby are various, of course, and each has a different story to tell, but if you speak to enough of them, a certain overall theme does seem to emerge. They are, almost all, currently waiting out the period that extends from one life to another. They have, most of them, left (or been expelled from) marriages, jobs, homes, institutions, or, occasionally (as one dapper, if tipsy, gentleman put it) have simply run out of the patience required of them to live as they'd been living.

They are, almost all of them, waiting for a next era to begin. Hopelessness is rare among them, though few seem to have specific dates in mind, or to be possessed of a plan that extends beyond the vision of vaguely improved circumstances. They are waiting for a check to arrive or a divorce to be finalized; they are waiting for a niece or nephew to come for them; they are expecting a huge cash settlement from the company that rendered them unable to work.

They languish there, in the lobby of the Hotel Duncan, as one of the several desk clerks (they are alike-looking as brothers—mild-faced, bespectacled men who might be forty or might be seventy) tends to hotel business, seated in the lobby's singular pool of bright light (from its lone overhead fixture), behind the imposing old mahogany front desk.

The man in room eleven never comes to the lobby. He never leaves his room, which is on the top floor, facing the street. Reclusiveness, however, is not a crime. The only disturbance he's ever caused has involved a handful of New Haven citizens who, over the years, have complained about a man staring down at them from the window of room eleven, his face obscured by wispy curtains. Unless the laws of New Haven change, however, staring from windows at people passing by on the street below is not cause for intervention by the police.

Still, several people have been sufficiently disconcerted by the man's gaze that they have, in fact, called the police. Their complaints, though, not only fail to involve any actual assault, but those who call the police always find themselves unable to be specific about what, exactly, they believe the man to have done to them. They're simply convinced that he shouldn't be there; that he's (as one Yale football player put it) "up to no good," or (as reported by a woman who works as a cashier at the Rite-Aid) "he's just sort of . . . creepy . . . I just feel like he's doing something *wrong* in there."

The police consistently inform these people that citizens are entitled to look as if they're up to no good (as long as they merely look that way), and that if there were laws against creepiness, a considerable portion of the New Haven population would be in jail already.

The man in room eleven is respected by the management and staff, in large part because he pays faithfully, in cash, the money neatly inserted into an envelope he slips under his door at the beginning of every month, and because he requires virtually nothing of the hotel's employees.

He plays the cello, quite well, but never after ten p.m. He apparently keeps a snake, which creates no disturbance of any kind. The snake's existence is apparent only because the boy who delivers the man's daily meals (there have been different boys over the years but all are respectable looking, well dressed, if unknown to any staff member who lives in or near New Haven) leaves, along with the man's food on a tray (ordinary food, chops and roast chickens and the like), a live rodent—a white rat, a hamster, a guinea pig—in a little cage, placed carefully beside the tray.

The following mornings, the tray and the cage, both empty, always appear in the hallway just outside room eleven.

The Duncan has its history of incidents, like any hotel. Even the Connaught in London, even the Ritz in Paris, has seen mortality do its work—how could it be otherwise, when so many come and go?

At the Duncan, there was the sudden disappearance of the room service boy (many years ago, when the Duncan offered room service at all), with no notice; without so much as leaving his uniform behind.

There was the porter (back when the Duncan employed porters) who came down in the elevator (no one was ever sure from which upper floor), walked purposefully through the lobby to the front door, and did not appear for duty the next day, or ever again.

There was the expression on the face of the man found dead in his room of a coronary occlusion. There was the single woman who'd said a cheerful good night to her two women friends, gone up to her room, and been found hung from the shower rod, by a silk stocking, the next day. There was the young man, stopping over on his way to Albany, who seemed to have been bitten, over and over, by . . . some small animal, probably a dog, though dogs have never been allowed at the Duncan.

Such events are not unusual, not in any hotel.

The only genuinely strange occurrence is a recent one, and it took place not inside the Duncan but on Chapel Street, in front of the hotel.

A young woman, a junior at Yale, had been walking back to the campus rather late at night, having been at a party on Dwight Street. According to her friends, she'd been entirely herself when she left the party: cheerful, bantering, and only as intoxicated as it's possible to become after imbibing two Miller Lites. It being Chapel Street, a mere few blocks from the campus, no one thought anything of her walking home alone.

She was found less than an hour later, standing on the sidewalk in front of the Duncan, staring up at the building, frozen in place. She was alive, and unharmed, but remains catatonic three weeks after the incident.

No one is able to speculate about why she'd stopped before the Duncan like that—it's hardly a New Haven landmark— though a faculty couple who had just walked past the young woman on Chapel Street do claim to recall the sound of someone knocking on glass, from above. They did not look up at the source of the tapping sound (it seemed so clearly meant for the young woman), and in fact thought nothing of it at all until they read about the young woman's hospitalization in a police bulletin on Yale's website.

The girl did briefly regain consciousness, in her bed at Yale–New Haven Hospital, the day after she was found on Chapel. She opened her eyes, but did not seem to be aware of her surroundings. She merely stared up at the ceiling of her room and said, "All those little teeth," after which she emitted a hissing sound that, according to the attending nurse, did not sound quite like a noise of which the human voice is capable.

She spoke so softly that the nurse, who was the only one present at the time, is not entirely certain that the girl said, "All those little teeth." The nurse believes it might have been, "All those little *teas*," which would probably have referred to the Master's Teas held in Morse College.

The latter version, of course, makes more sense. The nurse, however, is certain about the inhuman sound that followed the phrase; she says it resembled the hiss of a snake but was deeper and more penetrating, more like (according to the nurse) the sound of gas escaping from a valve.

At any rate, by the time the girl's parents arrived from Grand Rapids, the girl had lost consciousness again, and has not regained consciousness a second time.

The girl's parents have had her moved from New Haven to Grand Rapids. The doctors there are, as they say, guardedly optimistic. CAT scans have revealed nothing amiss in the young woman's brain. There are, have always been, unsolved medical mysteries, and people who, like the Yale undergraduate, fall abruptly into catatonic states and sometimes return from them, just as abruptly, wondering where they are, assuming themselves to be still on the bus or in the room or wherever they were when they passed out of consciousness, days or weeks or months earlier.

Still, if you find yourself walking past the Duncan on Chapel Street, it's probably just as well to focus your gaze straight ahead, either toward the lights and joviality of the Study Hotel or the brutalist bulk of the architecture school, depending on which way you're headed. There's plenty to see on Chapel Street, at eye level.

There are, after all, people who, for unknowable reasons, want to see things they'd be better off not having seen at all. These people seem simply to want to know that mysterious forces are alive and well.

There are zealots of another sort too. You could probably think of them as religious, in their way, though the message they want to impart is different from that of street-corner Christians. This other body of evangelists wants us to know that hell and damnation are inevitable, that we do not go unwitnessed by the evil eye, that it's only a matter of time until our final destination is revealed to us.

So why take chances? There are, after all, unsavory presences at large in the world, and they sometimes manifest themselves in the unlikeliest of places. So, really, there's no particular reason to glance up as you pass the Hotel Duncan. The man in room eleven has only proven dangerous to those who hear him tap on the glass, look up, and see . . . whatever it is that they see. It's best to stare straight ahead, and go on about your business, especially if someone overhead, in the Duncan, seems to want to attract your attention.

THE QUEEN OF SECRETS

BY LISA D. GRAY

Bradley Street

On Saturday when my mom and Aunt V picked me up from ballet class, the last dregs of their argument stunk up the car like chitlins at Thanksgiving, thick and spicy. We were headed down Whalley toward Aunt V's apartment, and while we waited for the light to change, my mom asked her, "Vanya, you did make the appointment for Thursday?" My aunt didn't answer and her eyes slid across my mother's face like a slap.

I waited a few minutes before leaning over the seat and snapping on the radio. My aunt's hand gripped the door handle, her knuckles bulging like little hazelnuts as we passed the empty playground. A drizzle sprinkled the window, making the swings, slide, and jungle gym's bright colors all runny like in those French paintings at the museum. I love that place. All those paintings and beauty under one roof.

"Sit down, Janelle," my mother said as we pulled up in front of my aunt's brick apartment building on Kensington.

Before Aunt V lifted the handle to get out, she turned to my mom and said, "Yes, Olivia, Thursday. Night, Janelle." She smiled at me and then she was gone.

A huddle of boys shot craps against Aunt V's stoop as they waited for their customers to creep out of the shadows. She stopped for a second and spoke to them before they moved to let her pass.

"What's Thursday?" I asked my mom.

"I don't recall anyone inviting you into the conversation," my mom said, like she did anytime she thought I was minding grown folks' business. I wondered what they'd argued about, but not for long, because my mom and aunt bickered one minute and laughed the next. "That's how sisters are," my mom would tell me after one of their melt-into-nothing arguments.

Tuesday, I was wiping the table and counter after dinner when the phone buzzed. I answered it on the fourth ring.

"Hello. Hey Auntie, yeah, she's here." Aunt V's voice sounded wavy. "Mom, pick up the phone!" I hollered into the family room, but I didn't hang up.

"Does she know?" my aunt asked my mother.

"Of course not," my mom told her in her I-don't-want-to-say-I-don't-have-time-for-this-but-I-don't-have-time-for-this voice.

"I want to tell her, O."

I wanted to keep listening but they might hear the TV. I was watching the news for my homework and it was kind of loud, so I hung up the phone then tiptoed to the door and cracked it a smidge. Mom was still folding clothes. Hills of socks, T-shirts, and jeans covered the coffee table in front of her. She had tucked the phone between her ear and shoulder as she talked and folded. "V, you were doing so well. What happened?" That was all I could hear because Mom's voice got softer.

I swept the floor, fed the dog, grabbed a Coke from the fridge, then headed into the family room hoping to catch more of their conversation. My mom was still on the phone and she lowered her voice, her eyes tracking me as I crossed the room to the sofa. I picked up the remote and sank into its fat brown cushions. The couch was my command station, like Captain Kirk's on *Star Trek*. The TV popped to life and my mom whispered into the phone, "Let me call you right back." Mom didn't say anything to me; she just hung up and climbed the stairs.

On Thursday, I got home from swimming practice just before four. I was late and hungry. Swimming always made me want to eat. A note sat on the counter next to a covered plate: *Out for a bit. Home soon. Mom.*

I remembered Mom and Aunt V's chitlin-funky conversation in the car and figured she must be with her or out with her friends. She did that sometimes, had a girl's night. But six hours later she still wasn't back and I was getting worried. I'd finished my homework and was balled up on the couch, TV on, a bag of chips on the floor. I flipped through *Essence* and half paid attention as Janet Peckinpaugh said, *"The body of a man found at the Pond Lily Hotel several months ago has been identified and an explosion yesterday evening rocked a local women's clinic. Details at eleven."* I changed the channel.

Vanya and Olivia were sun and moon, oil and water, opposites with nothing in common, but they'd been best friends since they were pinkie-hooking secret sharers. At fifteen, Vanya was what her sister and friends called a "goodie-goodie." She'd won spelling bees and science fairs; she volunteered at the Hospital of Saint Raphael and earned straight As on most of her report cards. Sixteen-year-old Olivia, on the other hand, had managed to earn little more than a reputation. She skipped school, smoked cigarettes, and snuck into bars like Ernie B's and the Oasis over in Newhallville. Olivia and Vanya were still as close as they'd been as girls and had had to depend on each other after their mother died in a car crash. Their worlds circled each other's, in distant orbits held together by an invisible pin.

It started the year their mother died. She'd picked them up from school, and as they drove down Dixwell Avenue the car skidded on some ice and spun around and around. The girls screamed and held hands in the backseat even after the car barreled into a tree. Everything turned silent and snow sprinkled the windshield where a spiderwebby crack now crawled. Their mother didn't move. The girls tried to scramble over the seat to get to her, but they couldn't undo their seat belts. Faces peered in the windows, voices called out to them, and then they heard the sirens.

After the funeral, their father was as much of a ghost as they imagined their mother to be. He plunged himself into work at their school where he was a principal, and spared little time for them, his grieving girls. He never dated and spent his nights staring at the television. The girls didn't know what to do with their grief or their father's indifference and tried to win his attention in their own ways. The thing the girls held onto was each other, even as they started moving in different directions. At night after dinner they sat on their beds and gabbed about their day. On Saturday afternoons, they washed and pressed each other's hair, and on Sundays they cooked dinner while talking about books and boys. They reminisced about their mother as they prepared the recipes in the cookbooks she kept above the stove.

At seventeen, Vanya was a tall girl with high cheekbones, a broad nose, and almond-shaped eyes. She possessed a quiet, easygoing nature and was well liked, but had become a loner like their father. Girls in her class called her stuck up and snooty.

Olivia was petite with a nose that turned up at the end and ears that stuck out a little like their mother's. Her smile drew people to her and she reminded almost everyone of their mother, who had sparkled at the center of any group.

I woke up on the couch Friday morning, and potato chips and empty Coke cans littered the coffee table. The house was quiet. My mom would kill me if she knew I'd guzzled three cans while doing the rest of my homework. The TV was still on and a reporter stood in front of a charred building on what looked like Bradley Street near my school, Saint Mary's. People swarmed behind the reporter, a few of them waving while others seemed to just want to hear what she was saying. I spied my mom in the back of the crowd, wearing her faded jean jacket. Her eyes were puffy, her hair uncombed, and my mom did not do uncombed hair, ever.

The reporter introduced a tall man named Captain Johnson who stepped up to the mic. Sweat trickled down his pale, heat-reddened face as the camera zoomed in on him. Looking directly in the camera, he began, and I listened.

"*Yesterday, at approximately seven p.m., a Caucasian male entered the Planned Parenthood clinic and detonated an explosive device. It seems there may have been as many as twenty women in the building at the time. We will release names to the media after we've identified the victims and notified their families.*" He abruptly turned away from the camera and the reporter took over. I didn't hear a word she said.

My dad was out of town at a conference, so I couldn't ask him any of the questions swirling through my head. Not that he'd have answers; he and Aunt V had kept their distance since that first summer when she came home.

I ran to my room, stuffed my legs into a pair of jeans, and

threw on a T-shirt over my nightgown. It was still early and as the sun rose over the tops of the trees, streaking the sky a golden orange, I pedaled hard, my heart pounding in my ears as random thoughts about Aunt V floated in my brain. Shoes. She loved shoes and had over a hundred pairs. I knew because the week before she'd paid me fifty cents a pair to organize them for her, and I'd earned sixty-seven dollars. The shoes sat on the large closet shelf, each in a cloudy-white plastic box. I'd taped Polaroid pictures to each—red pumps, purple sandals, orange suede boots, pink high-top sneakers, burgundy penny loafers . . .

I got to Bradley Street and there were people everywhere—police, firemen, neighbors, kids. I scanned the crowd for my mother, hoped to see my aunt. Glass, paper, and broken furniture littered the sidewalk and street. Men in uniforms carried black bags like the ones you see on crime shows from the building and lined them up on the grass outside the front door. The smell of smoke filled my nose and throat, and the faint smell of burning hay wafted through the crowd.

Olivia and Vanya had always shared secrets, and in high school Vanya dubbed Olivia their queen. They'd reveal their confidences before hooking their pinkies, gazing into each other's eyes, and repeating a solemn phrase they'd learned from their mother: *Forever and Always*. Olivia told tales of the things she and Seth got up to when she snuck out to meet him at night. V didn't really like Seth. He was a know-it-all whose mother talked about Olivia, called her wild and worse. Olivia's biggest secret spilled out the night of her graduation, the night she left town with Seth.

Olivia threw clothes in a suitcase as V tossed her sister's blouses, skirts, and shoes out of the blue bag until she caught that gleam in Olivia's eye. She knew Olivia would not be stopped.

"Where you going?" Vanya asked.

"New York or Washington. Seth got into Howard and NYU." She stopped packing and added, "I'm pregnant. I thought about, you know," she touched her still slim stomach, "but I can't do it."

Olivia closed her eyes for a moment, then tossed a pair of faded jeans into the almost full bag.

"You gonna marry him?"

"Yes," Olivia answered.

"You know Dad's gonna try to stop you."

"When has he ever tried to stop me from doing anything?" O said. "When has he ever cared? Besides, it's gonna be our secret." She held out her pinkie, but V didn't take it. O closed her suitcase as a tear rolled down her nose. She walked to the door.

"Wait!" Vanya called. She hopped off the bed and went to her dresser where she kept her box of memories. It'd been the last Christmas gift she got from their mother. She pulled out a bunch of crumpled bills and stuffed them into her sister's hand. "Take this," she said, then extended her pinky.

Seth started at Howard soon after he and Olivia arrived in DC. They lived in a tiny apartment with furniture they found or picked up from tag sales, and Olivia hated it. After a while she started to hate Seth too, but she stayed. She lost the baby a few months after they left home; she tried to forget and found a job on campus answering phones for the English department. When Seth graduated, they moved back to New Haven, where Olivia worked at Malley's in the children's department while Seth went to law school and they tried to have another baby. She missed her sister.

Vanya graduated the May after Olivia left and went off to Spelman College. She made friends. She danced at parties and sipped fruity cocktails on dates. She studied for classes and talked to Olivia at least once a week. They still shared secrets but now Vanya's were juicier than O's. O had settled into a life with Seth while V had started kissing boys and skipping classes. By the time Vanya graduated, Olivia's little indiscretions tasted like dry white toast in comparison to her butter-and-jam-slathered tales. Vanya went home to New Haven for a week before moving to Montreal to study nursing and didn't return home for ten years.

You got off the plane wishing you didn't look as raggedy as you knew you did. You were ready to start again and go back to before everything had spiraled out of control. Olivia had called almost every day that first year you lived in Montreal, and you'd gab for hours about your new grown-up lives—your classes in nursing school, her relationship with Seth, the baby they never had. A year went by, then two. You finished nursing school and found a job as an ER nurse. Olivia chaired committees, and hosted dinner parties, and you spoke to her less and less. You were lonely, and tired all the time, and you wanted to talk to your sister. Most days you struggled to keep your eyes open, especially on night shifts—you started doing it as a way to stay awake, a way to feel something on the days when life was a gray cloud you trudged through. You told yourself it was no big deal. Lots of the nurses did it. A hit here, a toke there, and before you knew it, you craved its caresses like a lover's. Some days you didn't even go to work, and when days turned to weeks, they fired you. You'd stare at your cracked reflection in another broken mirror, in another bathroom, in another bar, and as you painted your lips, you'd wonder who that hollow-cheeked woman was. When it got bad and you couldn't pay your rent, you'd call your father for money but never told him you'd lost your job, or that your belly was growing, or that your home was a run-down hotel, or that you turned tricks for hits. You loved the act of preparing it, measuring it, grinding it, cooking it, but especially smoking it. The bittersweet acridness of the blue smoke, the crackle of tiny, quartzy rocks as you kissed them with flame. You'd close your eyes and inhale, hold the smoke in your lungs, and then blow it all out as the smooth, tingly sensation creeped from brain to toes. You loved that most of all until the baby kicked and you knew you had to quit. You called Olivia. She came and stayed five months, and you stopped, and when she left, you hooked your pinkies and whispered, "Forever and Always," before Olivia closed the cab door and flew home with the baby. It didn't take long for you to start again. You missed O, couldn't find a job, and the hole in your chest throbbed as you thought of your baby, her baby, and you smoked. The first time you landed in jail you told yourself it's no big deal. Ten arrests for solicitation later and you spent eighteen months in prison and they shipped you back to Connecticut. You'd missed your father's funeral. A heart attack took him and you hadn't found out until three months after it happened because Olivia didn't always accept your calls. She never came to visit, never sent pictures of your baby, her baby. No one picked you up from Union Station and you loaded your bags into a cab, reciting Forever and Always in your head because you wanted to tell her you were home and she was yours—but not yet.

I was eight the summer I met Aunt V. The sun slipped in and out of clouds as I played jacks on the porch. My mom talked about her, but she'd never come to visit. "Work," my mom told me. She sent me cards for my birthday and every Christmas. I sat on the porch, tossing up my jacks ball, waiting for her to come, and when a yellow cab pulled up to our curb, I skipped down the front walk to meet her.

"Nelly, it is a pleasure." She squeezed my hand then hugged me until I almost couldn't breathe. Her almond-shaped eyes and broad nose were like mine. In our baby pictures our cheeks and smiles are so similar, *like twins* people said as they flipped through the family album Mom kept on the coffee table. Her curly Afro bounced as her yellow heels clicked up the front steps. Aunt V didn't look as pretty as the girl in the photos, though. She was pencil-thin with a trace of ash around her lips. I was dragging her bag up the stairs to my room when she asked me, "Where's your mom?"

"In the kitchen." I nodded my head toward the open door, and after I put her bag on the second twin bed in my room, I ran downstairs. Mom and Aunt V sat on the couch in the living room and I settled on the bottom step to listen.

"Thanks for letting me stay. I start work at the end of July so I should be able to get my own place by September."

"I hope so, because Seth is not going to be happy if it's longer than that, and you have to go to the meetings, Vanya. And no more secrets. Clear?"

"Crystal." Aunt V's voice was crisp and gravelly.

I thought they'd be happier to see each other, but they circled each other like kids on the playground before doing battle, only breaking the silence when Aunt V gave a tight little laugh. "Guess I'm the Queen of Secrets now, huh?" The Queen of Secrets—I liked the way it sounded: mysterious, dark.

"You don't have to be," my mom answered her. "Just know I love you, V, and that we want to help, really."

"*We?* Seth too? That boy finally off his high horse?"

"Vanya, that's not fair."

"Well, he wasn't fair, and he's the guy who got his underage girlfriend drunk and knocked her up. Clear?"

"Crystal," my mom said, and they burst out laughing. They

talked for hours that night. I could hear their voices buzzing as I waited for Aunt V to come to bed.

Aunt V became my best friend that summer. We spent whole days doing everything and nothing. In July, we went to the beach and she taught me how to swim. She moved into her own place over on Kensington Street near the hospital in September, and that fall, we gobbled bunless hot dogs out of a thermos as we sat on the hood of Mom's car, feeling the airplanes roaring above us as they soared to foreign places like Australia and Turkey.

She smoked long white cigarettes, and at Thanksgiving she and Mom giggled as I imitated her by puffing on a straw and teetering across the front room's green carpet in her red pumps with heels as long as my pencils. Her chocolatey perfume tickled my nose when she whispered in my ear. Sometimes I'd catch her studying me as I watched TV or did homework, and it made my stomach wiggle.

She gave me a Polaroid camera that Christmas and the first picture I snapped was of her. I pinned it to the bulletin board in my room. She is sitting on the floor in the kitchen. Her feet are bare, and her legs, which are spread wide in front of her, are swallowed by the red-and-green puddle of her full skirt. A little red ball hangs in the air in front of her face, and her hand is poised to sweep up a gleaming row of jacks on the floor. A half-full martini glass sits next to her and an imprint of her red lips decorates its rim. She is laughing.

You tried to stay clean. You snuck a few drinks at first, craved a hit, but then you started the job, and NA, and you stopped. Three months later you moved into your own place, reconnected with old friends, went back to church, and stayed clean until He came. He found you at the hospital where you worked and where you and Olivia had once sat in hard orange chairs waiting for your mommy to walk from behind the washed-out green curtain. You'd waited and waited, but she never came. You became a nurse because of that night, and you loved your job, but after a while the long hours and the dying exacted their toll, and you couldn't breathe, felt like you were sinking, just like you had in those orange chairs the night your mom died. Some days you drank, and you craved a hit, just one hit. He followed you home from one of the NA meetings at the church where Olivia volunteered. You'd started going when It had called to you, when Its memory tickled your brain, and you tried to ignore It. He never said a word to you until the day he approached you at the bus stop.

"Hello," he said. "We need to talk."

You didn't remember telling him anything about home. You'd stopped seeing him when you'd told him about the baby. He'd wanted you to get rid of it and keep tricking, and you thought about it, but much like Olivia all those years ago, you couldn't do it.

"No," you'd said, and he left you alone. That's when you called O.

The bus eased to a stop, and you got on, leaving him standing there. Three days later, you spotted him outside the hospital, and a week after that he showed up as you got off the bus at O's house, and your body went cold.

"What do you want?" you asked him.

"To talk about . . . about . . . you know." His blue green eyes slipped to O's house and you knew he knew, so you agreed to meet him at his hotel.

You met him the next night at the Pond Lily, because no one would know you there. You guzzled three martinis in the bar before heading to his room. He offered you a drink and you nodded. You sat at the scratched brown desk.

"*How are you?*" he asked.

"*Better than some, not as well as others,*" you responded, then sipped the glass of warm bourbon. "*And you?*"

He shrugged his thick shoulders, his hands hanging at his sides. He needed a shave and his breath stank.

"*Where is she?*" he asked.

"*Who?*" you said, raising an eyebrow, gripping the glass.

"*I know,*" he said.

"*Know what?*" You thought of Nelly and your sister, even of Seth, despite him still acting funky whenever you visited.

You went to him and whispered in his ear, "*She died.*" You kissed him and he kissed back, and then you felt his warm fingers at your throat, squeezing.

"*Liar.*" He let go and you gasped for air, then sucked down the rest of the bourbon. You slipped your hand in your purse and felt it there, and you knew you would do it. You apologized to him in your head and kissed him before pulling him to the bed. You would do it.

When you woke up, he was still sleeping. You slipped on your clothes and wiped the glass, the desk, the bed frame. You pulled a syringe from your purse and filled it with the insulin you'd taken from the hospital. Forever and Always, you thought as you eased the liquid into him. You left and started again. One time, one hit, you told yourself as you left the Pond Lily. When you got home you bought a package from the boy on your front stoop.

That day melted into months, and now you were strung out again, about to lose your job again, the Queen of Secrets again. You sat on the toilet, your mouth dry, your palms sweaty, your head pounding as the blue line on the end of a white plastic stick stared at you, and you wondered if you could do this again. It was the same as before—the same guy, the same blurry emptiness like those impressionist paintings Nelly loved. You wanted to tell Olivia but couldn't take Seth's condemnation, not again, so you told your *diary. You chronicled everything between its pages: every booze-soaked night, every baby that died in your arms, that night with him, your daughter and how you dreamed of her and you together knowing it could never be.*

My mother talked to a policeman. Emergency workers scurried around, people chattered, reporters interviewed witnesses in the crowd. I dropped my bike and ran to Mom.

"What are you doing here?" I asked her, knowing the answer, wanting to be wrong.

"Janelle." Her glassy red eyes held mine.

"I saw you on the news. Where's Aunt V?"

"You shouldn't be here, baby."

"Where is Aunt Vanya?" I pulled her arm, my voice rising.

Olivia dropped you off at six forty-five. On the ride over, you'd wanted to tell her everything. You'd tried the night before. You'd spent the night so you could get to the clinic early and maybe avoid the people with the posters chanting, "Baby Killer!" as you walked into the clinic. You'd wanted to tell her before you went to bed in Nelly's room, but you could not find the words. As you got out of the car, she matter-of-factly uttered, "Call when you're ready." No smile of assurance, no hug for strength. Five or six protesters lined the sidewalk and you tried to ignore them, tried not to see the tiny baby parts splattered across their signs.

Inside, your eyes wandered the room and you noticed you were the only one not dressed for a workout or an afternoon at the mall. A tall man wearing jeans and a T-shirt walked in, and you wondered if he was picking up his wife or daughter. He sat down. You felt out of place in your bright dress, but this time you'd at least kept up your appearance and you wouldn't let it go now. You dressed how you wanted to feel. The girls waiting with you appeared no

older than Nelly. You could have been their mother. One side-eyed
you, her eyelids squinched, her lips pursed, her arms crossed tightly
over her chest. You sat up straight, hands folded in your lap, legs
crossed at the ankles. The chair was cold and hard underneath
you, and you thought back to the hospital the night your mom
died. You hoped no one there would recognize you, which is oddly
enough something you never thought about as you gulped martinis
in dark bars, sniffed coke in bathrooms, and checked into seedy
motels off 91 with men like Nelly's father, this baby's father. The
man shifted in his seat and tapped his foot against the linoleum
floor. They called your name and, in a tight, dimly lit room, a nurse
walked you through your options, and you gazed out the window
and thought about tomorrow and starting over again. You took a
breath and began answering her questions. Heat seared your skin
and you were melting. You tried to run but had no legs, and rubble
rained down on you, and you thought of Nelly, your baby, her
baby, and you saw him lying in the bed next to you, his face, her
face.

A snatch of color caught my eye. I squinted and focused on
it—a shoe. A scorched, light-green slingback. A pale pink
rose bloomed from its toe. I knew the shoe because I had photographed it only a few weeks earlier. My mother walked in
a tight circle, hugging herself. A breeze blew and carried the
reporter's voice to me as I stared at the shoe: *"Now, back to
the studio . . ."*

I'd had to ride my bike home as my mom finished talking
to the police. When I got there I lay down on the other bed
in my room where Aunt V had slept the night before and felt
something hard under her thin pillow. A diary with *The Queen
of Secrets* scrawled across its worn cover in Aunt V's spidery
cursive. I opened it and started reading.

ABOUT THE CONTRIBUTORS

AMY BLOOM is the best-selling author of three novels, three collections of short stories, a children's book, and a collection of essays. She has been a finalist for both the National Book Award and the National Book Critics Circle Award, and has won a National Magazine Award for Fiction. She lives in Connecticut and taught at Yale University for the last decade. She is now Wesleyan University's Shapiro-Silverberg Professor of Creative Writing.

STEPHEN L. CARTER is the William Nelson Cromwell Professor at Yale Law School. He is the author of eight works of nonfiction, most recently *The Violence of Peace: America's Wars in the Age of Obama*. He has published six novels under his own name, others under a pseudonym, and over eight hundred short stories, articles, op-eds, and reviews. He could do none of this without the love, support, and deft editing of his wife, Enola Aird.

Mikhail Nazarenko

JOHN CROWLEY is a recipient of the American Academy and Institute of Letters Award for Literature and the World Fantasy Lifetime Achievement Award. His sci-fi novel *Engine Summer* is listed in David Pringle's *Science Fiction: The 100 Best Novels*. His books include *Little, Big*, the Ægypt Cycle quartet, *The Translator*, *Lord Byron's Novel: The Evening Land*, *Four Freedoms*, and several volumes of short fiction. He teaches fiction writing and screenwriting at Yale.

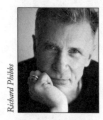

Richard Phibbs

MICHAEL CUNNINGHAM is the author of the novels *A Home at the End of the World*, *Flesh and Blood*, *The Hours* (winner of the PEN/Faulkner Award and Pulitzer Prize), *The Snow Queen*, *Specimen Days*, and *By Nightfall*, as well as the nonfiction book *Land's End: A Walk in Provincetown*. His latest book, *A Wild Swan and Other Tales* (illustrated by Yuko Shimizu), was published in November 2015. He lives in New York and teaches at Yale.

Lisa D. Gray

LISA D. GRAY's writing tackles issues of race and class while highlighting the intersections between identities and groups. She currently teaches at Mills College and earned her BA from Spelman College and her MFA from Mills College. She's attended VONA, completed a residency at the Vermont Studio Center, and received the Joseph Henry Jackson Award for distinguished writing from the San Francisco Foundation.

David Dimico

CHRIS KNOPF's latest Sam Acquillo novel, *Back Lash*, received a starred review from *Booklist*. *The Last Refuge, Two Time*, and *Black Swan* were reviewed by the *New York Times*. *Dead Anyway* drew starred reviews from *Publishers Weekly, Booklist, Kirkus*, and *Library Journal*, was named a Best Crime Novel of 2012 by the *Boston Globe*, and won the 2013 Nero Award. *Kill Switch* was short-listed for the 2016 Derringer Award.

Sigrid Estrada

ALICE MATTISON's most recent book is *The Kite and the String: How to Write with Spontaneity and Control—and Live to Tell the Tale*. She's the author of six novels, including *When We Argued All Night* and *The Book Borrower,* and four collections of stories, including *In Case We're Separated*. She lives in New Haven and teaches fiction in the MFA program at Bennington College.

KAREN E. OLSON, a New Haven native, received the Sara Ann Freed Memorial Award for *Sacred Cows*, her mystery debut set in her hometown, and a Shamus nomination for *Shot Girl*, the fourth in the Annie Seymour mystery series. A long-time journalist, she was an editor at the *New Haven Register* and is currently working at Yale while writing her third crime series and enjoying the best pizza anywhere.

Maggie Swanson

CHANDRA PRASAD has written several award-winning novels, including *On Borrowed Wings*, a historical drama set at Yale University. She is the originator and editor of *Mixed*, an anthology on the multiracial experience, which was published to international acclaim by W.W. Norton. Prasad's shorter works have appeared in the *Wall Street Journal* and the *New York Times*, among other places. Her first young adult novel, *Damselfly*, will be published by Scholastic in 2018.

Susan Rich

DAVID RICH splits time between writing movies, television, plays, and novels. He wrote the feature film *Renegades,* starring Kiefer Sutherland and Lou Diamond Phillips, as well as episodes of *MacGyver* and other shows. Forsaking Los Angeles for small-town Connecticut, David turned to fiction, writing *Caravan of Thieves* and *Middle Man*, featuring Marine Lieutenant Rollie Waters and his con-artist father.

ROXANA ROBINSON is the author of nine books: five novels, including *Cost;* three collections of short stories; and the biography *Georgia O'Keeffe: A Life.* Her work has appeared in the *New Yorker,* the *Atlantic, Harper's Magazine,* the *New York Times,* and elsewhere. She teaches in the Hunter College MFA Program and divides her time between New York, Connecticut, and Maine. She has received fellowships from the NEA and the Guggenheim Foundation and is the president of the Authors Guild.

David Ignaszewski

HIRSH SAWHNEY grew up in Orange, Connecticut, and currently resides in New Haven. He has also lived in New York City, London, and New Delhi. His debut novel, *South Haven,* was a Barnes & Noble Discover Great New Writers selection. He is the editor of Akashic's *Delhi Noir* anthology, and his articles have appeared in the *New York Times,* the *Guardian,* and the *Times Literary Supplement.* He is an assistant professor at Wesleyan University.

Hemant Sareen

JESSICA SPEART is the author of the highly acclaimed narrative nonfiction book *Winged Obsession* about the world's most notorious butterfly smuggler. The book was an Indie Next pick and has been optioned for a feature film. Speart also penned a mystery series featuring US Fish and Wildlife Service agent Rachel Porter. The series was created after years of investigating wildlife and drug-trafficking crimes for publications such as the *New York Times Magazine.*

George Brenner

JONATHAN STONE does most of his writing on the commuter train between the Connecticut suburbs and his advertising job in Manhattan. He has published eight mystery/suspense novels, including *The Teller, Two for the Show,* and *Moving Day,* which was an Amazon Kindle First. His short stories have appeared in the 2013 and 2014 Mystery Writers of America anthologies, and in *Best American Mystery Stories 2016,* edited by Elizabeth George.

Sue Stone

SARAH PEMBERTON STRONG is the author of two novels, including the noir homage *The Fainting Room,* "a masterful exploration of longing and its consequences" (*Publishers Weekly*). She is also the author of a book of poetry. To write "Callback," her story in this voume, she drew on seventeen years' experience working as a plumber. She currently teaches writing at Quinnipiac University and lives in Hamden, Connecticut.

Khem Spearman